WHERE THE SUN SHINES OUT

Also by Kevin Catalano

The World Made Flesh

WHERE THE SUN

SHINES OUT

a novel

KEVIN CATALANO

Skyhorse Publishing

First Edition

This is a work of fiction. Names, places, characters, and incidents are either the products of the author's imagination or are used fictitiously.

Skyhorse Publishing books may be purchased in bulk at special discounts for sales promotion, corporate gifts, fund-raising, or educational purposes. Special editions can also be created to specifications. For details, contact the Special Sales Department, Skyhorse Publishing, 307 West 36th Street, 11th Floor, New York, NY 10018 or info@ skyhorsepublishing.com.

Skyhorse® and Skyhorse Publishing® are registered trademarks of Skyhorse Publishing, Inc.®, a Delaware corporation.

Visit our website at www.skyhorsepublishing.com.

10 9 8 7 6 5 4 3 2 1

Library of Congress Cataloging-in-Publication Data is available on file.

Cover design by Erin Seaward-Hiatt

Print ISBN: 978-1-5107-2199-9
Ebook ISBN: 978-1-5107-2200-2

Printed in the United States of America.

For Megan, Cameron, and Sam

AUTHOR'S NOTE

The following stories first appeared in:

"Where the Water Runs North" as "Ceremony of the White Dog," *Exigencies*, 2015; "Henderson Lovely, Last of the Munchkins," *Booth: A Journal*, 2012; "Where the Sun Shines Out" as "Into the Lake," *Terrain.org: A Journal of the Built + Natural Environments*, No. 26, 2010; "Overtime," *Aethlon: A Journal of Sport Literature* 28, No. 2, 2013; "Overtime," *Atticus Review: The Sports Literature Issue*, 2014; "The Unreturned," *Fiddleblack Annual #1: Apparitional Experience*, 2012; "Snow Man" as "Unbounded Natureless Chaos," *REAL: Regarding Arts & Letters* 37, No. 1; 2013.

CONTENTS

THE UNRETURNED

What a small song. What slow clouds. What dark water.
Hath the rain a father? All the caves are ice. Only the snow's here.
I'm cold. I'm cold all over. Rub me in father and mother.
Fear was my father, Father Fear.
His look drained the stones.

—Theodore Roethke, *The Lost Son*

Summer, 1992

DEAN WOKE TO A soft, hot ear branding his cheek. Tears, not Dean's, slicked down his jaw and dripped off his chin, leaving behind a frigid, electric itch. He recognized the creamy-sweet scent of the skin as Jason's. Dean first believed he and his little brother were at home, in bed, hiding from imagined ghosts under covers, sharing air. But the stench of gasoline and car exhaust, differently sweet, said otherwise. A crowbar or wrench or jack jabbed his spine with each thump, digging a wound the size of which he could only imagine. He tried to move his feet to relieve the pressure, but wire cut into his ankles. Same with his wrists. Panic flickered in his chest.

Dean inched his face into Jason's neck and found comfort in his brother's smell—it was like applesauce and milk. Each inhale stilled his heart a little against the fear.

The car bounced and the boys thudded against the ceiling of the trunk. Jason groaned, then sobbed. Dean wanted to say something to Jason that comforted as much as his scent, but the words tossed around in his head like stormy water.

The line was long and the heat blazed under the tent, despite the industrial fan wheezing in the corner. Dean, Jason, and their father were the last ones in line, having waited until the end of the day to meet the Munchkins. Dean could just now make out the actors sitting at a table signing photographs. Their tiny bodies and wrinkly, melted faces had frightened him years past when they'd come to his elementary school to speak. Chittenango was the birthplace of the author of the Oz books, and so the village hosted an annual event, to which the remaining Munchkins always came. This year, Dean had won a prize for creating a poster project on the Munchkins for his fifth grade class. Since then, he'd become obsessed, which was his nature, and he was excited to meet the actual people who had played them.

Dean, Jason, and their father had already watched the parade—the many tin men and scarecrows and lions waving from floats. They'd been on the few rides that were crammed into the gravel parking lot of the Chittenango Fire Department—the Octopus and Tilt-a-Whirl and Pirate Ship. They'd eaten their foot-long fried dough with cinnamon, hot and greasy in its paper sleeve. They'd hurled rock-hard basketballs at hoops and tossed bouncy rings at jugs trying to win a giant animal, but came up empty-handed. The brothers did, however, win fourth- and fifth-place ribbons for the best Munchkin costumes. They were the Lollipop Guild, dressed in striped shirts and suspenders and knee-high, candy-cane socks. They'd slicked their dark hair back with mousse and memorized the song in case they were called upon to sing it.

Dean's costume had placed higher than Jason's, probably because, due to the bruises around his eyes, Jason was forced to wear their dad's aviator shades. Defeating his brother in the contest was yet another betrayal to add to a long list.

The brothers killed the time waiting in line by playing games. Dean's hands twitched in Jason's palms, anxious for Jason's move. He saw it coming, but Jason was too quick and he slapped Dean hard. Jason laughed. This was the tenth time in a row he had got him, and the tops of Dean's hands were red and puffy. After a few more failed turns, Dean became frustrated and jammed his scalding hands into his pockets.

Then his dad addressed him. "Hey Dean-O, I need to use the bathroom. I want you to keep an eye on Jason, okay?"

Dean squinted to make sense of this. His dad had never put him in charge of his brother, even though he was almost three years older than Jason. In fact, it was Jason whom his dad typically favored. Dean wasn't comfortable with this sudden change in rank, but he didn't know how to say so.

"I'll be five minutes." His dad pulled his leather wallet from his tattered jean shorts. He gave Dean a twenty. "If you get to them before I come back, you can each buy an autographed photo."

There were only two times when Dean had held a twenty—his First Communion and his tenth birthday.

"You'll be right back?" Dean asked.

"Yes, but you'll be fine." He turned to Jason, who, even with the oversized sunglasses, looked confused. "Behave and do as your brother says, got it?"

"Why can't I hold the money?"

"Because Dean is older than you."

"Barely."

"It doesn't matter. He's still older."

"You can hold the money if you want," Dean said.

"No," his dad snapped. "I'm telling *you* to hold it."

He gave Dean a hard, uncomfortable look, eyes saying this was about more than the money. It was probably because of yesterday, but Dean couldn't figure out the connection. Before leaving the tent, his dad turned back and nodded, and then he walked off into the sun-bleached crowd.

The bill felt heavy in Dean's hand. He didn't want to participate in his dad's plan, whatever it was. He didn't want to change the order of things between him and his brother. So Dean handed the money to Jason, who eagerly took it.

A large, broad lady in a purple dress came up to the boys. Her fatty arms jutted from her sides like a weightlifter's. At first, she simply stood there and hummed the Lollipop Guild tune. She had a shiny, almost translucent face, but a kind smile. From beneath her sunglasses, tears leaked down her cheeks, though she didn't seem at all sad. She suddenly looked down at them as if just now seeing they were there.

"Well, lookit how precious you two are," she said. "I bet your mama spent a lot of time on your costumes."

Dean wasn't sure how to respond, while Jason was busy snapping the twenty over and over.

"Where is she, your mama?"

"At home," Jason said.

"Y'all are alone?" She pushed the glasses up to rub her eye with her knuckle.

Again, Dean waited for Jason to answer for them, which he did without missing a beat: "Dad's going to the bathroom."

The lady's voice went lower, became eager. Dean thought she would try to steal the money. Instead, she said, "My name is Carol. I'm an assistant to the Munchkins. I think you two are just precious in your costumes. Would you like me to take you to the front of the line to meet them?"

This time, Dean knew what to say. His stomach or heart or prickling skin told him. But, like their game, Jason was quicker. "Yes!" He was so jubilant, Dean lost faith in his instinct.

Carol quickly ushered them out of the tent, a heavy hand on each of their shoulders. She told them they'd go around the other side to avoid the crowd. But then they were approaching the overstuffed Dumpsters behind the Fire Department, and Dean felt a door in his stomach open to a deep, cold fear that froze him stiff and silent.

An ice cream cone melted at his foot. A black ant was caught in the creamy puddle, its legs a furious scuttle. A tear slithered down Carol's bluish face. Jason snapped the twenty.

The car stopped. A door opened and closed. There were two voices.

Dean wanted to hear from his brother before it was too late. "Jason?"

"Yeah?"

Dean had no plan of what to say and no time to choose his words. "I liked your sunglasses."

"I can't find them." Jason seemed panicked about this, as if the missing sunglasses were the main source of his fear. Dean went to feel around for them, but the pinching wire reminded him that he was restrained.

The trunk groaned open. Two silhouettes peered in against the night-blue sky. It was Carol and a gaunt, long-armed man wearing an oversized Knicks jersey.

"You're awake already." Carol's motherly tone and the man's gold crucifix made Dean partly believe nothing bad would happen to them. But then she yanked Dean out of the trunk. The man pulled Jason out, and his head slammed against the hood. Jason grunted; his body flopped limp.

"Oops," the man said, tossing Jason over his shoulder. "Sorry 'bout that, Pumpkin."

"Doesn't matter," said Carol. "This is the one I want anyhow. That one could be trouble—lookit his eyes."

"What'd you get both for?"

"They were together. Can't just take one while the other goes off telling people."

Carol held Dean in her arms like he was a child. He felt her large, sagging breasts under her dress. He kicked and punched and squirmed, but she squeezed him so ferociously he saw dazzles in the night air. They walked up a gravel driveway. There were no lights anywhere, nothing other than a black wall of trees fortressing them in. An occasional lightning bug lit the night, and the woods buzzed with crickets.

"What we going to do with this one then?" asked the man.

"Figure something out, Christ's sake. Just don't tell me about it."

Dean screamed. Carol jammed her pillowy hand on his mouth and mashed his nose. She put her lips to his ear and hummed a gravelly lullaby, pimpling his neck and legs. She carried him up the creaking porch steps of a dim cabin. She bumped the front door open with her hip. She said, "You're home, baby."

Jason combed his fingers through Dean's hair. Dean swooned from the hands working mousse into his scalp. Jason was silent in concentration, just his measured breathing and sour-sweet breath. Dean steadied on Jason's lips, fuller than his own, perfectly pink. He had always envied Jason's features—the wider nose, almond-shaped eyes, straighter teeth. Then he felt a tickle of guilt for looking so long.

Dean looked past Jason to the bathroom mirror. His hair was helmet-slick, stuck in shape. Jason had already pocked Dean's nose and cheeks with freckles using a makeup pencil. He loved how different he looked. He loved changing shape.

Banging on the door made them jump. It was their father.

"Jason! You haven't finished your eggs."

"But my stomach hurts."

"Eat, or you're not going."

"But I'll barf, I swear."

"Goddammit, Jason." The door thumped again.

Dean thought he saw the beginning of tears in Jason's eyes. He took Jason's hand and gave it a reassuring shake.

"We'll be there in a second," Dean yelled.

"No, right now." More banging. The lightbulbs rattled over the mirror. "Or neither of you are going."

Their mother's voice from downstairs: "Karl, just give them a minute."

"Don't worry about it, Rene." Their father's voice lowered. "Dean-O. Do the right thing. Open the door so your brother can finish his breakfast."

Dean let go of Jason's hand. His head felt heavy as he studied the tile floor.

"Dean-O," his father sang.

He fought to control the shiver in his jaw as his hand raised toward the doorknob.

The house smelled like the bottom of a shoveled hole. The floors popped and snapped as Carol carried him through a hallway, past a kitchen with a woodstove and plastic patio furniture. The man was taking Jason, still unconscious, down a different hallway. Dean twisted to see where, but Carol restrained him. She brought him into a small room at the back of the house. A Batman poster was tacked over a bed crowded with oversized bears. The whites of their big, vacant eyes showed pink. There was no other furniture in the room.

She set him down on his side. Sweaty mousse seeped into his eyes, stinging. Dust and grit clung to his face. She knelt beside him and kissed his earlobe. Her leaking eyes slimed his cheek.

"You're my baby," she told him. The moon's glow cast through the window on her wide, oily face.

"Where's my brother?" Dean asked, shivering.

She smiled and shook her head. "He's not your brother anymore, honey." She walked toward the door. "I'll be right back with some clothes and dinner."

Dean screamed his brother's name, holding the *–son* until his throat burned and the name died out in a croaking rattle. There was no reply. When his voice was useless, he attempted to break free from the wire, but it bit back against his wrists. He inched toward the wall and put his head to it for leverage as he got himself on his knees. He could just see over the windowsill. A pier bobbed in a vast, black lake, where a hint of moon reflected just as perfectly still as the one in the sky. On the other side of the lake was a spray of lights, a town or neighborhood, something familiar. If they hadn't been driving too long, then maybe this was Oneida Lake. That would mean Chittenango was nearby. Dean couldn't know how long he'd been unconscious in the trunk of the car, however. They could be in Canada, and Dean suddenly pictured the map of New York State that his teacher sometimes pulled out, revealing with a pointer how close a whole different country was to home.

He rested his chin on the sill and his stomach began knotting up and he fell back to the floor. He wanted to call out again to Jason, but his voice was too raw. Instead, he cried.

"Oh, none of that." Carol was back and she had clothes under her arm and a plate of something steaming. All Dean could make of it in the half dark was chunky gravy over rice.

"Now, I'm going to take your costume off and put these on you," Carol said, kneeling and displaying the outfit on a hanger. It looked like something his grandmother's antique boy dolls wore: a white silky shirt, red vest, and bow tie.

"Please don't," Dean tried.

Carol took hold of the waistband of his shorts, but Dean kicked the floor to slide back. She smiled, grabbed his calves, and yanked him to her. The wood scraped at his spine, reopening the wound from the trunk.

"Be still now." She unclipped the suspenders and pulled his shorts down to his ankles but frowned at the wire that bound them.

"Wayne?" she called over her shoulder.

"Yeah?"

"Bring me the scissors." As she waited, she put her hand on the bone of Dean's hip. "You're a skinny one, aren't you?"

Dean's breaths quickened like rapidfire. He didn't want to be alone with Carol, even if that meant wishing for the man named Wayne and his scissors.

Wayne returned, handing over rusty shears. Dean could now make out his face. It seemed Wayne should have worn a beard or very recently had shaved one off. His was a narrow face with a jutting, somehow obscene chin. Dean avoided looking directly at it.

"That other one's a real shit," he said. "Scratched up my whole arm. Lookit."

His lean forearm was shredded, like he'd reached into an animal's cage.

"I told you we don't need but one. This one is nice and gentle."

"I'm getting to it, Pumpkin."

Their insulting Jason, her assuming Dean wouldn't fight like Jason had fought, and the last thing, *we don't need but one*, whatever that exactly meant, stung Dean with a sudden rage. He cocked his knees and kicked Carol's face. Her head flung back and blood streamed from her nose. There was a quiet moment when she sat there, peacefully tasting blood with her tongue. Then she shrieked. She smeared the hot plate of food into Dean's eyes and mouth. She yanked his hair, whipping his head around, and then put her mouth on his temple and growled, tickling a part of his brain that made him urinate. It seemed to Dean like something wild was attacking him—a lion or bear—and he was helpless against it, no longer human, but rather small, mousey prey to be consumed.

Wayne finally pulled her off, toppling her backward, on top of him. He sang *Pumpkin* into her ear, until the fury deflated from her.

"Let's just take a break," he said, helping her up.

"I don't need a fucking break." But she was breathless.

Wayne walked her out of the room, petting her thick hair.

Dean's eyes blazed. He turned over on his stomach and retched. He had this image of himself mangled like a gnawed-on chicken wing. He hoped that he was worse off than Jason, that he was taking on the torture that could have been leveled on his brother. But Carol was proving to him that the suffering was limitless.

Wayne returned a minute later and crouched beside Dean. He used his fingers to swipe the food from Dean's face.

"Sorry about that, son," he said. "But you shouldn't've done that. Good boys don't do those kinds of things. When she comes back, you'll want to apologize." He pulled on his long chin. "From here on, I'd like you to call me Papa. Or Pop. Just don't call me your old man."

"Don't kill him," Dean said, but the sting in his throat thinned the words.

Wayne twisted up his mouth. "Call me whatever you want." He then ducked out of the room as if embarrassed.

Dean felt drowsy, but he feared slipping into this, as if death waited for him. He instead focused his energies on getting his shorts back over his waist. As he arched his butt off the ground, he kicked something that clattered on the floorboards.

"Because of the grass? Your brother's over there beat up because of the grass?"

"Karl."

"No, Rene. I want to hear this. He's always getting off too easy."

"This isn't the time to *yell* at him."

His dad paced the kitchen, the floor whining in the familiar spot in front of the refrigerator. Jason sat on top of the counter, Mother holding a bag of frozen peas to his eyes. His mouth was red and slobbering, but his breaths were now controlled.

Dean felt he was sitting in the middle of the kitchen, displayed for public ridicule. He was unable to look at his father, at anyone. Especially Jason, since it was now obvious that Dean had betrayed him in the worst way. The cruelest part was his father forcing him to explain it, which he couldn't even to himself. So he shut down, closed all the doors on his interior so that the Dean at whom everyone was staring was just the shell. He hoped he could maintain it, as he felt a sad rage collecting in his stomach.

His dad bent over, trying to get his face into Dean's vision. "You love your brother, don't you?"

Dean's face bunched up; he fought back desperately.

"Then why didn't you do anything?"

"Dammit, Karl. That's enough. He gets it."

"But I don't!" His dad lifted a kitchen chair and slammed it on the floor. Dean jumped.

"Dad, stop," Jason said.

Their mother charged past him, smashing the bag of peas into their father's chest. She crouched beside Dean and pulled his face into her, brushing his hair and shushing him. Dean allowed her to, but the main part of him resisted. This was the last thing he wanted, to be mothered like a child. It made him feel even weaker than his father did.

His dad sighed and tossed the bag around in his hands. The thawing peas rattled the silence. "Look, Dean-O. I'm sorry. I just wanted to—"

"Sorry is enough," his mother snapped.

He joined Jason, patted his back and squeezed his shoulder. "Sorry. Really, everybody."

"We can still go to the Oz Festival tomorrow, right?" Jason asked, both eyes swollen almost entirely closed.

That night, Dean and Jason were allowed to have the TV in their bedroom. *Dumbo* was on, which they'd never seen. When the black crows began singing, Jason got out of his bed and climbed into Dean's. They went under the blankets. Jason's bruised eyes swelled like a frog's, the openings mere slits; Dean could just make out the gleam of his pupils. He put his arm around Jason. Their knees collided. They tickled each other's feet with their toes. Forehead to forehead, they rehearsed their Lollipop Guild song, giggling through each verse.

A sudden crash like the collision of a screen door on its frame rattled the window. Thumping came from just beyond the wall, outside. Dean squirmed to his knees and looked out the window. Wayne shuffled down the pier with Jason slung limp over his shoulder. With his free arm he dragged a sack of rocks or bricks, which thudded over each plank. Dean's instinct was to call out, but instead he fell back to the floor. His thoughts were frantic as he rolled over the shears, trying to get them in his hands.

Carol entered. Dean froze. She knelt beside him, wheezing. The peacefulness in her face reminded him of old church paintings in which saints look heavenward.

"I know why you didn't eat," she whispered, voice quivering. "You wanted something else."

She untied the top of her dress, reached in, and pulled out an enormous breast. It poured from her grip like a bag of sand. Blue veins spidered through its moonlike breadth. She bent over him, pushing the purplish nipple onto his lips. He jerked his head away, but she grabbed hold of his face and yanked him back. She pinched his nose, and when he finally had to breathe, she filled his mouth. The nipple was bitter. He tried to roll his tongue back to his tonsils, but there was no escaping.

"Just hush now and drink."

He flipped and twisted the scissors underneath his body, nipping his fingers as he worked them into cutting position. He realized, however, that he couldn't both try to free himself and resist. He puckered his lips, put his tongue under the nipple, and began to suck. His mouth knew instinctively how to do this, though he had to fight back the vomit inching up his throat. Nothing was coming out of Carol's breast except briny sweat.

"That's a real good boy."

For a moment, he was delivered to a place that seemed too far back to remember. It was his mother—the taste of her skin, her warmth that became his, the rhythm of her heart that controlled his. Dean's eyeballs rolled back. A cone of heat spiraled from his chest to his crotch. He melted and stiffened, until Carol's moan snapped him from this strange reverie. He came out hating her.

He had the scissors in position, wedged up on the wire. The harder he tried to cut, the fiercer he sucked. The moment he felt his hands free, a single drop of something rich and sweet blossomed his tongue.

Before he could think it, his arm flung up from under his back. Carol screamed, and something hot coated his hand. She looked at him, befuddled, eyes gushing water. The ears of the scissors poked out from the side of her belly. He tried to get up, but his feet were still bound. His heart was going crazy, like a stampede of hooves hammering his chest. He grabbed the scissors and yanked them out. Her stomach let out a sigh followed by dark blood. She was sitting back on her legs, eyes following him as if watching a film.

He attempted to cut the wire at his feet, but he kept fumbling the blood-slicked scissors. The whole time he thought there was a bird in the room, cooing just above his head, until he realized it was him, whimpering. He dried the scissors on his shirt. Now he could grip them, and he chomped at the wire. It took two attempts, but he was free. Dean scrambled past Carol, who was wilting forward. He heard her crash just as he left the room.

He scanned the unfamiliar kitchen: table, chairs, stove—a screen door. He barged into it.

He was in the vast, purple daybreak. Bright, crisp air, the whispering of the trees far above, the murmuring lake. He saw Wayne's silhouette at the end of the pier, crouched and pulling the sack around Jason's body. His legs went numb.

Jason and Dean were playing basketball in their wet driveway, carefully dribbling the ball around puddles. It had just stopped raining, and they were allowed outside on the condition that they not go on the grass.

Their dad had explained that their clothes would get muddy, and they could ruin the lawn.

Dean dribbled behind his back—a move he had been working on—and drove by Jason to score a layup.

"Aw, man," Jason said. "Good shot."

Basketball was the only thing Dean was better at than Jason. His younger brother could draw better, was funnier and quicker, and certainly more fearless. Still, Dean didn't like to beat him. The guilt that followed never made it worthwhile.

Only one more basket and he'd win, so Dean deliberately took a long, wild shot. The ball bounced high off the rim and landed in the grass with a slopping thud.

"Darn it," Dean said.

Jason scrambled onto the lawn and grabbed the ball. He didn't immediately return to the driveway. Instead, he was distracted by something in the grass.

"Whoa," he said. "All these nightcrawlers are oozing out of the ground."

Dean looked back at the house, at the windows. "Hurry up," he said. "You're not supposed to be out there."

Jason gasped as he dug his fingers into the ground. "Look at this." He held up a pointed rock. "It's an arrowhead! Holy cow, a real arrowhead like from the Indians."

"Bring it here so Dad doesn't catch you."

Suddenly Mark D, the fourteen-year-old from the other side of the village, zoomed past on his bike, tires spraying a line of water up his back. He never came around here unless he was looking for someone to pick on. He braked and turned in a controlled skid, then pedaled hard toward their yard. He did a wheelie, landing his front tire on the grass a few feet from Jason.

Mark had the shadow of a mustache and was rumored to have access to his father's gun. He had once shown Dean and Jason his throwing star in a rare gesture of solidarity, right before trying to chuck it at them.

"What're you doing, dipshit?"

"Get off our lawn." Jason puffed out his chest.

"Or what?" Mark threw down his bike and stomped on the grass. He towered over Jason, who did not flinch.

"Jason," Dean called. "Come here. I have to tell you something."

Jason did not turn. Mark grabbed Jason's hand and yanked the arrowhead from him, then chucked it an impossible distance. Jason tried to get it back, but Mark shoved him to the ground. Jason popped up, the backside of his shorts and shirt soaked. Jason karate-kicked at Mark's leg, a move he and Dean had practiced often on each other, but Mark grabbed his foot and tossed him down again. This time, Mark jumped him and pounded at his stomach.

"Hey!" Dean called, still standing in the driveway. He felt stuck to the asphalt, no more mobile than the pole of the basketball hoop cemented into the earth. He could only watch like a tortured spectator. Even when Jason screamed, tilting his head back, making eye contact with Dean, eyes pleading for help, Dean couldn't move. Mark pressed his thumbs into Jason's eyes. Jason squealed a sound Dean had never heard, not in all the years of their own fighting and taunting. Still, he did not go to him.

When Mark was finished, he used Jason's head to get himself to his feet and then spat on Jason's mouth. He then climbed his bike and sped off. Jason held his face, knees up to his chest, rocking back and forth on the lawn. The toes of Dean's sneakers were at the lip of the driveway, grazing the wet blades of grass.

Just beyond Wayne's head, across the lake, the trees were silhouetted against the dawn sky. Wayne looked up from the sack. His dangling crucifix bounced over the heap like a tethered moth. "What're you doing out here?"

"I think I killed her." Dean's voice was chapped, cracking in the giant, open night.

Wayne stood. "What?"

"That lady. Your wife. I didn't mean to."

"Pumpkin?"

Wayne stumbled over the sack, hurried toward him. Dean waited, his feet apart and his hands closed to fists. Saying aloud what he'd done, killed a person, had given him a peculiar courage. He felt emptied out and hollow, with no reason to fear this man. But Wayne walked right by Dean—who felt a strange, singing panic in his throat—and went into the house.

Dean was alone. The trees, the sky, the lake, quiet, like held breath. The motionless form of his brother punctuated the end of the pier. Dean's legs revived. His feet pounded the planks. The soft air whistled in his ears as though he was speeding down a runway, preparing for flight. And what if he took off, gliding through the twilight sky, making small life's troubles? But this could never be made small, no matter how high he soared.

He stood over Jason, whose lower half jutted from the sack. The striped socks from his costume were loose and sagging at his ankles. Dean knew this leg, even if he couldn't make out its details: the wispy blonde hairs, the scar above the kneecap from a bike jump, the three moles on his calf that Dean had once connected with a pen as Jason squirmed and hooted. Dean hovered his fingertips over the shin, then touched. He fell back. His ears rang. His throat swelled against his tonsils. He looked into the sky, where the dark blue was becoming purple and pink, and settled on the crescent moon. The white began to bleed into its surroundings like a thumbprint smudge, then it retreated far back into the atmosphere, becoming nothing more than splintered light alone in a cold corner of space.

A chill sliced through Dean.

The screen door slammed open, sounding like gunshot. Wayne stepped onto the pier and growled, "You little shit!"

Dean stupidly watched Wayne approach until he realized he was still present in his body. He pulled Jason's legs from the sack and rolled him into the lake and then fell in after him. He snatched Jason's suspenders and then kicked like mad trying to keep himself and his brother above water. Wayne shouted or wept from the end of the pier. And then Dean heard nothing but his own wild breath.

Dean got a good grip on Jason, holding him with one arm and swimming with the other. His burning muscles found a rhythm. He was headed for the waning lights on the far shore—miles, it seemed, to go. To his left, the sun had come up full over the trees, warming his cheek. Out towards the center of the lake, his body went numb from the exertion. Under him, two kicking legs collided with two others—Dean couldn't tell them apart. He squeezed Jason to be sure he still had him, but there was no sensation. A sudden fantasy flashed through his brain: maybe Dean was not the one who had survived; instead, it was Jason who was now carrying him.

Jason cutting quicker through the lake.

Jason at the shore, draping Dean over his shoulders, fighting through morning woods and fields.

Jason shivering at the front door, collapsing into Mom's arms, who assured him he was home, he was safe, and Dad looking on, relieved to find that of his two boys, it was Jason who returned.

Dean held that vision in his mind as he moved his brother through the lake, inch by inch.

A BOY'S WILL

Summer, 1992

———◆———

ACCORDING TO THE FBI brochure that the lady from victim assistance handed him, Karl was not allowed to question his son about the abduction. He was not allowed to blame him, either, or show extreme emotions or correct him if he did talk about the incident. But Dean didn't talk about the incident. He barely spoke. Not to Karl anyway.

What Karl was supposed to do was remind Dean that he loved him. He was supposed to give Dean small choices to help him regain some control. He should create an environment of normalcy. He should work closely with the victim specialist to assist with reducing Dean's trauma.

Stuck to the fridge with an orange and blue '92 Big East Champs magnet, it was impossible for Karl not to read the brochure as a personal rebuke, as though the authorities—and his wife—were conspiring against him. He wanted to scream. He wanted to break things. He had broken things earlier in the week, the leaf of the kitchen table that belonged to Rene's grandmother.

"Oh, that's just great," Rene had said.

Mostly, Karl was angry at Dean, whom he wanted to shake into articulation. He wanted information, the same information the FBI and Madison County Police wanted: what did the abductors look like, other than one being a man and the other a woman? Where had they taken them, other than the woods on Oneida Lake? What was the color of the vehicle? Dean wouldn't even say whether it was a sedan or van or truck. And because of his silence, four days of it and counting, the goddamn abductors could be in Canada by now.

So yes, Karl wanted to blame his son. He did not want him to choose between spaghetti and fish sticks for dinner. Nobody had a goddamn appetite in this house anyway. And an environment of normalcy? His youngest was dead. They'd buried him yesterday. He'd looked like a waxen doll in the casket, not eight years old but five. And fuck, *fuck* the brochure because during the wake, Karl filled St. Patrick's with his wailing. Dean sat just beside him stiffer than his little brother. Rene pulled at Karl's shoulders and when that didn't work, his face, tugging at his face until he was backward on the altar steps, crying and embarrassed. He spent the rest of the service in the car, smoking and drinking from a flask until he drizzled the gravel lot with pink bile.

That was when he met the victim specialist. She leaned on the open car door, straddling his pathetic vomit, and offered exactly what he needed: a Kleenex and a stick of Doublemint. Before she identified herself, he thought she might be a nun—for her generosity, not her appearance. She wore a navy-blue knee-length skirt and jacket, a shimmery royal blue blouse, a chunky necklace of yellow stones. She was black. Dark-skinned, a healthy sheen to her forehead and cheekbones. African or Haitian, he thought, until she spoke without accent.

"Can I get you some water?"

Her perfume filled the family station wagon, a vanilla-lemon scent that called to mind an airy back porch, ceiling fans, and rocking chairs.

"No, thank you."

She held out her hand. "I'm Lena Johnson."

He was ashamed of his hand, nicked and calloused from the six days a week at Mohawk. Hers was soft and impossibly cool in this humidity. Karl pulled himself out of the car. His brain felt like a dry, hard sponge, his knees like gelatin. He shut the door and leaned on it.

"How are you, Mr. Fleming?" Her soft voice entered directly into him, pooled his chest with a fluttery light. It was the first time anyone had asked him this. Everyone else—the neighbors, his parents, the guys at Mohawk—they all inquired about Dean first, then Rene, whom he'd never even thought to resent. Until now. Until this Lena Johnson asked how he was. It seemed a question that required no answer. Instead, it was an invitation into her eyes, a warm brown like something sweet had just come out of the oven.

This could be a tactic, something the FBI trained their female agents to do to get into the heads of suspects.

He looked away, attended to his gum to try to get his guard back up. From here he could see the nearby shopping center, mostly empty on this Wednesday afternoon.

Lena Johnson must have sensed the shift in him, as she adjusted accordingly, crossing her arms under her chest, but loosely, both hands cupping her elbows. She wore many gold rings, but there was no diamond.

"I understand if you're tired of talking to officials," she said. "I want you to know that I'm not an investigator. I'm trained in child psychology, and I've worked with several children who've experienced trauma like your son's."

Karl kicked some stones around. He'd neglected to polish his only pair of dress shoes, the ones he was married in twelve years ago, at this very church.

"Tomorrow I would like to come by the house and talk to Dean. I understand he hasn't been communicative."

Karl laughed, then immediately felt guilty. There'd been a lot of guilt; people were pushing it on him, forcing him to wear it. He didn't want to. He didn't feel he deserved it. The *Herald Journal* told of how he left his boys alone at the Oz Festival, and then they were kidnapped, as if it were a cause-and-effect situation. As if his leaving them alone so he could piss made the abductors want his boys. But that was how everyone seemed to interpret it. What about the others in line? Why the hell didn't they do anything when some strange lady stole his boys away in broad daylight? And the abductors, everyone treated them as if they were just a part of life, an unfortunate reality—like drugs or drunk drivers. *It's your fault, not theirs, if you don't take proper precaution.* And

Dean . . . Karl still bristled thinking about him in that instance. He should have known better than to go off with a stranger. How many goddamn times had he talked to both his boys about that?

"Mr. Fleming?"

There was that soft, musical note of her voice again. This time, he felt his skin reach for her, as though she were magnetic.

"May I come by?"

He was saying, *Yes, of course*, but to what exactly? To her helping his troubled son open up, or to that voice, those eyes, that warmth that he wanted to cocoon himself in?

She smiled, and before leaving, reached into the bag he hadn't noticed on the ground beside her feet.

"In the meantime, take a look at this." She held out a glossy brochure. "It could help."

He wakes to screams. He's up before he knows who he is or anything about his life. There's only darkness through which he trudges like walking through tar. Pieces of himself shoot like stars from the pitch, so now he knows he's Karl Fleming, that he's in his room in his house on Race Street in Chittenango, New York. And there are the screams, no stars yet, no light, except for a dimness around the impression that it's a child, his child, Dean, who has colic, who wakes so often in the night.

He stumbles through his door and down the hall, wondering why Rene hasn't gone to the baby the way she always does, immediately when Dean begins to cry, Karl pleading for her to wait, *just wait*, let him cry some and see if he can put himself back to sleep. *If you go right away, he'll keep crying every night. He won't learn.* But she'd ignore him, swoop up the child and bring him into their bed, nursing him back to sleep while Karl fumed. And here he is, going to the baby. But it's no baby. He's awake now. The door of the boys' bedroom is open. No, just boy. Just Dean. And Dean is lying in his bed, eyes open staring at the ceiling. Rene is standing in the corner, heaving and blubbery, pulling at the front of her nightgown as though it burns.

"What's going on?"

Rene doesn't answer. She is looking at Dean as though he's a stranger or ghost who suddenly appeared, unwelcome, in this room.

"Dean-O?" Karl tries, but his son's eyeballs don't seem to see. They move in frightening, mechanical jerks, as though he were a robot malfunctioning.

"We need help," Rene spits at Karl, shrinking to the floor. "God help us, we need help."

Lena Johnson brought her vanilla scent into their living room. She sat on the edge of Karl's ratty blue recliner, somehow giving it class. Rene had made her hot tea—she didn't drink coffee—and she settled it in her lap like those British ladies on PBS shows. Her hair was pulled up tight on her head, revealing the lovely roundness of her face. Today she wore black pants and a white-collared shirt, the top two buttons undone to reveal a simple gold chain and a taunting inch of cleavage.

Their house had ceased to be theirs since the abduction. News vans parked in the street, reporters littered the front lawn, a regular stream of uniformed officers went in and out the front door freely, while the FBI, always in their suits, invaded the family room with recording equipment.

None of it mattered to Karl; it was better than being alone with Rene and Dean and the way they both judged him. He'd given up trying to talk to either, since Dean would ignore him, and Rene would find fault with even his simplest utterances. It had gotten to the point that she no longer slept in their bed but instead cuddled up with Dean every night in his room. Until last night, that is, when Dean had done *something* that Rene wasn't talking about. When Karl got the message that there was nothing he could say to her, she judged his silence, as if she knew all along that he would give up on her and their son.

Dean was on the couch across from Lena Johnson, scratching intently at a scab on his shin. Mesh shorts and a Syracuse Orangemen T-shirt were all Dean had wanted to wear. Karl had been charged with dressing him, as Rene had announced that morning that she needed her space from Dean. So Karl tried to abide by the brochure and gave Dean the choice of outfit, which was more for Lena Johnson than his boy. He wanted to be able to boast, if given the opportunity, that he was trying to do the right thing. He wanted her approval, her smile, maybe a touch on his wrist as she said, "Good for you."

She didn't do any of this. Instead, she'd informed Karl and Rene that she wanted to speak to Dean alone in the living room. It was okay that they listened in from the kitchen, but under no circumstances were they to interrupt if Dean revealed something "unpalatable." Karl enjoyed watching Lena Johnson tell his wife what to do in her own kitchen. Looking at her side-by-side with this perfectly elegant woman, Karl was ashamed of his wife, who at ten a.m., still wasn't dressed, hadn't put on her makeup, or done her hair.

"I also have to inform you that unlike other therapists, what Dean reveals to me is not considered confidential. My purpose is to assist Dean with the healing process but also to get information pertaining to the incident. For that reason, I will be recording our conversation. I hope we have an understanding."

"Yes, of course," Karl said, perhaps too eagerly. Rene shot him a look and then sat at the kitchen table and put her head in her hands. A dismissive gesture with her fingers was her consent.

Lena Johnson looked sadly at Karl. He shrugged as though he couldn't fathom Rene's behavior.

"When I'm through, maybe we can all talk." Then she left.

Now, Karl leaned against the kitchen counter sipping burnt coffee, concentrating out the window, on the creek that cut through the backyard, as a way to hear the conversation in the family room. Lena Johnson introduced herself, then asked Dean how old he was. He couldn't make out Dean's response, but he must have answered since Lena Johnson echoed "Ten," and then asked his birthdate. This time he made out his son's voice, no words really, just a low rhythm of sound.

"And your brother, how old is he?"

"Eight." Clear and definitive, as though Dean was proud of this.

"His birthday?"

"August 12, 1984."

"His favorite food?"

"Cheeseburgers without pickles."

"Your favorite food?"

Dean's voice went low again. He mumbled something syllabic Karl couldn't match with a familiar word. What was his favorite food? Dean ate everything without complaint, whereas Jason was picky. That cheeseburgers were Jason's favorite surprised Karl. Rarely did Karl grill burgers, and more rarely still did he take the boys to Burger King, though he would have. When he could, Karl enjoyed spoiling his boys with food Rene wouldn't buy. He'd take them out on the weekends to local events, most often the state fair, the Firemen's Field Days, the Oz Festival. There he'd splurge, treating them to ice cream and fried dough and sausage and peppers. They'd bond over the food—talking about what they'd eat beforehand, humming to it during, and on the way home, their stomachs full and a little queasy, agree on what they wouldn't tell Mom they'd eaten, though usually Jason, hopped up on sugar, would spill it anyway.

Karl's face got hot realizing that he'd never get to do this again. He bit down on the inside corner of his mouth to distract himself.

Rene turned on the faucet and clanked dishes around in the sink. She reached into the cabinet underneath and brought out Comet and doused the sink with it. She scrubbed, putting her tiny weight into the job. Karl got the image of her trying to remove a blood stain from a shirt.

"Last night," Rene said without turning around. "He . . . touched me."

Karl wasn't sure she was speaking to him and when it became clear she was, he didn't understand the words.

Rene stopped cleaning and leaned over the counter, her spine and shoulder blades protruding through the thin gown. "When I woke, he was rubbing . . . me. I thought he was asleep. I pulled his hand away, but he was strong. I didn't know he was so strong." She was nodding to something in the sink, her short brown hair mussed in the back. "He was fighting me, climbing on top. Karl, he wasn't wearing underwear."

She fisted the sponge, squeezing the milky cleaner over her knuckles. She raised her fist to slam the counter but thought better of it and let the sponge drop. Her hands went to her head, and she pulled it down and buried her face in the sink. There, in the bleachy hollow, Karl heard her mumble, "Fuck, fuck, fuck."

Karl's head buzzed and his ears rang and things were going dark and he had Rene's small wrist, jerking her around to face him. Her eyes were lit up with fear. He could smell her coffee breath and the sweet stench of her armpits. He didn't understand himself, why he wanted to hurt her. His wife's neck so frail, arms so thin, sternum that he could cave with a stab of a finger. He was trying to say, *What did he do to you?*

She tried to get by him, but he wouldn't allow it. He had her pressed against the counter, could feel her hip bones on his thigh, could feel every other contour of her body through the thin nightgown, and now the anger was mixing with arousal. Was this how his own son felt about his wife? This desire to both punish her and . . . Karl was furious at himself, and he leveled it on Rene, pressing her harder into the counter until her pubic bone was hard on his thigh.

"Move away from me or I'll scream." The venom in her voice, in her eyes, was so convincing that he wilted away from her. She escaped from the kitchen, marching through the family room where he heard her stomp up the stairs.

Karl pounded the countertop, rattling the silverware in the drawer below.

He was of no use at home, that much was clear, so he set the alarm for four thirty a.m., woke the next morning to it, and with the stealth of a burglar, stole out the door. He sat in the truck and started the ignition and thumped the shift into reverse, and then sat there in the dark feeling like a fugitive for going to work. He hadn't informed Rene because he couldn't bear how she would look at him. But he was more anxious about leaving without telling the authorities. It maddened him that he had to run his life by them now. Still, he didn't want to arouse any more of their suspicion. The memory of the last time he was questioned—interrogated, really—still prickled his spine. So he jammed the truck back into park and went into the dark house.

The morning after the abduction—when the boys were still missing—Karl had been summoned very early to the station in the village. Chittenango chief of police, Earl Bell, was there, as was the county sheriff and two FBI detectives. They all crammed themselves around the table of the multipurpose conference room, cluttered with a dusty TV-VCR on a cart, a copy machine, a dry-erase board on wheels, an overhead projector, and, in the corner, a refrigerator and coffee pot and a greasy box of doughnuts from Lynch's bakery.

Karl could see in their eyes, they'd been trying not to reveal that he was a suspect: their overly nice tones, their trying to make him feel relaxed. The FBI suit who seemed to be in charge of questioning had some kind of deformity where he lacked a neck, his ears touching his shirt collar, his double chin pressed against the knot of his tie.

"Just tell us one more time, just go through the day, even if you think something's insignificant."

How many times he had to repeat the story, to go back over every detail of a single moment, testing his memory, quizzing his reliability. An hour in, he remembered new details but withheld them because he didn't want to appear like he was changing his story. How much did they really want to know? That Dean had been angry at Karl that morning because Karl had yelled at Jason for not eating his breakfast? Did he need to reveal that part of the reason he'd left the boys alone was to give Dean some responsibility, Dean whom he felt was overly mothered, too meek, whereas Jason, the younger one, had far more gumption, and Karl did not feel that was right? The older brother should look out for the younger, not the other way around.

What he would not say, what he quickly lied to himself about, changed the truth in his head almost immediately until he mostly believed it, was that when he left the boys, he hadn't even used the bathroom. And then he'd become suddenly afraid in that hot, stale-coffee-and-doughnut-smelling conference room, that someone had seen that Karl never went into the Port-A-John. That he'd only walked to it, and when it was occupied, stood behind it looking at his watch, and occasionally at the group of high school girls and their tanned, toned legs that tauntingly developed before any other part of them.

"How long did you leave them there?"

That accusatory phrasing, everyone using it: Rene, the papers, the news.

He'd left them there.

"Ten minutes. Tops."

"You didn't go anywhere else?"

"No."

"You were in the john for ten minutes?"

Why did it matter? He hadn't kidnapped his own sons. Karl's ears and neck began to get hot.

A little before nine a.m., Chief Bell walked him out to his car. Bell was a short man with hairy arms and a thick blond mustache. He had a reputation for being cruel to teenagers, taking their presence in the village as a personal assault on law and order, or his version of it. Karl had gone to high school with Bell. They'd played varsity basketball together, though it took a lot of figuring to have called them friends. Still, Bell acted the ally.

"Government dicks complicating this whole thing," said Bell, holding open Karl's truck door. "But if you do think of something, call me first, would you? Best to keep this local."

It was Bell who, not a half hour after the questioning, phoned Karl. "We found your boys," was the first thing he said, and Karl's knees quit him and he was on the sticky linoleum floor of the kitchen, so goddamn relieved. Bell must have recognized his mistake, and immediately added, "I'm sorry, Karl. Only one of them made it."

At this point, Rene had snatched the phone, singing hysterically into it. Karl was stunned, pressed to the floor as if being sucked into the center of the earth. His mind was either blank or overloaded, but it dared not try to guess, to wish, which boy had survived. Soon, Rene had joined Karl on the floor, crying into his chest, punching his arm—crying and punching a faraway body—and they remained in that pathetic mound while two suits waited awkwardly in the living room.

A man is fishing in a boat off the southern shore of Oneida Lake. The sun is bright on the lake when he thinks he sees movement in the water. He first thinks it's an otter or beaver, two-headed and strange. When he sees it's boys, he knows instantly that one is dead by the moon-white skin, the eyes unblinking, the open mouth taking water. And the back of the head caved in. The live boy, the one tugging the other along in grunts, does not stop at the boat. The man fishing has to yell down at him, and even then the boy keeps swimming, keeps grunting. The man reaches over the side and grabs his shirt, careful not to tip the boat. Like a wind-up toy, the boy continues his arm stroke, despite the missing water. The man can't hoist him in while he holds the body.

Let go, son.

The boy is spooked. He hollers, flails. The man fishing knows which fish to fight and which to free. When the boy drops back into the water, he continues his slow stroke as though nothing has happened. The man decides to row beside him the rest of the way to the shore. Once there, the boy tries to stand, but his legs, purple and wrinkled, are jellied useless. So he sits his butt onto the stones and tugs the arm of the body until it is up between his legs. Then he moves backward and performs the same pull. A dog has come sprinting and barking from the side of a nearby house. It sniffs the dead boy's head, then screech-barks the primal way dogs do when afraid. The man thinks it might attack, so he swings his oar at the dog, thumps its skull. It runs off twenty yards, stops at a tree, and picks up its desperate barking. The boy continues to move the body one sad foot of ground at a time. The dead one's skin is coming loose at the calves like wet tissue. When its blank eyes happen on his own, the man fishing sprints past the dog toward the house. To call someone. To get away.

Lena Johnson was troubled. If Karl were playing poker with her, he'd have discovered her tell: rolling her gold chain between her thumb and finger. She was weighing her words, testing them in her head, it seemed, before releasing them on Karl. Dean had gone upstairs. Rene hadn't come back down. For a moment, Karl didn't trust the two of them up there alone. But seeing his son climb the stairs, using the railing to pull himself up as though his skinny legs lacked the strength, he was already doubting Rene's story. In any case, he didn't dare tell Lena Johnson what Rene had dared to tell him.

"At first I thought it was regression," she began, still playing with her necklace. "What I've come to find in other kidnapped children is that they refuse to speak about the encounter because it's too painful for them to recall. So they regress to a state of infancy, to a pre-speaking part of their lives. It's a coping mechanism. This, however, is not the case with Dean."

She looked across the table, her eyes weighted in their sockets. There was an open package of Chips Ahoy! between them, which Karl had lamely offered when she asked to talk.

"I'm hesitant to speak too prematurely about this before I review the case with my superiors, but I'm getting the impression that Dean is taking on Jason's identity. For example, he couldn't tell me anything definitive about himself but he was very confident in answering questions about Jason. I can't tell for sure whether he believes he's Jason or if . . ."

She seemed suddenly distracted, looking toward the sink, the overturned canister of Comet.

"What?" Karl urged, restraining his impatience.

"I also get the sense," she continued, "that he's toying with me. Or at least that he's aware of the power he now holds; we want information from him, and he's enjoying withholding it."

Karl muttered, "He's fucking with us." He glanced again at Lena Johnson's eyes, the bags underneath that his son had put there. In only a few hours' time, Dean had wrecked this woman's beauty.

"Mr. Fleming—"

"Karl."

"I doubt very much that his intention is malicious. This may be another way for him to regain some control. We need to remember that he may have witnessed his younger brother's murder, and—"

"Is that what he told you?"

"And according to the witness, Dean was intent on returning Jason's body somewhere. I believe it was back home. Here."

Karl sat back. "Why would he do that?" he asked quietly.

Lena Johnson tipped her head. "Why do you think?"

Pinned to the corkboard above the phone were expired pizza coupons and a calendar that needed its page turned to June, and the boys' school photos. People had always told him that Dean and Jason looked identical, but Karl had never seen it. Dean was narrower, a long neck and face. Jason would always be shorter, but he'd be thicker, stronger, get more girls.

Lena pulled her chair closer, put her elbows on the table and clasped her hands together. Her bracelets clamored on the tabletop. "Karl," she began, and he suddenly regretted suggesting she call him that. "You got to talk to your son."

He felt his heart beating in his throat. She'd think he was staring at her, but he wasn't.

"Hey, I get it," she said. "It ain't the man's job to talk. It ain't easy."

Why was she talking this way? Like she would at home or out with friends?

"But this is something I can help you with. I can mediate between you and Dean. I'll make it painless, I promise."

Karl put his elbows on the table, raked his hands down his face, sighed. The ringing was coming to his ears, competing with Lena Johnson's words. All just words.

"What I'm saying is that I'm here for you, too. This situation puts a strain on the entire household, not just the victim. I firmly believe that if Dean sees you open up, he'll feel more comfortable doing it."

Karl stood up from the table and returned the chair to its appropriate position. He put his hands in the pockets of his jean shorts, showing her that she was mistaken about him, that he could be composed and open-minded about her advice. That he defied the stereotypes of a stubborn, uneducated working-class guy, more complex than what all her degrees and training were trying to reduce him to.

"The problem here is Dean," he said, clear and controlled, "and the fact that there are two dangerous people still out there." He raised his finger, pointing to the kitchen window dusted with pollen. He dared to meet Lena Johnson's eyes, so she could see how serious he was, how stable and sure. There was no resistance to her expression, no condescension either. Instead, she looked tired and sad, like a mother at the bedside of a very sick child, one who might not make it.

Karl's bottom lip twisted and flexed beyond his control. He said *excuse me* or *good day*, something terse, then rushed from the kitchen. He bumped into a suit in the living room. He shoved open the screen door.

A reporter turned from her conversation with a police officer and rushed to Karl. "Mr. Fleming. Please, Mr. Fleming."

Vision blurred as though his eyeballs were coated with Vaseline, Karl pretended to scratch a stubborn itch on his eyebrow, moving quickly to his truck.

"Has your son provided any new information?"

He hurried into the truck and escaped down the road. He got no farther than the vacant high school parking lot two minutes away. There he parked and ducked below the truck's windows just in case, and punched and kicked everything he could reach, and allowed the agony to do what it wanted with his face.

On the morning of June 6, five days after the incident at the Oz Festival, the male abductor turned himself in. His name was Wayne LaFleur. He'd seen the constant alerts on the news and got scared. He'd called up the hotline, said who he was, gave his address—an uncle's house in Oneida—and waited on the front porch drinking a can of Genny Cream Ale. That simple.

Karl wanted to see the man right away. Bell explained that he was being questioned by the FBI, but that he'd get the chance to the following day. In fact, they needed Dean to come by the station to identify Wayne and confirm his confession.

"What about the other one?" Karl asked on the phone. "The lady?"

"He claims he doesn't know where she is. But the dicks won't let him off that easy. And if they do, I'll take a turn on him."

Rene couldn't stand the thought of being near Wayne, and she had remained aloof with Dean. However, she had begun taking him to morning mass at St. Patrick's. But the way she made him sit in the back seat of the station wagon, and how when they got home she rushed out of the car and into the house, leaving him in the back seat, told Karl that this was not her way of reconnecting with Dean. She was simply escorting him to church. He bet that they didn't even sit in the same pew.

Lena Johnson, on the other hand, insisted that she herself accompany Karl and Dean to their meeting with Wayne. This could be a traumatic encounter, and she wanted to be there in case something happened. She didn't specify for whom it would be traumatic.

The three of them drove to the station in Syracuse where Wayne was being detained. Dean was wedged between Karl and Lena Johnson in the front seat of the truck, his bony knee pressed against Karl's leg. Lena was trying to bait Karl into opening up—"Karl, how do you feel about seeing the kidnapper?"—which Karl ignored. Yes, he needed to try to reach out to his son, he knew that, but he wanted to do it on his own. His attempt was, "Hey Dean-O, want to listen to the radio?"

Dean turned the volume knob until the classic rock station became audible, Lynyrd Skynyrd's "Simple Man." Karl nodded and tapped the steering wheel. Dean jammed the next channel button and looked at Karl while he did it. Fucking with him. He then pressed the other buttons, one after another without even waiting to hear what was on them.

"Dean, please," Karl said with restraint. "Just pick one."

So Dean mashed the third button, static. He raised the volume, then sat back and crossed his arms.

Karl could feel Lena Johnson looking. She was expecting him to lose his patience. He proved her wrong, saying nothing, focusing on the road.

The agent without the neck met them in the lobby of the precinct. He said hello to Dean, smiling as though they were pals. He led them down a bright hall, through a security checkpoint where Dean and Karl got visitor badges in exchange for Karl's driver's license. A heavy door buzzed, unlocked with a clang, and they passed through. Karl was aware of the cuts on his hand from the tantrum in the truck. He didn't want to hide them, but neither did he want to showcase them to the agent. The wounds blazed as he kept his hands in his pockets.

The agent stopped at an open door. He had to swivel his shoulders to turn to them. "Don't worry, the man's not in here." He gestured them inside. "We'll be able to watch him through a secret window."

The room was small and dim, a few chairs and a table and that large window looking into the interrogation room, which was empty. His partner was there, sitting on the table, looking like a model from a Sears catalog. He wasn't wearing his jacket and had his sleeves rolled up. He smiled and greeted them.

"What can we get you, Dean?" the handsome one asked. "Chocolate milk? Pepsi?"

"How 'bout a candy bar?" the other offered.

Dean said, "Coffee."

The agents looked at Karl.

"He'll have chocolate milk," Karl said, putting his hand on Dean's shoulder. Dean twisted away.

While Handsome was out, his partner filled them in.

"We'll bring the man into that room. He won't be able to see us. All you have to do, Dean, is say whether he's the bad guy that hurt your brother."

Karl saw Lena Johnson roll her eyes. "If he's the kidnapper," she interpreted without the patronizing tone, "all you have to do is nod yes or no. That's it. Then we can go home."

"Well," the agent fumbled, not looking at Lena, "we might like to ask a few more questions. If you're up for it."

"I'll take you out for ice cream after," Karl said. But the invitation hung thickly in the air like a bad smell. Thankfully, Handsome returned with an armful of drinks and snacks. He unloaded them on the table like confiscated weapons: candy bars and bags of chips, cans of soda and the milk. Nobody made a move for them.

"Are you ready?" Lena Johnson asked Dean.

"Yes," he said, so clear and confident that for a moment, Karl thought there was an older boy in the room.

No-Neck nodded to his partner, who grabbed his jacket before leaving. The others stood watching the window, the barren room on the other side ugly with neon light. The buzzing tension of waiting for the space to be filled, filled with this man who murdered his boy. Panic suddenly ignited Karl's chest. He had not prepared himself for this moment. He'd been preoccupied with Dean, wondering if he'd comply, if he'd be willing and able to identify this Wayne and how he'd react. Karl had to look down at his work boots, fearing the suddenness of Wayne's arrival. He felt like a child on a haunted house ride at the fairgrounds, sitting in the cart on the tracks waiting to be thrust into the dark, keeping his eyes on his feet to endure the upcoming fright.

And then came a hand on his back, a little tug on his shirt. It was Lena Johnson, reaching from the other side of Dean. It was just a touch, and when he turned to her, a reassuring nod. When he looked back at the window, Wayne was there.

He was as he should be, nothing new or extraordinary about him. It was as if Karl had cast him in the role, and the man simply assumed position. This Wayne looked the part of a white trash abductor of children. His hair was slicked back off his wide forehead. He was thin but strong, arms and neck roped with veins. There were the obligatory blue, homemade tattoos etched on his wrists and hands and running up into the short sleeves of the khaki jumper.

The handsome agent stood behind Wayne, pointing to a place on the floor where he wanted him to stand. This was directly in front of the window.

"Is he in there?" Wayne asked over his shoulder, keeping his small eyes on the window. "The boy, is he there?"

"Christ, Steve," No-Neck muttered as if his partner could hear. "Get him out of there."

"The hell is he doing?" Lena Johnson said to the agent, pulling Dean close to her.

"He's there, isn't he?" Wayne continued. He then moved toward the window. The agent grabbed his shoulder, and that was what set Wayne off. He lunged toward them, shouting through a gummy, toothless mouth. "I'm sorry! I'm sorry! I didn't want to kill him."

The agent-in-charge was out the door and, a second later, in the adjacent room, swiftly getting Wayne in a rear choke hold. Wayne kicked and screamed, and then two officers were there to help.

On this side of the glass, a similar scene played out. Karl was pulling Dean away from the window, Lena Johnson assisting. Dean was laughing and fighting. He kicked at the window. Karl lifted Dean from behind, squeezing to restrain his wild son. He remembered what Rene had said. *He was strong.* He kicked and flailed and screeched, and Lena Johnson took a sneaker to her chest. She was on the floor at the same time that Dean tossed his head back and smashed Karl's chin. Dean rushed to the window, pounded the glass, hollered inside.

"Come back!"

But the room was empty.

It was Wayne who provided the only details of the abduction. They were mostly unconfirmed, however, since Dean still refused to cooperate. But Karl took the narrative as fact.

Wayne's partner stole the boys away from the festival, drugged them, then put them in the trunk of her car. Wayne then met her at one of the long-abandoned summer cottages that vacationers used to rent in the fifties. There they intended on keeping only one of the boys. She liked the more docile of the brothers; the other she didn't like for his feistiness. Wayne took this one into a separate room, gave him a cupcake, and while he was eating it, brought an aluminum baseball bat down on the back of his skull.

Wayne remained stubborn in his refusal to out the lady, presumably his wife. No amount of bargaining or threatening would get him to reveal any identifying information. He wouldn't even say whether she had survived the stabbing, which seemed to madden the officers the most. But he came clean on everything else, including the location of the lake house.

The FBI and local authorities scoured the cottage, substantiating half of his story. They'd found the aluminum bat, the sack with the rocks, even the scissors. What they didn't find was any trace of the woman, no fingerprints or blood, not even a strand of her hair. Wayne explained that he scrubbed everything clean with bleach in the way he'd seen on TV. Any evidence that might have been on Dean or Jason had been washed off in the long swim through Oneida Lake. Wayne didn't want her found. Asked repeatedly why he was protecting her, he said simply that he loved her.

Lena Johnson had carefully reviewed Wayne's account with Dean, but he wouldn't say one way or the other whether any of it was true. Luckily, they had enough evidence to convict Wayne without Dean's assistance.

What stuck with Karl the most was how Dean, in order to escape, had stabbed his captor. While this detail concerned Lena Johnson, since it exacerbated Dean's potential psychological damage, Karl was optimistic: with his back up against the wall, his son had found it in him to fight back.

Things had gotten quiet around the house since Wayne turned himself in. The news vans and police cruisers were no longer parked in the street, and the suits had removed their recording equipment. Lena Johnson still came by in the afternoon to talk to Dean, though she'd given Rene the number of a child psychologist in Syracuse, suggesting that she, too, was moving on.

With the house empty save for Rene and Dean, Karl decided it was time to return to work.

Not two days later, Chief Bell showed up at Mohawk Steel & Die. Karl was in his office talking to a distributor on the phone while looking out the window, down on the factory. That was when he saw Bell walking the lane between the giant stamping and punching machines, turning his head left to right, oblivious to the overhead crane in operation. No one, not even a cop, was allowed near the machines without a hard hat or goggles. If injured, Karl would be in a shitload of trouble. He hung up the phone and hurried down the steps, then brought Bell back up to the office where they could hear each other.

"The dicks are moving on with the investigation," Bell said. He refused to sit, and there wasn't much space in the cluttered office to move around, though he tried. He seemed hopped-up on too much caffeine or something stronger. "They're not closing the case until the lady's body is found, but as far as they're concerned, it's cold."

"What does that mean?"

"It means," Bell said defensively, "that I think that lady is still alive."

Karl had been uncoiling a paper clip, but this stopped him.

"A mortal stab wound bleeds like a fucking faucet," Bell continued. "Maybe that asshole scrubbed inside the cabin, but what about outside? The porch steps, the grass, the driveway to the car? There should be more blood, but there wasn't. And since nobody else wants to admit that she ain't dead, it's on me to find out . . . and you."

"What can I do?" Karl offered as innocently as possible.

"I'm glad you asked." Bell sat down. "We need a legitimate detail to jumpstart the case. A name, just a first name, would be best. But details about her face would be good, too. An identifying mole, tattoo, something like that."

There were witnesses at the festival who had claimed to see the woman, but the only details they could agree on was that she had brown hair and was overweight. One report had her dressed as Dorothy. Another said she wore a purple nightgown. Someone thought she was crying. No one remembered her face.

"Haven't we tried that already?" Karl asked. At least twice that he remembered, an officer put a binder in front of Dean that contained pictures of different types of eyes, noses, mouths, and hair. You could match various combinations of these facial features to create the composite of a face. Dean had flipped the pages around for a while until he'd produced a ridiculous, mixed-race amalgam of features.

"Yes, but Dean hasn't been to the cottage yet."

Karl looked at Bell's illusion of a mustache, so blond it could be mistaken for a swollen upper lip.

"I want to bring your boy to the scene, see if that jogs his memory."

Karl fiddled with the paper clip. He shook his head and smiled. "That FBI lady would not be okay with that."

"You're going to listen to what some black *bitch* says about your boy? She don't care about you. She don't know how we do things here. Maybe that's what they do in the city, where those people kill each other every night. Out here we got to teach our boys different, to stare down their demons so they don't follow them along the rest of their lives."

Karl was hung up on what Bell had called Lena Johnson. He hadn't called her the other word, but he probably wanted to. In no way was Karl innocent of thinking or even saying racist things. If he scoured his conscience, he'd find that he didn't really like black people. There were very few in Chittenango, and only a small percentage of the employees at Mohawk were black. But the experiences he had with them confirmed the stereotypes.

Still, Bell's disrespect of Lena Johnson was uncalled for. As for the other thing, the facing of demons, that point held some traction.

Bell leaned forward, put his eyes too hard on Karl's. "Aren't you afraid that the kidnapper is out there looking for another kid to snatch? I know other parents who are. You should spend an afternoon in the station. The amount of phone calls I get about whether this lady's been caught. Mothers who don't want their kids walking to school no more. Who don't want them going to the goddamn park. Pat Pratt talked my ear off for an hour saying we couldn't have no more events in Chittenango until we find that lady. The prick'll make sure that happens, too. No more music or carnivals or goddamn bake sales on the church lawn." Bell put his hands on Karl's desk. "Look, nobody blames you for leaving your boys alone. But dammit, if we don't get Dean to talk, I don't know what they'll say."

It was then that Karl remembered a basketball practice back in high school. At over six feet, Karl had played center. Bell was point guard, quick as hell and a marvel handling the ball. Bell had dribbled into the lane and was trying to get a shot up over Karl, who wouldn't fall for Bell's tricks. Bell got frustrated, lowered his shoulder into Karl's stomach to create space, then shot a fade-away jumper that went in. Karl charged Bell, cocked his fist back ready to pound his smart-ass face. But the coach stepped in. Bell smiled at Karl from behind the coach, taunting, a look Karl could still see now, especially now.

Karl could hear Rene's light snoring from the hall. She was asleep on an air mattress in the playroom, a tiny, awkwardly angled space in the corner of the house where the boys played Nintendo. He'd many times offered to switch—give her the master—but she ignored him, her way of aggravating his guilt. Karl continued to Dean's room, pushed the door open cautiously, not sure what he might find. He found nothing. Two perfectly made beds. He wasn't nervous, not yet, but his frayed, practiced nerves were at the ready. He noticed the bathroom door was closed. He only got it open an inch when it met an obstruction. His heart thumped in his throat. He reached the light switch, and there was an elbow on the floor. Karl pushed the door open, and Dean groaned and scratched his nose. A quick scan of the tile floor confirmed he was only sleeping. Still, Karl's heart was going fast.

"Hey Dean-O."

Dean opened his eyes.

"Let's go," Karl whispered. "I'm taking you to church this morning."

Dean blinked. "Why?"

"Just because. Come on."

Dean leaned on him as Karl helped him stand. His face was still stained by sleep, and he stood on shaky legs, rubbing his eyes. Karl put his hand on his small shoulders and noted that Dean didn't jerk away.

"Do you need to pee before we go?"

Dean nodded. He pushed his mesh shorts down in the front and sprayed the seat before finding the bowl. Karl fought the urge to say something. But while Dean was in this state of waking, he allowed Karl to be his dad. Karl didn't want to interrupt that.

Karl picked Bell up at his house, which was in one of the newer neighborhoods up past the high school. Three days had passed since their conversation at Mohawk. While Karl had been convinced almost immediately of Bell's point, he didn't want to appear that he'd given in to him so readily.

Bell came out wearing plainclothes: a pair of jeans, gray sweatshirt, Syracuse Orange hat, and sneakers. He looked smaller than he did in his uniform. He climbed into the station wagon, didn't acknowledge Karl, but tossed a greeting into the back seat. Karl spied Dean's reaction in the rearview. He lifted his head off the window, squinted his eyes at Bell.

"Where are we going?" Dean asked, for the first time.

"Your dad is giving me a lift to the lake."

Karl's face went hot. He didn't want Bell to speak for him.

"I don't want to go there." Dean sounded like the boy he was only one week ago.

"Don't worry about it," was all Bell said, looking to Karl to drive.

"I don't want to go there."

Karl's hand remained on the shift.

"Come on already," Bell said.

Karl put it in reverse and headed toward Route 5.

What he had told himself last night, and was repeating to himself now, was that this was for Dean's own good, and the good of all other children in the area. It was unfortunate that Bell was the voice of this rationale. It was even worse that he was sacrificing his relationship with Lena Johnson, since she would find out somehow—she wasn't stupid—and when she did . . .

But Dean had to confront his fear and help catch the lady, because Karl couldn't begin fantasizing about going back in time to that moment and doing things differently.

A breath of steam hovered over the lake. It had rained the night before, leaving the tall grass and trees beaded and heavy. The sun dazzled the wet leaves and spider webs and wild flowers that crowded the gravel road. The brush was so overgrown, they missed their turn. There was no space for a turnaround, so Karl had to reverse, tossing his arm behind Bell's seat, cranking his neck to see out the back window. He caught a glimpse of Dean, who had his eyes on his lap. Karl also noticed that Dean was sitting behind the passenger seat, where Jason always sat. For a terrifying moment, with the boy's head down and just his dark, straight hair visible, he thought it was Jason.

Karl slammed on the brakes. The boy's head popped up, and it was Dean. Karl's heart slammed so hard, from his ears to the bottoms of his feet, that for a few seconds, he couldn't catch his breath. Bell shot him a look. Karl couldn't speak to explain. He continued to reverse, trying to avoid looking at Dean.

Karl found the turn. This road was even narrower. Gravel popped under the tires, branches groped at the side windows. They passed a number of identical cottages, each varying in decrepitude, a few so neglected they'd sunk in on themselves like shrunken faces. Yellow police tape told which was theirs. Bell got out to unknot the tape from a tree so Karl could park in the front. This was the first time Karl had been here. He'd imagined a bigger house, an old Victorian with lots of rooms, furniture covered in dusty white blankets. This, however, was the size of a detached garage, a front porch that could fit a straight chair and nothing more.

Bell opened the door to the back seat. "We're here," he said to Dean, as if here was Disney World.

Head down, Dean looked like he was dozing or praying.

"Come on," said Bell.

Karl finally got out and told Bell over the roof to give him a minute.

"Just pick him up and carry him in."

Karl stuck out his chin and held Bell's small, green eyes until the officer looked away. Bell took off his hat to swat at a cloud of gnats in front of his face. He jammed the hat back on and walked toward the cottage.

Karl opened the back door.

"Hey, Dean-O. We're just going to pop in for a second, okay?"

"I don't want to," Dean said to his lap.

"It'll be fine. I'll be right next to you."

"No."

The overgrown grass licked Karl's calves, leaving him chilled.

"Are you afraid?"

This sounded so stupid; it was why Karl never talked in this way. Trying to explain feelings was impossible, pointless. They weren't meant to be explained, just felt, and anyway, he didn't have the vocabulary for it. When he tried, it sounded too obvious. Of course his son was afraid, why make him say it? Of course Karl was angry, at his family, at God. Of course he despised his wife. Of course he wanted to leave her. Of course it was his fault . . . all of it.

All of it.

Then Lena Johnson arose like a specter from the murk. There wasn't a message she had, no memory of a profound statement she'd made. It wasn't even a picture of her face. It was just her, the lemon-vanilla gush of warmth and light in his chest, slinking down to his stomach.

"Goddammit," Bell shouted from the porch. "I'll take him in if you can't do it."

Karl got into the back seat. His hand found Dean's knee, dry and prickled with tiny hairs losing their down.

"I killed your brother." Once it was said, Karl forced himself to repeat it, like a teenager who'd finally worked up the nerve to say he loved a girl and he wanted to say it again, and again, before the opportunity was gone. "I killed your brother." His face fell onto Dean's head. There was a smell to his hair. Something like honey and dog. It wasn't entirely pleasant, but it was familiar. Familiar, maybe, because Karl could finally see that Jason had known the scent of his brother better than anything else. Jason wore Dean's hand-me-downs from the day he was born, and so that smell was his entire universe. "I killed your brother."

A slamming door made them both jump. Bell had entered the cottage, the screenless screen door bouncing on the frame.

The jarring noise or Karl's blunt announcement or some other mysterious willful source compelled Dean to cry. And even though Dean's sobs were violent, a spite directed at Karl, accompanied by "hate you, hate you" with strong bone-fists, it was enough to open the floodgates in Karl, to dampen his son's hair with snot and tears while restraining him with an embrace, to change Dean's smell into something new and strange, unrecognizable to anyone other than his father.

WHERE THE WATER

RUNS NORTH

Winter, 2001

—◆—

THE EGG HUNG IN the morning air as though winter had frozen it midflight. It had funneled through the fog of marijuana smoke that ghosted over Chittenango Creek. Brett peered into this smoky cone and saw through it, on the opposite bank, a slowed-down Dean, unwinding frame-by-frame from his pitcher's hurl. He could clearly see the tattoos peeking out from Dean's coat sleeve. He could clearly see Dean's chapped lips and the mouth twisted into a crooked smile. This was Brett's moment of peace, before the world tipped into its sudden violence, and the rock-hard, frozen egg crashed into Brett's face.

The pain blazed; every inch of him sizzled. He was positive his head was halved like a melon. He writhed on the ground and held his face together. His legs flopped and thrashed as he swam in the bloody slush.

Dean was laughing. Brett heard the scrunch of his retreating footsteps. Then silence. Footsteps coming, and Dean's voice was above him.

"Don't be a pussy. Get up." Dean kicked his leg. "Come on, you're not hurt bad." Dean's breathing trembled Brett's nerves like thunder. "You better not tell your dad. Or you're dead."

Then Dean was gone. There was only the burble of water slithering beneath crisps of ice. Brett didn't want to move. He would allow his body to empty itself into the creek and curse it.

Then, a voice fell down on him. It was a girl's "Hey," shrill enough to cut through the cloud of oncoming unconsciousness. But it was familiar, part of the soundtrack of his neighborhood.

"Hey." A dog barked, and Brett knew.

Angela Ruggero struggled down the steep bank, cursing Cauliflower too freely for a twelve-year-old. "Come on you bitchass dog or I'll punt you into the cocksucking creek."

Don't touch me, drummed in Brett's head, hoping it was loud enough for her to hear. He felt a damp nose chilling his ear, wet hairs tickling his cheek.

"Get the fuck back," and Cauliflower yelped. A pressure on his shoulder warmed him through. "Brett?" Her voice was suddenly silk threaded, as if another girl spoke for her. "Can you hear me? Hello?"

He thudded his boot to the ground over and over, meaninglessly. She must have given it meaning; she tugged at the shoulders of his coat, grunting, the dog nosing the back of his head.

"No," Brett managed to say.

"You'll freeze." Angela yanked his chest off the snow. Her strength was unbelievable, and again, he wondered if there were two girls. "Fucking help me, goddammit."

Brett put his arms under him in a push-up. Once on his knees, he expected his head to roll off his shoulders and shatter. The damage was unknowable, other than the blood goring an unsettling circumference in the snow, like the inksplot of a giant pen.

Brett was on his feet, though unsteady. Cauliflower was lapping at the red snow, his white muzzle crimsoned like a clown. Brett felt Angela holding him, guiding him up the slope.

"How bad is it?" Brett asked.

"It's steep."

"No, my face."

As if he were a camera, her head came into frame, a close-up. Her grayish eyes squinted; her narrow nose scrunched. Puberty was shaping her—a zit on her forehead, a thickening of her eyebrows, the thinning of her cheeks. The end of a fat, brown braid was in her mouth. When she spoke, it remained tucked in her cheek like Skoal.

"You look like a caveman," she said. "I think it's an improvement."

Cauliflower led the charge up the bank, fighting against the leash's length. Brett focused on Angela's breathing, the occasional grunt. When he stumbled, she jerked him up and cussed. They reached the top, but they still had Russell Street hill to climb. Brett's face had gone numb. Blood leaked off his nose and chin, speckling the snow. He drifted in and out, held fast to Angela's shoulder.

He thought of last summer, a neighborhood picnic when their block was closed off and neighbors grilled hot dogs and Italian sausages in the street, and macaroni salad had warmed in the sun, and the baked beans had strips of burnt bacon in it, and the jello had walnuts and fruit. Angela was all girl then, round-faced and squealy. She rode her bike swinging a sparkler in the twilight. Brett chased her on his bike—one of the last times he would ride. They'd circled the adults who were drinking their Gennys. At the end of the block, Brett cut her off, rammed his tire into hers, and sent her hurling over the handlebars. When she caught sight of her palms and wrists, slashed and bloodied, she began to cry. Brett took off toward his house, where he locked himself in his room and waited to get an earful from his dad.

He hadn't spoken to her since but often wondered about the extent of her scars—whether they would look like a suicide attempt, and how that would alter her. Whether from here on, people would see her as tortured.

They were on his doorstep. He couldn't remember getting there. Cauliflower was chewing bald a patch just above his tail.

Angela asked, "Is your dad home?"

When she again came into his camera view, one side of her knit hat and face were slathered red. She didn't seem to notice, or care. A fantastic tickle flooded Brett's chest, as though someone had opened a liter of soda inside him.

She snapped her fingers in his face. "Hello? Caveman?"

"You're picking at it again." Brett's dad dropped another package of oyster crackers into his clam chowder. "Didn't the doctor tell you to leave it alone?"

Brett sighed and crashed his arm on the table, bouncing the silverware. The fat, stitched wound zippering up from the tip of his nose into his hairline had given him the habit. Like chewing the inside of his mouth or stabbing the tender skin at his thumbnail, pressing the hardening scar sent a dazzle into his brain.

He looked out the drafty window of Auntie Em's Café. Across the street, outside the pizzeria, loitered three kids he knew from high school. They all three lived in Mohawk Manor, the nearby trailer park, and seemed to hang out together for that singular reason. One was a girl, a ninth grader who had gotten her boobs early and wasn't sure how to handle the attention. The other two were seniors, jocks from the wrestling team who were in opposite weight classes. The large one snuck behind, bear-hugged the girl, and lifted her off the ground. She tossed her head back and laughed, but tried to wriggle free. The small one grabbed for her legs, but she kicked at him.

"What is this?" Brett asked the drafty window. "This place, these people?"

"You're not going to eat your chowder?" His dad took another bite, his jaw clicking louder than the crackers he crunched. His bald, orange-fuzzy temples collapsed and bulged at each chew.

Brett put his face over the snotty bowl of soup. He stirred it to release its steam and inhaled. There was no smell. He dipped a spoon into it and licked. There was no taste either, just hot, slimy cream coating his tongue. Brett eyed the other patrons in the poorly lit café, gnashing their burgers and fries and special-of-the-day shepherd's pie. They ate ferociously, grease glistening their lips and fingers, mouths so full their cheeks ballooned like horn players.

Brett pushed the soup away. "Hurry up so we can go."

"Will do," his dad said, lowering his bald head closer to the bowl. He looked up suddenly. "Are you in pain?" He reached into the Rite Aid bag that was in the chair next to him and retrieved an orange bottle. "This'll make you feel better." He placed a Percocet beside Brett's Coke. Then he lifted Brett's chowder and brought it carefully to his side.

"Sandy?" he called to the pear-shaped waitress, rolling silverware into napkins at a nearby table. "Can I get some more crackers, please?"

"No problem, Mr. Mayor."

She said it with a touch of irony, but his dad didn't notice. He seemed pleased when people announced his position in the village, as if being the mayor of a tired, forgotten place like Chittenango was the pinnacle of existence.

"Take your pill."

Sandy came by and one-by-one placed the packages down on the table.

"Why? So I can be numb like everyone else here?"

"What're you talking about?"

"Not to mention Mom."

"Your mother was just experimenting."

Brett blew air from the side of his mouth. "Okay, Patrick."

His dad wiped his lips with a napkin. "I've been meaning to talk to you about your . . . incident."

"Incident."

"The doctor told me that you don't get an injury like that from falling. He said it looked like someone threw something at you. And I have a good idea who did."

Across the street, the second boy managed to restrain the girl's legs, holding her like a wheelbarrow. The jocks swung the girl. She was laughing, "No." She squirmed so hard she fell to the sidewalk. She hid her face between her knees. The smaller one put his hand on her shoulder. The girl snapped, hurled fists at him. She stood, then punched the bigger one three times in the arm, and ran off.

"He's a menace, Brett. Why you hang around with him is beyond me. I want you to stay away from him, understand?"

The jocks shoved their hands in their coat pockets and didn't look at each other.

"If you just admit that it was him, I could probably put him in jail."

"Of course you could. Medicate your son and lock up anyone who causes you problems. I wouldn't expect anything less."

Brett sat back in his chair. He pulled his sweatshirt's hood over his head and tucked it behind his ears like a girl does with hair. Brett had the sensation of being alone in a dark theater, watching his life on a movie screen.

"Come on, Brett." His dad delivered the lines predictably. "Just tell me it was him."

Brett examined his deformity in the bathroom mirror while masturbating. His reconstructed nose was purple and bloated, halved by a centipede of black stitches. His eyes were a pus color underneath, and the whites were like shit stain. His shiny-swollen brow did, in fact, resemble a caveman's.

He ejaculated without orgasm.

Brett leaned his forehead onto the mirror, pressing the thick, other-feeling wound against the cold glass until his head tingled. Light swarmed behind his eyelids, lasers and orbs. There was wisdom in pain, he was realizing. Perhaps like an incantation, it could deliver him from adolescence, where he had begun to believe he didn't belong. It was embarrassing that he fell into the category of teenager, all those moronic movies and commercials and music videos targeted at him. There were decades to go, it seemed, before he'd put behind him this miserable demographic.

He left the bathroom, snuck across the hall so his dad wouldn't notice, and went into his bedroom. He circled the cramped space, three or four times, like something caged. There was an overwhelming, unnamable desperation. He looked to his desk for answers: empty Skoal canisters, unopened textbooks, tattered and dog-eared paperbacks of Leibniz and Wittgenstein. He homed in on a protractor, pens, and lighter. He sat and snapped a pen in half. He blew clean an ashtray, then emptied black ink into it. He lit the pointed end of the protractor with the lighter, blackening the silver. The underside of his left arm was soft and pink. He pressed the point into the skin just below the wrist until the flesh popped and blood bubbled. His hand shook as he dragged the needle through. He then lifted the point, punctured a different spot near the other, and tore a second line. His arm burned as if set aflame. Blood slithered in rivulets. He sopped it with a pair of boxers, then smeared the ink into the cuts. He repeated the design on the other wrist. When he was finished, he laid his two arms on the desk, admiring the two emblazoned xs.

Brett returned to the creek in search of Dean, the first time since the "incident" one week ago. It was early morning, the snow on the banks glowing purple. Normally, Brett would meet Dean here for their morning routine—smoking a bowl of mediocre weed, then enjoying a refreshing tobacco dip on their walk to school. Today, Brett sat under the bridge on the cold cement landing and packed a bowl, though he had no intention of smoking. He wanted to remain clearheaded now—avoid numbness whenever he could. He scratched through his coat at the crusting tattoos. He was eager to show them to Dean, an ink enthusiast, who'd begun his collection with similar homemade etchings.

Instead of the Skoal, he lit a stale cigarette he'd found in a forgotten quarter pack in his sock drawer. The bowl was for Dean.

There remained evidence of the assault, if it could be called that. It looked like a deer had been slaughtered—brown-red smudge and the imprint of a carcass. There was no drip-trail up the bank, which Brett took to mean a part of him hadn't survived.

He couldn't say he was surprised about what Dean had done to him, considering his history. Still, Brett had always thought himself an exception to Dean's erratic behavior and wanted to see him again to know how true that was.

Growing up, Brett had known Dean was different—somewhat dangerous—and that he should be left alone. Dean loitered at the Byrne Dairy, stealing money from the kids who came with hopes of buying candy and soda. He had been known to break into cars, and one time the high school, where he spray painted his name across the basketball court. He set the maintenance building at Sullivan Park on fire, which nearly ignited the forest.

No one at Chittenango High got close to Dean, who was a second-time senior, inching on twenty years old. Brett, a woeful, fifteen-year-old ninth grader, was the closest thing to a friend Dean had and, most likely, vice versa. This might have had something to do with Brett's dad, and the fact that Chief Bell had to turn his head away from Brett's public marijuana use, and therefore, Dean's. Brett hoped this was not the case—that Dean saw something else. Maybe it was that Brett reminded Dean of his brother. Brett would like it if that were the case but now feared it wasn't.

Ten years ago, Dean and his little brother had been abducted. The story—now part of Chittenango lore—went that Dean managed to rescue his brother's body, swimming him two miles through the lake. When Dean appeared on his parents' doorstep in the early morning, cradling his wet, stiff brother, he'd apparently said—though Brett had his doubts about this—"We're home."

There was a side of Dean, however, that only Brett saw, or so he wanted to think. Sometimes, out of nowhere, Dean seemed to revert back to a younger self. Brett knew it was happening when Dean got a soft, wet-eyed look, and wouldn't speak for a while. He'd appear lost and quietly frightened, as though he had suddenly found himself in a different time. What triggered this shift Brett didn't know, but he liked to think that Dean was gifted, like a troubled superhero, with the ability to move through his own history with a simple glance back or forward. Dean usually came out of this trance by punching Brett in the arm or recruiting him to vandalize something. Or, just as often, Dean would leave unannounced, as if Brett had never been there.

Out of boredom, Brett stood and began searching for the egg that had damaged him. He raked his boot across the surface of the snow, which scattered like billions of sand-sized crystals. This meant it was getting warmer—the first sign that winter might actually pass. He found nothing but some pinkish slush. So he climbed the slope, crossed the bridge, and descended to the other creek bank. There, he found a cache of eggs, plugged into a mound of snow in a neat, violent row, as orderly as they would appear in their carton. Brett plucked one out, harder somehow than rock. What had given Dean the idea to freeze and weaponize eggs? Would he have hurled one at the first person who came down here to the creek, or had Dean been waiting for Brett specifically?

He wound up and whipped the egg across the creek, aiming for his old self. The egg smacked into the bridge's support and then thumped to the ground, whole but dented.

"Get up, you pussy," Brett called in a different pitch. "You're not hurt."

He grabbed another one and hurled it harder.

"You better not tell your dad or I'll kill you."

There were many more eggs, and endless self-loathing, but no more time.

He climbed the bank and left the packed bowl for Dean.

His first day back to school was torturous. When he passed girls in the hall, they scurried from him, gag-laughing. The guys treated him like a minor celebrity, crowding his locker and seeking details of the assault as if he had fingered one of the girls from the JV soccer team. Where once Brett would have been thrilled by this attention, today he was repulsed. He might have hurled at them an old favorite: *You think, therefore I am not.*

Dean hadn't shown. He wasn't in the corner of the school parking lot where the smokers smoked and compared butterfly knives. Nor was he lifting his baggy jeans over his butt in the back of the football field, where the chain-link fence divided school grounds from the cemetery, the designated spot for fights. On the way home, Brett walked by the Byrne Dairy, then the creek again—but there was no sign. The bowl hadn't been touched.

He did, however, see Angela.

She was at the top of Russell Street, tugging at Cauliflower, who was chewing his ass. When Brett saw her, he stopped, considered turning back. But she looked up. He pulled his hood down as far as it could go and tucked it behind his ears. He walked past her—Cauliflower nipping his boot laces—and said, "Hey."

"Hey?" she said. "I save your cockass and all you can say is 'Hey'?"

Brett stopped. The cool gray of her eyes seemed to reflect into her hair, giving it an unnaturally silver tint.

"Want to lick my scar?"

"Gross."

He smiled, and she quickly added, "Maybe I'll French kiss it instead."

Brett laughed before he could call it back. He didn't like to laugh.

Cauliflower saw a squirrel and growled. The dog darted for it, but Angela yanked so hard Cauliflower somersaulted. She crouched down, grabbed his muzzle, and said, "I hate you, fucking dog." Cauliflower got hold of the fingertip of her glove and pulled. "Goddamn stupid cockbitching . . . ," and that was all she had.

"So you're a dog person."

"He's Trent's dog." She put the icy-stiff end of her pigtail in her mouth and sucked. "He just got him, but he's too lazy to take care of him."

Trent was Angela's mother's boyfriend who had moved in a year ago. He worked nights tending bar at the Ten Pin. During the day he drank beers in the garage while painting historical murals of the village for the upcoming bicentennial. These were commissioned by none other than Brett's dad, who—like everyone else in the neighborhood— had noticed Trent's skill with the brush.

"Why don't you let me take care of Cauliflower?"

Angela squinted.

"I'll tie his leash to the bridge and toss him over. It'll look like a suicide."

Her eyes got wide—with more light, the gray turned green. She said, "We could give him some TUMS, see if his stomach explodes."

"Pour honey into his ears, then dump fire ants inside," Brett added. "Watch him get eaten inside out."

"Dip his paws in gasoline and set them on fire. See how fast he runs before burning up."

Brett was in love.

Cauliflower had his leg up in the air and was licking his fuzzy prick.

"Well?" Brett said.

"Well what?"

"Which is it going to be?"

She sucked hard at her pigtail, tired eyes staring at the curb.

"Trent gives me ten bucks a week to look after Shit-for-Brains," she said. "I'm not going to off my only source of income, not in this economy."

Again, Brett laughed. A twelve-year-old who watched the news? He wanted to make a joke about the foot-and-mouth disease in England but couldn't piece one together. What remained was an awkward space to fill. A car drove by and a high school jerk leaned out the window. "Fuck her in the butt!"

Cauliflower barked, which, for once, was welcomed.

"I gotta go," Brett said.

"Yeah." Then Angela added when Brett's back was turned, "If you think of other ways to torture a dog, let me know."

"Will do." Brett cringed at his father's stupid expression. He wished he had asked her about her wrists, if she in fact was scarred, if she looked like a suicide victim. He could have shown her his tattoos, a kind of overdue apology that she just might understand.

March came, which usually meant another month of snow. But long icicles fanged from the roof and dripped. Snow water streamed down the street and into gutters. Patches of lawn were visible. Thawing winter always reminded Brett of St. Patrick's Day as a boy, when he propped rocks with sticks around the yard and baited them with saltine crackers in hopes of trapping a leprechaun.

Brett sat on the sofa looking out the bay window at Trent, who was in his garage drinking beer and preparing his paints. Cauliflower was in his pen next to a space heater, gnawing on rawhide. Without being able to hear it, Brett knew that Trent was listening to a classic rock CD—Rush or Van Halen. Trent squeezed paint onto a dinner plate while rocking out. He wore a red grilling apron as a smock, and black, fingerless weightlifting gloves. Two cigarettes were tucked under a frayed Buffalo Bills knit hat. Trent downed the rest of his Genny and belched. Cauliflower barked weakly at the rude interruption.

Trent's favorite subject used to be dogs set against woodsy landscapes, which Brett deemed as little more than paint by numbers. Now, his focus was horses pulling carriages down dirt roads, men and women in nineteenth century clothes, babies in spoke-wheeled prams. Brett found these depictions of Chittenango impossible to believe. Where were the Deans of that time, the Bretts?

Trent was about to put the brush to the wide, blank canvas when Brett's dad pulled into the driveway. He got out of the car and called hello across the street. Trent ignored him.

"Okay then," Patrick said. His awkward smile turned into a frown, and he barged through the front door, yelling for Brett.

"Right here."

"Oh." He regained his anger by positioning himself before the couch and putting his hands on his hips. "What the hell's gotten into you?"

"Should I answer that or wait for the rest of your act?"

"Dammit, Brett." He kicked the leg of the coffee table, knocking over a vase of fake tulips. He began gathering the dusty flowers but then righted himself. "I was in the middle of an important conference call, and I had to drop everything to talk to your principal." Patrick waited, tipping his bald head forward, and then continued, "She said you were cutting up your arms in class. Is that true?"

In reply, Brett took off his hooded sweatshirt and displayed his arms. The *x*s on his wrists were scabbed, but fresh, oozing lines of bloodied ink extended the length of his forearms like rivers on a map.

They'd been discussing *Huck Finn* in class, and Brett, sitting in the back, felt himself dissipating. He imagined being a storm cloud, emptying itself of its moisture, then thinning out, becoming air. He could have stood up from his desk and walked out. But he needed the immediate reminder, the grounding of pain, to secure him back to his body. He'd bent a paper clip back and forth until it broke in half, leaving a jagged tip. He'd made the first line without anyone noticing. During the second, the nodding-off girl who sat beside him screamed and leapt from her desk. Miss Cavallo hurried to investigate, but upon seeing Brett's arm, she had to sit her wide butt on the floor to keep from fainting. By that point, Brett was alive again.

His father brought his hand to his mouth. "What in the hell's gotten into you?"

"You already used that line." Brett returned his attention to Trent, who had painted something chocolate brown along the bottom of the canvas.

"I don't know what to do with you anymore," he heard his dad say. "I think I'm going to have to call your mother."

This got Brett's attention.

"I'll ask her to come stay for a few days," Patrick continued, emboldened. "She might know how to get through to you."

"That's a stupid idea," Brett said. "Don't invite that woman here."

His dad went to the phone, pretending not to hear.

"Patrick."

He dialed.

"Dad. Think about what you're doing. She's toxic."

Their eyes met, and Brett thought he might have gotten through to him. Too late. His dad's tone went an octave higher: "Hi, Karen?"

Brett pressed his hot, throbbing scar to the cold windowpane.

Brett woke to his windowsill pillowed with six inches of snow. Heavy flakes fell as though the clouds had exploded into pieces. People would soon be out in this, pre-coffee, heavy coats thrown over pajamas, armed with shovels as their cars warmed to escape for work.

Someone trudged through the street, phantomed by the flakes that whitewashed his form. Cigarette dangling from lips, the long skeleton stride, the hoisting of jeans up over the butt—it was Dean.

Brett scrambled to get his clothes on. He'd still yet to see Dean since the assault, let alone speak to him, and that lack of communication grew more torturous by the day. The extent of his yearning confused him. There was nothing he could compare it to. But he thought, he hoped, he'd be given some clarity now.

He darted to the front door, jammed his feet into his boots, and stumbled outside before they were fully on. The falling snow made a curtain of white and gray, impossible to see a distance. He high-stepped down the driveway to the street. Dean's boot tracks were already filling. Brett hurried after them, but the flakes were dizzying. He could no longer tell which direction was which, whether his house was behind him, or if it was ahead. The immediate scent of cigarette smoke made him expect to collide into Dean at any moment. He called to him, but the snow muffled his voice as if he had yelled into a pillow. Tried again, and thought he heard a response. The deep snow thwarted his attempts to run, tripping him, taking him down. His bare hands were hot with cold. Brett tried to get up, but he felt cemented. In the swirling white ahead, there might have been a form, and it might have been coming, or going.

When she came into the house, not three days after his dad phoned her, his mother wore movie-star sunglasses, a lot of perfume, and diamonds in her ears. She was Carolina-tanned and no doubt had gotten a boob job. She'd definitely done what she could to remove the Chittenango from her.

She had perfectly wrapped gifts in her leopard-print suitcase. For Brett, a Carolina Tar Heels sweatshirt. For Patrick, a Duke Blue Devils hat. It was this kind of perplexing gesture that reminded Brett why he hated her—adorning father and son in the colors of the most vicious rivalry in college sports, and performed with such graceful innocence so as to cast doubt on whether she was aware.

She was aware.

The house hadn't had a female in it in two years and didn't look right with one now. Neither did she seem to know what to do with herself, even though the house had been hers for over a decade. She had brought her own wine and poured herself a water glass of it. She said she had to make a phone call, which she did in the bathroom, and then Brett and Patrick heard the bath running. This was how she had occupied her time in the months before she left. She'd be angry at both of them for no obvious reason, which she showed by stomping around the house, slamming cupboard doors in the kitchen. His dad had quit asking *what's wrong* because he never got an answer. Brett would catch her sneaking into her purse and tossing back a pill. Then, into the bathroom she'd go, from where Brett sometimes believed she'd never emerge. He wouldn't have blamed her if she hadn't.

Now, Brett and his dad sat quietly in the family room watching a Saturday afternoon Nicolas Cage movie, the volume high to distract from the haunting roar of bathwater.

The talk came two days later. Brett was in his room, looking out the window at Angela smacking Cauliflower on the snout. She was jabbing a finger at him, which the dog licked. The snowbanks lining the street and driveways were already shrinking, and the asphalt was visible and dry.

"So your dad says you're not taking your painkillers," Brett's mother said, sitting next to him on the bed.

"My *dad* has given you correct information."

"Why not?"

"I don't know," Brett said to his chapped hands. "Don't want them."

She used to call Brett Butterbean. Everything ended in Butterbean, even when he was around his friends, back when he had friends. She'd call him Butterbean and tickle-kiss his neck.

He had loved her once, far more than his dad. She was the cool mom, until he was old enough to judge her mothering. Offering him sips from her vodka tonics when he was four; letting him stay up until midnight watching slasher films when he was six; giving him one of her Percocets when he was nine and had crashed his bike and cut up his knuckles and knees—he'd needed his stomach pumped. Mom had told the doctor he had stolen one of her pills, which Brett confirmed.

"Does it hurt?"

She lifted her hand to touch his face. He closed his eyes, his heart flittered. He waited for her to comb his hair from his forehead, run her fingertips just over the wound. On rare occasions, she would sing him to sleep—Christmas songs mostly, even in summer. These would flood his chest with warm, cinnamon mood, and he'd drift easily into sleep.

She had also told him, one rainy morning, that she had tried to kill him when he was a baby. She had terrible postpartum depression, she'd explained. She had held him under the water in the bathtub, and at the last minute, changed her mind. She never told anyone, and she had felt it was time he knew. He was twelve.

He had never told his father anything. His dad was always away, always working toward his provincial political career. Brett had blamed Patrick for leaving him alone with her, which he felt he had done on purpose.

Brett opened his eyes to find her digging something from under a fingernail. He kicked off the bed and moved to the farthest corner of the room.

"No, it doesn't hurt," he said. "Nothing hurts. We have no feelings in this house."

"Come on, Brett. Don't be that way."

"What're you even doing here? Trying to appease your conscience before you go back to your better life? Well, let me help you." Brett clasped his hands to his heart. "You have filled me with so much love, Mother. I was lost before you came, but now I will go forth into the world with direction and purpose. I am going to study, get into a good college, and make a name for myself. Maybe I'll even marry a woman with great big fake tits. All because of this little visit."

"Oh screw you," she said, brushing by, her perfume gagging him. "You're just like your father."

She walked out, and Brett slammed the door behind her.

Trent tipped the rest of a can of beer into his mouth and then went into the mini-fridge for more. Brett knew it would be empty. He'd been counting on it. Trent set his brush down on the work bench and put on his Bills coat. He checked his pockets for car keys and wallet. Cauliflower lifted his head from his paws. Trent spoke to him, then got into his rusted Crown Victoria and drove off. Brett had also counted on his leaving the garage door open. The Trents of the world were predictable.

Already in his coat and boots and with a red duffel bag under his arm, Brett hurried outside and across the street. The neighborhood was quiet, everyone at work. Brett had skipped school for this. When he stepped inside the garage, Trent's presence smacked immediately, as though he hadn't left. It felt like Brett was occupying someone else's body, a creepy sensation that nearly caused him to turn right back around.

The prominent mural distracted him. It was in its touch-up stage, an obvious depiction of the Erie Canal. A longboat laden with crates barely rippled the water. Three dusky men in overalls stood on the bow, their faces shadowed by wide-brimmed hats. A line of rope stretched from the boat to a pair of leaning horses on the towpath. On the other side of the canal were a row of red buildings pocked with windows, and a sign: NONE-SUCH MINCEMEAT, MERRILL-SOULE CO. A looming smokestack reflected in the brown water.

The image was tugging Brett back to his childhood at Bolivar Road Elementary when his class was taken—at least once a year—to the excavated dry docks at the Boat Museum. It could be, however, that he was being delivered even further back to the event itself, the nostalgia was that potent. Chittenango's past mingled too easily with its present; one could traverse time with a mere surrendering. Just ask Dean.

Brett wanted to stay and examine the mural further. But he was there for a different purpose.

Cauliflower watched as Brett unlatched the door of the cage. He put his hand under the dog's tender belly, lifted him out, and then placed him inside the duffel bag. Cauliflower seemed to expect this.

Brett hurried out of the garage. When he was a couple houses away, he quit his half-jog and continued casually toward the creek. He tried to empty his head. He had already convinced himself that this was the right thing. Angela needed to be unburdened, and he knew she wasn't capable of doing it herself. He could then find a job, give her fifteen dollars a week instead of ten.

The snow was wet, slicking his way down the slope. The creek had nearly overcome the ice—it would any day now. When it did, it would flow north. Everyone born here knew that. Which way other water ran in other towns, Brett didn't know.

He set the bag down on the stony bank. When he opened it, Cauliflower's twitching nose emerged, sniffing hard. Brett's temples thumped as he put his hands around the dog's muzzle. The delicate bones underneath the fur felt like a smaller creature's—a squirrel's maybe. Cauliflower licked Brett's palm as he squeezed. The cold gums slimed; the teeth felt like a string of wet pearls. The black, glistening eyes looked at Brett as if to say it understood why it should die, that its existence was torturous.

"What you got there?"

Brett fell over the duffel bag. Cauliflower barked at Dean who was sitting in the shadows under the bridge. A dense cloud of smoke circled his body like aura. Dean used both hands to get to his feet, then pulled his jeans over his butt. He walked dreamily forward. His eyes under his baseball cap were wide and teary. "A dog?"

Brett was soaked from the snow. He got to his knees and held the dog's collar so he wouldn't escape. He said, "It's my neighbor's."

Dean sat cross-legged in front of the duffel bag. He put his dry, purplish hand on the dog's head. Cauliflower licked Dean's wrist and Dean smiled.

"Can I hold it?"

"Sure." Brett's voice was small.

Brett wanted to play it cool, show Dean he could take the violence without hard feelings, and maybe take other things. He didn't know. What he couldn't take was Dean abandoning him again. He needed him, wanted him, wasn't sure why, but needed to find out.

Dean pulled Cauliflower from the bag and embraced him. He nestled his face into the thick fur of Cauliflower's neck. A low purr came out of Dean. Brett remained still, mesmerized, as if witnessing a rare natural occurrence. Dean gazed into the blue, cloudless sky— or through it, into another place. His jaw was working something out, as if he were reading to himself. Brett watched carefully as Dean's eyes began to narrow and harden. His lips clenched into a thin line. He noticed the dog, squeezed him, smirked. He then looked at Brett, who could see Dean was returning from wherever he'd been.

"The fuck happened to you?" said Dean, staring a hole into Brett's face.

Brett raised his hood and tucked it behind his ears. He couldn't meet Dean's eyes. "You did this."

"The egg?" Dean laughed. "Damn, that really fucked you up."

Brett sank deeper into himself.

Dean held Cauliflower away from him and swung the dog's legs from side to side as though it were dancing. "This is a shit-ugly dog," he said. "What're you doing with it?"

Brett wiggled a stone free from the icy ground and tossed it at the creek. "I'm going to kill it."

Dean's expression froze, where Brett thought he might have been disturbed. Then, a smile crawled up into his cheeks and his eyes twinkled. He simply said, "Yes."

Things began moving quickly.

Dean brought Cauliflower to the creek and kicked a hole into the thin ice. He plunged the dog in. The water was only deep enough to submerge Cauliflower's head and shoulders, while his hind legs fought against Dean's chest. Dean was unsatisfied with this and removed him. Cauliflower licked the water from his muzzle.

"Hey, dipshit," Dean said, not even looking at Brett. "Get me the bowl."

This wasn't going how Brett wanted, even though there hadn't been a plan. At the very least, he was the one who needed to decide Cauliflower's fate—for Angela. If it wasn't him, it defeated the whole purpose. Still, refusing Dean was nearly impossible.

He brought the bowl to Dean, whose arms were full with wet, shivering dog.

"Light it for me."

Brett held the pipe to Dean's mouth and fired the lighter. Brett watched Dean's sucking lips. He tried to remain casual, but his belly was flipping at the thought of how far this could go.

Dean held Cauliflower by the neck and spit a thick fog of smoke into his face. Cauliflower bared his teeth and growled. Then he whipped his head from side to side and barked in high pitches as though badgered by fleas.

Dean laughed. "What else can we do to it?"

Cauliflower was panting, looking in Brett's general direction but at nothing really.

"Hey, Brett." Dean said his name without irony, as though he'd been saying it for years—longer than they'd known each other. As though they shared a bedroom and parents, and this was how Dean would have always addressed him. "What else should we do to this dog?"

Brett scratched at the arm-scabs through his coat. "Zip him inside the bag," he said darkly. "We'll stone him."

Dean was giddy. He pressed Cauliflower into Brett's arms and then searched the ground for rocks. The dog shivered but was otherwise listless. Brett placed him inside the duffel bag and felt each zipper tooth clicking in his fingers as Cauliflower disappeared.

A rock smacked the heel of Brett's boot.

"Get out of the way." Dean was about to hurl another.

Brett joined him and watched as Dean missed. He tried again—throwing so hard he fell forward. The rock landed in the creek.

Dean said from the ground, "You were easier to hit than that fucking thing." He smiled. "I got you first try."

As though his head were stuck inside a colossal clock tower bell at noon, Brett was deafened by a riotous clang. His body knew it, but it took his brain a frantic moment to understand how furious Dean's statement had made him. He was struck dumb by it, wrenched from the scene and ringing as he watched Dean from a distant place.

Dean brushed away snow, revealing a rock the size of a cinderblock. "This will do it." He stood and bent his knees to lift. He waddled to the bag with the rock knocking between his knees. The bag bulged at one end, and Brett heard—beyond the thrumming adrenaline shaking him—the scraping of claws on nylon. Dean grunted the rock up to his chest, then, like an Olympic weight lifter, pushed it over his head. Dean wavered, stepped backward to regain his balance. His boot hit Brett's, who had come up behind him and grabbed hold of the rock. Brett's hands overlapped Dean's; his nose grazed the back of Dean's neck.

"The fuck?" Dean grunted through biting teeth.

Brett said to the back of his head, "Why'd you do it?"

"What?"

They both wobbled underneath the rock's weight.

"Did you want to get rid of me?"

Dean's elbows rattled. Brett began to relinquish more weight to him.

"Brett, come on."

"Did you want me dead?"

"Jesus, Brett."

He let go, and the rock dropped square on top of Dean's head. What came from Dean, as if out of his stomach, was a guttural *huhn*. He pitched backward into Brett, and both fell to the ground. Dean was face down and contorted like a corpse. Brett was strangely calm. Someone like Dean couldn't die that easily. He'd been through far worse than this, and maybe his life had already been taken all those years ago.

Still, Brett turned him and put his ear to Dean's chest. The heart was strong. It lulled Brett, softened his insides. When else had he been this close to Dean? To any other person for that matter? Brett's head gravitated toward Dean's face, the excuse being—if anyone was looking, or if Dean happened to wake—that he was listening for breath. Dean's cheeks were ashy, stubbled with acne and whiskers. Brett couldn't smell him, but imagined that the scent was sharp, tangy sweat and marijuana. He positioned himself over Dean, shivering so hard he was afraid his clattering teeth would rouse him. Brett shuddered as he grazed Dean's flaking lips with his.

A blossoming in his stomach reached between his legs, into which he was succumbing, losing himself. He pressed his mouth onto Dean's, pushed his tongue inside. He ventured deeper so that their teeth clinked, so that he could lick the throat. His erection was violent, and he thrust into Dean's crotch. Not enough, not nearly. He unzipped his jeans, unzipped Dean's, put his erection into Dean's zipper, the slit of his boxers. His nudged Dean's moist, deadened pearl-head. His jabbed and bullied it awake. His fought and fought, looking to kill and the thrill that comes from it. By the time Dean's penis began to react, to grow against his own, Brett was already coming into Dean's thick coils of pubic hair.

Brett was heaving into the hot yawn of Dean's mouth. He tasted copper. He looked at Dean's lips, at the bloodied teeth marks he'd left there.

When his senses returned, he half-expected Dean to be awake, to acknowledge what they had shared. But his jaw was slack, eyeball whites peeking like moon slivers. Dean's arms were outstretched, palms up Christ-style. The tattoos were visible on his wrists—chunky blue chain-links—ordinary, even crude as they lay vulnerable to inspection.

Brett draped Dean's limp arms over his back. He put his legs up on Dean's so his entire body lay flush on his. He nuzzled his head just under Dean's chin and tried to allow the slow, deep heartbeat to carry him away. It was then that Brett noticed the rock laying smack in the middle of the duffel bag. He watched it for many heartbeats, but there was no movement.

The doorbell. Angela stood on the front porch, manically zipping her coat up and down, chewing her pigtail.

"Where's my dog?"

The fear wetting her eyes, the panic raising her voice—she was still a girl. The world was still a good place. She had a long way to go to thirteen, when things would begin to unravel and the ugliness would be revealed.

A single look told he'd misinterpreted her, terribly.

"Tell me the truth. You didn't take him and kill him, did you?"

Brett focused on her chubby wrists. Warmer weather would reveal if he'd scarred her.

"You're a sick freak." She flung around, pigtails whipping dramatically. She marched down his driveway and across the street to her yard.

Though, did he really need spring to confirm that he'd scarred her? Brett wished he could call out to say he had Cauliflower in the house. He'd invite her in and reveal the dog, wagging its stub of a tail. Angela would give Brett a long, honest hug, then go to Cauliflower. There was a tin of cocoa mix in the cupboard left over from when his mom still lived there. He'd make some for Angela the right way, on the stove with milk, and that would be the beginning of something. It would be their strange story of how they found each other.

It was the last night of her visit, and his mother was cheerful. She danced and shook her butt in the kitchen as she attempted to make the family dinner—a strange meal of boiled shrimp and goat-cheese grits served over uncooked arugula. This must have been what she ate with her new, wealthy boyfriend, a real estate agent, Brett guessed, specializing in oceanfront property on the Outer Banks—some yuppie-redneck amalgam named Kenton or Tyler or Connor. She'd never said whether she met someone else and she wouldn't. She'd find a backhanded way to reveal it, and then make them eat it.

That night, Patrick's teeth grinding kept Brett awake. His dad had given Karen the master bedroom, so he slept in Brett's bed and Brett slept on the floor beside him.

Suddenly, his dad farted so loud it woke him.

"Who's there?" Patrick said, sitting up and startled. He looked down at Brett, who was grinning.

"Good thing I can't smell."

For the next few minutes, they laughed the kind of laugh that pains the stomach, stops the breath, heats up the face. The kind that could pass for crying.

His mother was gone in the morning, but the house still buzzed with her presence. Her hairs in the tub, her perfume in the towels, leftover grits in the fridge. Brett looked in the bathroom medicine cabinet and saw that she'd taken his painkillers.

How much blame could they really put on her for leaving? Patrick was no kind of husband; Chittenango was no kind of place for dreamers. Either she left, or she filled her stomach with a bottle of pills and haunted the bathroom. Like everything else, this was made clear without a word. For Brett, anyway. Not the case for his dad. For the first time, Brett actually felt sorry for him. He'd sleep tonight in the bed that she had been sleeping in. He wouldn't change the sheets. He couldn't. Not until her scent had been sniffed out of the fabric, at which point, he'd still swear he smelled her, when in fact, he'd be smelling himself.

These mornings brought long shadows, birdsong, and mosquitoes. The moon was a milky stamp in the bluing sky. Amazing how his small world could change in a few short weeks.

Brett leaned over the rail of the bridge, looking down on the creek. The water had broken through the ice and foamed in its rush. A crowd of birds riddled the bank on the other side of the creek, pecking at the thawed, rocky ground. They fought each other for something, hopping and biting, flinging white chips like confetti. It was the eggs, broken open and runny. Brett could only imagine the terrible smell that brought the swarming fruit flies competing with the birds. On the opposite bank, a single egg was split, spilling its snotty, black innards. Three birds pecked hungrily at this rotten meal.

Brett had come back for the duffel bag and its contents. He'd considered leaving it, fearing this return, but decided he didn't want Angela to stumble on the body of her dog. The bag wasn't there, however. In its place was the large rock, which radiated the memory of Dean. He could hardly look at it without cringing. As far as he was concerned, that had never happened. He hoped any evidence of the event, including that which hid inside him, had gone with winter.

Something spooked the birds on this side of the creek. Dean emerged from under the bridge. He held Cauliflower in his arms like a football. The dog was very much alive, his cottony tail flailing. Brett stepped back so Dean wouldn't see him; he didn't want to know what Dean remembered, if anything at all. Dean stooped, and Cauliflower leapt from his arms and sniffed the split egg, then sneezed. He spotted the multitude of birds on the opposite bank. Cauliflower darted into the water up to his belly and barked, high-pitched and crazed.

The birds took off into noisy flight. Collectively, they skimmed the water going northward, then darted up above the budding trees. As they ascended high into the atmosphere, their shape accordioned—thinning out, then bunching—as if they were showing Brett how to breathe.

HENDERSON LOVELY,

LAST OF THE

MUNCHKINS

At this writing, only nine little people from the film survive, and one of us will have the sad distinction of being the 'last of the Munchkins.' I am the oldest of the group, so I doubt it will be me. As Coroner, I have averred enough of us over the rainbow as it is, and I don't care to be the last one standing when the music stops.

—Meinhardt Raabe, *Memories of a Munchkin*

Late Spring, 2001

———◆———

PATRICK PRATT WOKE FRANTIC with the thought that it was raining. He was at the window, drawing the curtain, before fully awake. Long shadows of trees and mailboxes cut across the neighborhood lawns. His heart lifted. This was the day he'd been waiting for since he'd become mayor, and, somehow, in the last few weeks, it had snuck up on him.

Pat's knees and ankles crackled as he crept past Brett, who was asleep on the couch. He accidentally looked full-on at the scar that gnarled his son's forehead like a gouged-out third eye. Pat shivered and quickly occupied his thinking with the song. *The dreams that you dare to dream really do come true.*

Pat's heart was fluttery with the kind of panicked palpitation that rendered him light-headed. He'd described this to his doctor a few years ago, who had prescribed him blood pressure pills. The doctor told him to take it easy, jog, or meditate or do simple breathing exercises. Instead, Pat would sing lines from "Over the Rainbow" to himself, imagining Judy Garland's round, cherubic face looking wistfully at the sky. It usually helped.

Unsure of what his houseguest, Mr. Lovely, ate for breakfast, Pat set out English muffins, grape jelly, Raisin Bran, bananas and oranges, and an Entenmann's coffee cake. It wasn't until now, seeing the food displayed on the counter, that he realized he'd imitated a hotel's disappointing Continental breakfast. He'd offer to make Henderson an omelet, though something told Pat that the old man's morning meal would be Wild Turkey spiked with coffee.

Pat spooned Chock full o'Nuts into the filter and heard Brett stir.

"You coming to the parade today?" he asked over his shoulder, accidentally scattering grounds on the floor.

"What do you think?"

Pat mopped the linoleum with his hand, then brushed off the grit over the sink. He went into the family room, keeping his eyes steadied on the tip of Brett's nose, a respectable distance from the scar. "I would like you to come."

"That's not going to happen." Brett pulled the blanket over his head.

"Please. It's important to me."

Brett flung the blanket off and said to the ceiling. "It's important to Dean, too, but you wouldn't know that."

"After all I've done to make this day happen, and you're concerned about Dean?"

"That's funny, Patrick. I could have sworn you dedicated the festival to him."

Pat absently scratched below his pajama bottoms, conjuring an itch on his tailbone. "I need to get Henderson up."

Pat hurried down the hall to escape a comment Brett was sure to hurl. He knocked on the bedroom door. "Good morning." No answer. He knocked again, put his ear to the door, then entered.

Henderson was in bed, awake. He stared at Pat, milk-blue eyes sharp and clean as though he'd been waiting for him all night.

"Did you sleep okay?" Pat asked.

Henderson licked his toothless mouth like some half-frog creature. He cleared his throat. "Let's get this over with."

A demented couple had swiped the kids in broad daylight during the '92 Oz Festival, right from under everyone's noses. The national media painted Chittenango as a bunch of dumb hicks for allowing it to happen. *Seems like someone would have noticed something,* the stylish newscasters had said, shaking their heads, clucking their tongues. Almost ten years later, Chittenango still hadn't recovered.

Pat was the festival's eager coordinator at the time. He was also the village historian, specializing in the life of famous resident and Oz author, L. Frank Baum. While Pat was not blamed for the abduction, it was his beloved celebration that quickly got the ax. Parents in the village had passionately argued that continuing the festival would be imprudent and too horrific a reminder. There hadn't been an Oz Fest since.

Pat sought to change that. He'd become mayor two years ago, winning the election 568–392 on the campaign promise that he would renew Chittenango's tarnished image, which would bring much needed revenue. The best way to do that, Pat had assured, was to resurrect the Oz Fest, making it twice as big as the previous ones in order to get the attention of the entire state of New York. After all, this was the new millennium, a time for change and new beginnings. Of course, Pat would do the right thing and dedicate the festival to Jason *and* Dean Fleming.

It was not an easy sell. There was very little money to fund a festival, since the village—like most of Central New York—had been enduring a recession. Nearby Mohawk Steel & Die, which employed many in Chittenango, had laid off a quarter of its force and was looking to cut even more.

But the biggest obstacle, to Pat anyway, was that the Munchkins who usually attended the event were all gone. Five of the original movie Munchkins had always appeared at the Oz Fest: the Coroner, one of the Lollipop Guild, a Sleepyhead, a Trumpeter, and a Villager. They were the main attraction. However, during the ten-year hiatus, they had died. Most casual followers of the film believed that these were the last of the Munchkins. Oz enthusiasts—including Pat Pratt—knew otherwise.

Cast as one of the many soldiers of Munchkin City, Henderson Lovely had never made a single public appearance affiliated with the film. Pat understood that if he really wanted to convince the village about the festival, he needed to lure Henderson to Chittenango.

While waiting for Mr. Lovely's big arrival, Pat misted Windex on a framed, original 1938 photograph of the Munchkin actors posing in front of the Culver City Hotel. He'd recently won it on eBay for three hundred dollars—a staggering price considering his meager wage. Pat hadn't been able to resist the purchase. It was the perfect addition to the extensive collection of *Wizard of Oz* memorabilia that ornamented his home: original movie posters, autographed headshots of Judy Garland and Jack Haley, ceramic figurines and commemorative plates, and throw pillows with film scenes stitched into them. Pat believed the photo would impress his special guest, who would be here at any moment.

"Has it occurred to you that everything's hung too high for a midget?" Brett said, leaning in the entranceway of the family room. Ever since Pat had corrected his son's use of that word, Brett had been saying it twice as often. Pat had suggested, as subtly as possible, that Brett stay at a friend's house for the weekend, forgetting that the only person his son hung out with was Dean Fleming. He'd even considered sending Brett down to North Carolina to stay with his mother. No way in hell Brett would go for that.

"Couldn't you put on a collared shirt, just while Henderson is here?"

Brett wore a yellow *Limbaugh for President* T-shirt. Pat wasn't sure if it was ironic, whether anything his son did was ironic. Like the disturbing homemade tattoos on his arms—were those made in earnest, or was he just trying to be different?

"How about," Brett began, putting his finger to his lips in mock thought, "I slip into one of Mom's old dresses and pretend I'm Dorothy?"

Pat stomped past him into the kitchen. "Right. Thanks, Brett."

"No, seriously," Brett said, following. "I'll shave my legs and put on some lipstick, and we'll show that tiny old midget what a freak show we really are."

Pat placed the Windex under the kitchen sink next to the garbage pail. He lingered, closed his eyes and inhaled deeply, taking in the odors of day-old chicken bones and Pine-Sol. Pat came up from the sink and smiled at Brett. "You go do that."

Over Brett's shoulder, a reflection of light came through the bay window and moved across the wall of the family room. A car had pulled into the driveway. Pat's chest flipped.

"Please be good," he said to Brett.

Pat rushed out to the front porch and watched as the driver got out of a black, dinged-up sedan. Henderson had insisted over the phone on being picked up in a limousine. Pat was disappointed to see that for the money—nearly one hundred dollars—the vehicle was a Lincoln Town Car. Apparently, Henderson was upset, too.

"What in the hell you got me riding in, Mayor?" His voice was strident and screechy, grating like a rusty door hinge. The frazzled driver fled the car to retrieve the wheelchair from the trunk. He glared at Pat as if blaming him for Henderson's behavior. "Why didn't you just rent a guldern Chevy Lumina. You ever ride in a Lumina, Mayor?"

Pat trotted down the driveway and ducked his head into the car.

Henderson Lovely wore a Tampa Bay Rays cap that half hid a long, severely wrinkled face. Big, drooping ears flanked the length of his head. His eyes were soft and blue, nearly ghostlike in their transparency. As expected, Henderson was tiny, though Pat was not prepared for the incongruity of size and age. Incredibly, he looked like an elderly eight-year-old boy.

"My apologies for the car, Mr. Lovely," Pat said in his official, mayoral voice—low and authoritative. This was the same tone he used during town meetings when fielding complaints about infrastructure or garbage pickup.

"Just get me in the guldern house. Need a drink."

Pat tipped the exasperated driver the contents of his wallet—six dollars. He grabbed Henderson's leather suitcase and wheeled the old man up the plyboard he had laid over the porch steps.

Brett was lurking in the shadow of the doorway, the light just catching his scarred brow.

"Jesus Christ," Henderson said to Brett. "You look like death warmed over."

"Thank you, sir." Brett smiled.

"The hell happened to this boy?" Henderson turned to look up at Pat.

It was a good question. Pat still didn't know, as Brett refused to talk about it. Inexplicably, Brett was loyal to his attacker.

"My father beats me."

Pat laughed nervously. "Don't . . . pay any attention to him." Then he perked up and said in a deep voice, "Pay no attention to that man behind the curtain." He waited for the reference to take, but Henderson freed himself from Pat and wheeled past Brett and into the house. He went straight for the kitchen, found the broom wedged between the refrigerator and wall, and began opening cupboards with its handle.

"Where you keep the bourbon?"

"I'm sorry, Mr. Lovely," Pat said. "We don't keep alcohol in the house."

"What kind of respectable man doesn't keep something stiff to offer his guests?"

Pat began to answer, but Henderson cut him off.

"Boy!" he screamed. Brett came into the kitchen. "Put some decent clothes on; we're going out. Surely there's a bar in this"—he omitted the obvious adjective—"town."

"Pat," Brett said, "the old man and I are going to get drunk. Give me your car keys."

Pat gave his son a look. He went into the refrigerator and pulled out a liter of Pepsi. "How about a nice cold soda?"

Henderson grumbled and spun the wheelchair around, gashing the drywall. He went into his suitcase and pulled out a bottle of Wild Turkey.

"Get me a glass with ice, Mayor."

Pat dropped a handful of ice into a commemorative Oz glass and displayed it to Henderson, who scowled and took it. With the glass in one hand, Henderson had to open the bottle's cap with his teeth. In doing so, his dentures flew from his mouth. The teeth landed on the carpet.

"Get those for me, boy."

Brett stepped back. "Um."

"Brett," Pat ordered, "get Mr. Lovely his teeth."

Brett shook his head.

They all three looked at the teeth glistening on the rug. Pat finally bent down and grabbed them, the slime shivering his neck and armpits. Henderson opened his mouth. Pat looked at Brett, who nodded, amused. Pat eased the dentures halfway into the hot, moist mouth, then pushed the rest in with his fingertip. It made a sexual, unctuous sound. Henderson sucked the dentures into place, then looked at Pat as if this were a test—and Pat had failed.

Tracking down Mr. Lovely had been surprisingly easy. He was living in a retirement community in Tampa, and it only took a few phone calls to the clubhouse secretary to get Henderson's number. Convincing him to come to Chittenango, however, was far more difficult. After attempting the nostalgic, sentimental appeal—which had absolutely no affect—Pat resorted to money. He offered Henderson $5,000. Henderson said no. He offered $7,500. Henderson said no. He offered $10,000. Henderson said yes. Pat hung up the phone that afternoon in December feeling shaky. Neither he nor Chittenango had anything close to that amount of money.

Pat woke the next day with an idea. He would raise the money, campaign for it, and inspire people to give donations. He had secretly missed running for mayor—politicking before small crowds, earning people's votes. He'd do it again: persuade the village that bringing Henderson Lovely here could draw positive attention to Chittenango. People from all over Central New York would come for the weekend-long festival to see the last living Munchkin. They would spend their money here; they might even return to see the Erie Canal Landing Museum or the Chittenango Falls State Park.

To help advertise his efforts, Pat would build a sign—a donation thermometer to mark the progression of the money raised. Trent Shirley, Pat's neighbor, cut him the eight-foot-tall wooden thermometer, and Pat painted it in his garage. He then strapped it to the roof of his station wagon, drove into town, and stabbed it into the snowy lawn of First Presbyterian Church, the location of the Oz Fest come June.

Chittenangoans were skeptical about paying so much to acquire Henderson, but they were willing to give it a shot, thanks to Pat's enthusiasm and rhetorical savvy. First Presbyterian held a few bake sales, the Rotary Club sold spaghetti dinners, and the local pizzeria agreed to have Tuesday night specials—two one-topping pies for ten dollars—the proceeds of which went to the fund. Pat himself sold raffle tickets at the Chittenango Bears basketball games. All of this amounted to *maybe* a thousand dollars. Pat had to make his case for the Oz Fest elsewhere.

He campaigned tirelessly over the next few months. He went to Canastota, Cazenovia, Oneida, Verona, Manlius, Fayetteville, and DeWitt, putting up flyers, talking to people outside grocery stores and banks, and, most thrilling, speaking at town meetings.

". . . This isn't just a cause for Chittenango," went the end of his speech. "This is a celebration for all of Central New York, to prove our resilience in the face of adversity. To prove to the country that if we can dream, then we can survive, and if we can survive, then there is hope for all of America."

Pat loved delivering this speech, and it grew more flowery the more he gave it. The response from the few who came to the meetings, sitting in metal folding chairs in church basements sipping coffee from Dixie cups, was a polite applause. A basket was passed around, a few dollars collected, and Pat inched closer to his goal.

One day, he drove into the village to fill in another segment of the *Bring Back the Oz Fest!* thermometer and found it had been toppled. Pat righted the sign and was met with a spray-painted FUCK YOU. He asked Chief Bell to keep an eye out for vandals, by which he meant Dean Fleming. Dean was making it clear that he did not approve of the festival. But Pat was too focused on money to worry about the blaring irony of trying to honor someone who didn't want it. One obstacle at a time, he told himself.

Pat's big break came when the *Syracuse Herald Journal* covered his efforts and included the story on the front page of the local section. Pat requested the headline, "The Mayor of Hope," but the editor stuck with the banal, "Chittenango's Oz Festival Returns, Wants Munchkin." The end of the article provided contact information for donations, and soon after, the checks began to arrive. By the end of April, the snow nearly melted, Pat stood on a stepladder and scraped the bottom of the can to get enough paint to fill in the rest of the thermometer. Many residents came out to view the accomplishment. They clapped and cheered.

The moment didn't last, however. An egg came hurling from nowhere and splattered the thermometer. The only thing anyone saw was someone across the street darting into the trees.

The evening of their guest's arrival, Pat assembled the lasagna while Henderson and Brett watched baseball in the family room. Every now and then Henderson would ask Brett about girls.

"You getting any snatch at school? Any pretty girls you can invite over here?"

Pat quietly spooned the ricotta on the noodles so he could hear Brett's answer. He knew little about his son's personal life. He'd quit inquiring about it after his wife had left.

Brett laughed off Henderson's questions and said something about calling up hookers and putting them on Pat's credit card. *Fat chance*, Pat thought. *My credit card's all maxed out.*

The lasagna was in the oven. Pat took the Munchkin photograph from the wall, careful not to smudge the glass frame. He crouched beside Henderson's wheelchair.

"Does this bring back any memories, Mr. Lovely?"

Henderson examined the photo, rattling his unsecured teeth around in his mouth. He then noticed the Oz memorabilia on the walls as if for the first time. He swallowed the rest of his bourbon, ice cubes crashing against his lip. "What kind of life is this?"

"I'm sorry?"

"This is the way your house looks all the time? All this horseshit?"

"Excuse me, but—"

"Where're the pictures of your boy or your wife?" Henderson looked gravely at Pat. "You got a wife, don't you?"

"She left us losers," Brett said.

"Christ on the cross, looks like a child's room in here," Henderson said.

Brett thrust back on the couch and laughed, kicking his legs in the air. Henderson joined.

"Okay," Pat said, standing and re-hanging the photograph. His hands were shaking. "Okay."

He fled into the bathroom and took deep, desperate breaths while pacing the small floor. *Someday I'll wish upon a star, and wake up where the stars are far behind me.* He sat on the toilet, fingering the triangle he'd folded on the end of the toilet paper. *This couldn't be the way it was going to go*, he thought. *No way.*

The three sat down to the table when dinner was ready. Henderson ate a couple bites of the lasagna and salad and then pushed it away and worked on his third bourbon. Pat hoped the old man was jollier in his intoxication and so he tried engaging him. "Do you have any interesting stories to tell about being on the set of the *Wizard of Oz*?"

Henderson grumbled and shook his head.

Pat slumped but during dessert—strawberry shortcake with homemade vanilla ice cream—he tried again, this time whispering a question into Brett's ear. Brett waited a moment, and then asked Henderson if he'd ever seen Judy Garland naked.

"What?" Pat slapped Brett's arm.

Henderson took the question seriously. "I sure wish. Had a fierce crush on her, yessir." He twirled the ice in his glass, making music. "Damn shame what happened to her."

"You mean, the interview on the Jack Paar show, when she said how unruly you all were, and every night you had to be rounded up in butterfly nets?"

Henderson glared at Pat and said very slowly, "I mean how she overdosed."

This sucked whatever life there was from the meal, but Pat was undeterred. He had Henderson here, and he was going to take every advantage, no matter how it wounded his pride.

Once Henderson and Brett migrated to the family room, Pat abandoned the dishes to the sink and snuck a cassette into the VCR. He then backpedaled to sit in the recliner and held Henderson's expression in his periphery. On the television screen, pouty-lipped Dorothy scampered down a dirt road with Toto. Pat fast-forwarded to Dorothy opening the door of the once-airborne house, the picture shifting to brilliant color, illuminating the flowers and yellow brick road.

They didn't get very far in the scene before Henderson shouted, "The hell is this?"

"I just thought we'd watch the scene in Munchkin City." Pat was sheepish. "You know, where you come on."

"No guldern way!" Henderson barked. "I never, not once, watched this stupid picture and I want to die knowing I never watched it."

"You've never seen it?" Pat turned to face Henderson, genuinely concerned. "This is the most magical, amazing, wonderful—"

"Dad." Brett never called him Dad. "He's serious. Turn it off."

The look in Henderson's needling eyes revealed he was beyond livid.

"Will do." Pat jammed STOP and sank into the recliner.

"Good," Henderson said. "Now, boy, turn it to *Law & Order*. It's just starting. And you." He shook his empty glass at Pat. "I could use a fresher-up."

The first time Pat had seen the film, he was six or seven. He sat on the bristly, industrial carpet in front of the television. The huge, colored bulbs on the Christmas tree were blinking. His father was smoking clove-scented cigarettes. His mother watched from the doorway of the kitchen, moving a dish towel around a plate. The songs and characters overcame Pat. He felt he was hovering just above the floor, disconnected from his home, his body. Afterward, his father had told him that the author of this story was born in their very own village. In a house that was walking distance from their own. Pat's heart pounded with possibilities. Of all the places in the whole wide world, the man who created the Scarecrow and Lion and Tin Man was born right here. What a gift! What a wonder! That night, when he found it impossible to lie still in his bed, he looked at the dusty globe that sat on his dresser. He got up and spun it on its axis, examining the continents and oceans. Suddenly, he lived somewhere. He, Pat Pratt—a boy who had very few friends, who wasn't good at sports or drawing, who wasn't the brightest in school—was now somebody.

They sat through two excruciating episodes of *Law & Order* during which Henderson demanded absolute silence so that he could follow the plot. It was eleven p.m., so Pat got out blankets for Brett, who would sleep on the couch, and dropped by Brett's room to make sure it was presentable for Henderson. No surprise, it smelled like marijuana. Pat sprayed the room with a can of Lysol until it gagged him.

Pat returned to Henderson to see if he needed help getting ready for bed. The old man's chin was on his chest, the wattle of his neck glistening with drool. He was asleep.

"Want some help?" Brett said from the couch, not even looking up from a book.

"No, I got it."

"Good."

Pat wheeled Henderson into Brett's room. He tried to jostle him awake, but Henderson was stubbornly unconscious. Pat rubbed his bald head and sighed. He unzipped Henderson's jacket and unbuttoned his shirt and worked them off his small arms. The skin sagged from Henderson's sternum like an oversized sweater. When he pulled off the socks, Pat was horrified by Henderson's feet—they were purple and curled as though they'd gone rotten. Looking at this withered, decrepit man passed out in the wheelchair, Pat wondered what kept Henderson alive. He seemed so shriveled and frail that the slightest nudge of nature could tip him into death.

He easily hoisted Henderson out of the chair and placed him into Brett's bed. In an unexpected memory-lapse of the reflexes, Pat tucked the covers under Henderson's chin, just as he used to with his son.

The next morning, an hour after wrestling Henderson out of bed and rushing him into the bathroom, Pat and Henderson drove into town. Pat had assumed that Henderson had a replica soldier costume from the film. Henderson explained that he'd never once participated in one of these stupid events, so why in the hell would he have a replica of his costume? Henderson elaborated on this point all through breakfast and on until they were in the car, just to be sure Pat had been thoroughly ridiculed.

They drove by the park in front of First Presbyterian. Tents, vendors, food trailers, and a few rides were set up and ready for the crowds. A massive, inflatable Emerald City Castle was coming to life. A stage and surrounding bleachers were being assembled where, after the parade, Oz scenes would be reenacted, and the best costume contestants would be judged. Chief Bell stood near the bleachers, arms crossed over his wide chest, chatting up one of the workers while scanning the park. *Stay alert*, Pat silently pleaded.

They passed under the banner that stretched across Genesee Street: WELCOME BACK TO THE OZ FESTIVAL! Underneath was written: FEATURING THE LAST SURVIVING MUNCHKIN, HENDERSON LOVELY. At the bottom, in smaller font: DEDICATED TO JASON AND DEAN FLEMING.

People were already claiming their spots on the curb for the parade. Pat winced at the green-brick sidewalks, which used to be yellow, and the FOR RENT signs hanging in many of the windows. In the last five or six months, many of the shops on Genesee had closed. Worse, it was the Oz-themed ones that hadn't survived: Emerald City Lanes, Oz Cream, and Auntie Em's Café. Pat had tried to persuade residents in the seasonal newsletter to eat and shop locally. To offer his own support, he frequented these places almost daily. He'd spent more money than he cared to admit bowling (alone), eating ice cream (in winter), and ordering the lunch special every day of the week (almost always shepherd's pie). Eventually, even he quit these pitiful routines, seeing as he was often the only person in these establishments.

Pat stopped the car to allow a convincing Wicked Witch cross the street. She wore a prosthetic chin and nose, crooked and warted. As she skirted by, she looked menacingly at Pat. Her eyeballs glowed white against the hunter-green of her skin. Pat waved, enthralled at the enthusiasm this woman had put into her costume.

"Isn't she great?" Pat said to Henderson.

"That's a grown guldern woman playing make-believe," Henderson said. "It's pathetic."

Pat suddenly feared that Henderson would be just as rude to the residents as he was to Pat. This hadn't occurred to him before this comment, since he'd assumed that Henderson's aversion was personal. After all, a lot of people didn't like Pat. He told himself that was the price of ambition, of being the catalyst for big change. It wasn't about popularity, though honestly, he hoped people would exalt him once they saw how successfully the Oz Fest went.

"Mr. Lovely, I trust you'll behave today." Again, Pat employed his mayoral tone. "We are paying you a lot of money to be here. So please—"

Henderson pinched Pat's thigh. Pat howled.

"Don't you dare try to make me feel guilty," Henderson snapped. "You're the knucklehead who squandered a mess of cash to get a wrinkled old fart to wave in your parade."

"Why are you even here then?" Pat was surprised he hadn't thought to ask before. So he asked it again, this time more commandingly.

Henderson looked out the window and rapped his knuckles on the glass. He might have been looking at the families setting up beach chairs and blankets on the side of the road.

"I resented all the others for putting on their ridiculous costumes and dancing around in all your parades and festivals." Henderson's voice was soft and pensive, while retaining a throaty edge, as though anger were a breath away. "Before we were in that picture, we all worked the freak show circuit in carnivals, travelling round the country so people could gawk at us. I was Bitty-Ton. I wore a rabbit pelt on my crotch and carried an albino python around my shoulders. I'd been doing that since I was seven years old. Didn't even know my real name. The one I got now I made up for the Oz picture. After the picture, I went back to being Bitty-Ton. You know the contract we all signed, how we were paid horseshit, got no royalties. Toto the guldern dog got paid better. And fifty, sixty, seventy years later, the only way we could make any kind of living was to dress up like clowns and come to your parades. Even after all this time, we're still little freaks."

Pat was taken by the story, but didn't understand its point. "So . . . why are you here?"

Henderson looked at Pat, disgusted. "I'm here. Isn't that enough?"

Pat turned into the large gravel parking lot of Oneida Savings Bank, where the floats and paraders were making ready. Pat found a spot and threw the stick into park. It went against his deep-seated code to inflict anger upon an Oz actor, but he had taken enough abuse.

"Listen to me, Mister Lovely. I don't give"—he searched for the right cuss—"two shits what you have against me. I sacrificed a lot to make this day happen. And I'm paying you handsomely for your services. So I'd appreciate it if you were a little bit more respectful."

"It's about the money?" Henderson shot back. He reached into his back pocket, pulled out a tattered wallet, and whipped out the check Pat had written him. "Here's the money, right here." He jammed it in Pat's face. "Take it. Take it and drive me to the airport. I don't need it, don't even want it."

A small noise escaped Pat's throat and bounced around his open mouth. He sucked his tongue in search of saliva. Just as he found a drop, there was a knock on his window. It was Maureen Benson, parade coordinator. She wore a headband with lion's ears, her nose was painted black, and she'd drawn whiskers on her cheeks.

Pat cranked down the window. "Hey Maureen, we'll be right there."

Maureen smiled at Henderson. She said to Pat, "We're behind schedule. Just waiting on you."

Pat rolled the window back up, slowly. He hoped the check wasn't still in front of him. Hoped it had never been produced in the first place. But it was, it had. *Where troubles melt like lemon drops, away above the chimney tops, that's where you'll find me.*

Pat looked through the imaginary check and said to Henderson, "All set?"

Henderson's glassy-blue eyes steadied on Pat's. He said nothing for a long moment, then smiled. Pat couldn't interpret it, but luckily, the check that had never existed was put back in Henderson's wallet.

Pat tugged the wheelchair out of the back seat and helped Henderson into it. Maureen was there to usher them through the motley crowd of marchers. Designers were making final adjustments to the dozens of Oz-themed floats. Marching bands tested their instruments. Girls dressed as Dorothies or Glendas and boys dressed as Scarecrows or Lions darted around them. Then there were the regulars who came from all over Central New York to participate in any parade; these were the Civil War reenactors, the rescue missions with their army of dogs, the bagpipers, and the Shriners in their tiny cars.

Then they reached their float. Pat was aware that the Boy Scouts and Girl Scouts had built it, but this was the first time he'd seen their work. A wobbly cardboard rainbow with only three colors, not even the primary ones, arched over the seats in which Pat and Henderson would sit. Behind that was a slipshod yellow brick road comprised of yellow and orange sponges. It took Pat a few moments to identify the sculpture of pantyhose and cotton stretched around a cone of chicken wire—the twister.

Maureen hurried them aboard before Pat could find more flaws. Pat climbed on, then yanked up Henderson. Maureen's husband, Rich, got into the black Ford pickup that would tow the float. He started the truck, and the stereo in the cab blasted the film's soundtrack. Maureen gave Rich the thumbs-up signal. There was a quick jerk, and they eased onto the road.

A group of twenty or so children dressed as Flower Munchkins surrounded Pat and Henderson's float, shouting along with the lyrics of "Ding, Dong, the Witch Is Dead." Their voices were discordant but earnest. Pat had been unaware of the addition of the children, but he was, at last, pleasantly surprised by something.

The float turned onto Genesee Street. A smattering crowd clapped and waved. Others looked on indifferently, talking on cell phones or hands shoved into jean shorts. A handful of out-of-towners who thankfully showed up, snapped photos of Henderson. The children were more interested in the Smarties and Dum Dums that the Flower Munchkins tossed. Pat spied a few kids perched on their fathers' shoulders who waved ardently at Henderson. They seemed to have been told about Mr. Lovely ahead of time and were excited about witnessing him. Maybe when they grew up, and hopefully remained in Chittenango, they would tell their own kids, "I saw the last living Munchkin."

Henderson appeared to be enjoying himself. He shook his little hand here and there, calling out a squeaky hello to those who yelled his name. His unwaving hand tapped his knee to the music. His face even ribboned into a wrinkly smile, one that made him nearly unrecognizable as the crank who'd been staying with Pat.

It was at this moment—when Pat saw that this impossible parade was happening—that his heart seemed to radiate the entire spectrum of colors. He felt he could open his shirt and out would arch the rainbow he knew lived dormant inside him, and all the riches of possibility would sprinkle at the feet of his people. If only Brett were here to see this moment.

But wasn't he?

Just ahead, standing in front of the closed-down video store, Pat spotted a pair of crazed-looking teenagers. They wore colorful, striped shirts with suspenders. Their hair was heavily gelled and slicked back. Their cheeks were thickly rouged. Their pants, which Pat could now see since the crowd had given them space, were rolled up to their hairy calves. It was Brett and Dean, and they were shouting unintelligibly at Pat.

Pat's rainbow went monochromatic, then retreated back into him and sat there heavy in his chest. He turned away and waved to the crowd on the other side of the street. Pat felt the float jerk to a stop. Brett and Dean were standing in front of the pickup truck. They held paper bags in their fists. The music had ceased. The crowd had hushed. Where was Chief Bell? Why wasn't anyone doing anything?

The two approached, eyeing Pat. Henderson didn't seem alarmed but, rather, amused. Maureen had ushered the Flower Munchkins away. Brett and Dean climbed into the bed of the truck with some difficulty, and when they stood—only a few feet from Pat and Henderson—they wobbled. They'd been drinking. Pat couldn't even look at Brett. At this moment, he wasn't his son.

Brett and Dean cleared their throats, stuffed one hand into their pockets, and out of the sides of their mouths, began their song. In a crooked and sadistic impression, they claimed to represent the Lollipop Guild, but it was clear to Pat that they represented something far more sinister. Eyes red and puffy, their feet unsteady as they imitated the herky-jerky kicks from the film—Pat was on edge waiting for the terroristic moment when this ruse would turn violent. He felt hostage, especially with Dean, not Brett, directly before him. What did he have in the paper bag? Would Dean . . . kill him, right in front of everyone? Surely Brett wouldn't participate in the murder of his own father.

Right?

Brett and Henderson appeared to be enjoying their moment, the old man's eyes sparkling with delight, Brett's with a playful wink.

At the conclusion of the little song, when they welcomed them to Munchkin Land, Brett and Dean formally offered to Pat and Henderson the contents of the paper sacks: two forty-ounce cans of Genny Cream Ale. The crowd remained silent as if someone had used a remote control to pause them. Brett and Dean continued to hold the cans of beer suspended. Henderson suddenly broke into laughter. He raised his arms and clapped. A few in the crowd joined in. Henderson took the beer from Brett. He cracked the top, raised the can to the crowd in a salute and then he drank. More residents whooped and hollered.

Pat finally acknowledged Dean, whose eyebrows were raised in invitation. But Pat didn't move.

Brett leaned over and said, "Take the beer, Dad."

Pat expected his son to fill him with hate. Wasn't this stunt sabotage? Or, perhaps like the launched dentures, another cruel test? But there was no resentment for his son, or Dean for that matter. If participating in this skit made the boys happy, as it made Henderson and the village happy, then why not? He didn't have much choice in this moment anyway. So Pat reached out and took the hefty can of beer.

Their offerings accepted, Brett and Dean clasped their hands together and pumped their fists over each shoulder in self-congratulation. The entire crowd cheered.

Pat felt a jab in his side. "Stand up, Mayor," Henderson said. "You're on."

His legs raised him as though being hand-cranked. When he stood, the residents cheered. Emboldened, Pat imitated Henderson: he raised the can, which Dean had already opened for him, and took a cautious sip. The beer was warm and slightly bitter, but the people roaring and pumping their fists made it tolerable. He took a bigger swig, the foam fizzing his nose, causing him to cough. The alcohol was already warming his blood. Henderson put an arm around Pat's waist, and they drank together.

Brett hopped off the truck, but Dean remained. He held out his hand for Pat to shake. Feeling good, feeling hopeful that anything was possible, Pat happily shook. After a vigorous embrace, Dean smiled and said, "I pissed in your beer." He jumped down to join Brett, and then turned to give Pat the finger. Brett shoved Dean, and Dean chased him down the street and through the crowd.

Pat fought back the urge to retch. His throat ached, his eyes watered, but he would not sully this moment by puking during the parade. He inhaled deeply through his nose and motioned for Maureen to get the float going again. She directed the Flower Munchkins back into position. Pat returned to his seat, trying desperately not to taste the salt in his mouth that now demanded attention.

"That was fun," Henderson said smiling. He tipped his beer and craned his head far back until he swallowed the last of it.

Pat leaned over the side of the truck and said to one of the Flower Munchkins. "Let me have one of those." He pointed at the girl's paper basket of candy. She happily handed him a package of Smarties. Pat thanked her and dumped the candies into his mouth. He then slapped the side of the pickup to get Rich going.

The truck started up again, and with it, the music.

KINGS OF THE CANAL

Spring, 2007

―――――◆―――――

ENERGY WAS HIGH FOR this time of day, though it was hardly day at four thirty a.m. A sliver of orange swathed the horizon, the only indication that morning wasn't far off. The rest was pure night, complete with moon and April cold and peripheral peace and lamps lighting up the parking lot of Mohawk Steel & Die. This was where the energy was highest, a group of diesel pickups and pimped-out hatchbacks defying the white parking lines. The drivers, the young who skipped college to work the factory for a time, which would stretch and stretch until one morning they'd wake at this same hour to find their knees and backs had gone to hell and retirement wasn't even close—these young men were fueled with youth and anger and amphetamines that they chased with Red Bull to endure the monotony of work and life. On top of that, they were jazzed by the promise of a fight.

Mark DeMartano was backed by his loyal Dozen, hissing and barking orders to *fuck that faggot up*. Mark, whom his friends called D-Mart, did his slow dance of intimidation: pacing, huffing, blowing breath into the cold air like an ox, staring down his opponent from under the shadow of his sweat-stained hat. He sucked snot into his throat and spit. Light from a nearby lamp cast his bearded face blue and mean, illumined the wolfy hairs overgrown on the back of his thick neck, gleamed on the vein that cut his bicep in half.

Dean was not prepared. His canvas sneakers seemed filled with sand, his arms limp at the shoulders, and worse, a smile was creeping into his lips. That he felt good was the problem. This was like watching a scene in a movie from his couch. He'd tried to keep away from the needle for the night, hoping that would summon the appropriate anger for this occasion, which had been more or less planned. Dean knew what he was walking into. He knew he didn't have to win. He only had to fight, and in the fighting, maybe there'd be some redemption. Maybe he'd be free of one of the many burdens that swamped him into that dark so dark.

He lit a cigarette, hoping to distract the smile.

"This isn't a smoke break, cocksucker."

That did it. That burst his mouth into laughter. And once it began, he couldn't quit. Maybe it was his nerves or the heroin warming him through, but he stood on that sacred battleground of asphalt, defiling it with silliness.

"The fuck's wrong with him?" someone asked.

"He's high," Mark answered grimly, stopping his dance.

"Beat him anyway." The Dozen were expecting violence; they wouldn't allow their miserable shifts to begin until they got some.

Yapping behind Dean from his dad's truck was the dog, a blur of white as it clawed at the window, either rooting him on or warning him to retreat before shit got ugly. He didn't know the dog's real name. Brett had kidnapped it and abandoned it at the creek. Dean kept the stupid thing, changing its name every few months, because what the hell? This month he called it Paddy for Paddy Ryan, the Trojan Giant, the King of the Erie Canal.

"Slap that fucking smile off his face," the Dozen chanted. "I'll do it if you don't."

"You come here to fight?" Mark shouted over the twenty feet of pseudo-night.

Dean had. He'd hoped that the situation would supply what he lacked. He'd hoped this, when—for the past twelve hours—he'd failed to summon what had been barnacled to him since he was a kid: self-loathing and doubt and depression and guilt and an anger unquenchable. And especially this person, D-Mart, who fifteen years ago was just Mark D, the bully who beat up Jason while Dean did nothing but watch—like he was doing nothing now. Despite the junk, anger should have been easy coming. This was his opportunity for revenge. So what was wrong with him? Standing on loose ground, giggling like a child, like the faggot he was.

The first time he saw Mark again, Dean was plenty ready to throw down. He should have done it and gotten it over with, walking up to him at Mohawk, asking "Do you know who I am?" and then clocking him in the nose. Done.

It was back in March, winter's claws still digging in, when his dad told Dean it was time to get a job, a real job this time, enough of this working on some loser's race car.

"It's a sprint car, and if he wins we'll split the—"

"And if he doesn't win? Or even if he does. Look. I can get you a job at Mohawk. You stay there one month, save your paychecks, you'll have enough to rent an apartment. I'll pay the deposit."

"And then you can get on with your life."

"Then you can."

Dean knew his dad wanted him out of the house so he could finally marry his fiancée, a lady from Oswego who refused to move in until Dean was out. His dad was a piece of shit, and he hated to give him what he wanted, but it would be nice to have his own place and some real money for once, so long as the work wasn't too hard.

It was. He was used to going to bed around two or three a.m., waking at eleven, smoking some pot, hanging around the house for a while, showering, then going out around four in the afternoon to drink beers in Clint's garage while Clint talked up his car, which at this point was just a high-bar chassis and tires he'd found in a junkyard. But the hours at Mohawk were absurd. His dad woke him at four a.m., he slept in the truck as his dad drove and listened to talk radio, and he stumbled into the factory and clocked in by five. The work itself woke him immediately. The plant with its enormous machines was ferociously loud, even with the earplugs. If Dean wasn't paying attention at the massive punch press, he'd lose a hand at best, and the edges of the sheet metal were so sharp they could slice through the gloves. The guy training Dean was missing the tips of his fingers on his left hand, and both hands were jigsawed with innumerable scars. His dad, who was also the floor manager, rode Dean's ass hard the first couple weeks to make sure he didn't fuck up.

There were, however, perks to Mohawk, which kept Dean going. One was the amount of drugs going around the factory. Speed was the most popular, for obvious reasons, but also painkillers of nearly every type and even some cocaine. It was like a pharmacy, and it seemed everyone knew about it except Dean's dad, who only came down from his overhead office to ride Dean's ass. And who was the primary dealer? That was the second surprise, for it didn't take long to discover that D-Mart was the asshole from his youth, Mark DeMartano, who'd regularly bullied him and Jason. When during lunch break he saw him, a broad-bearded, mean, Italian bastard with his loyal Dozen, Dean felt that old angry guilt return. Just like he was a boy again, the toes of his sneakers skimming wet grass. There was the emptiness that followed, the abandonment, later filled with the destruction. There it all was in Mark.

Who was actually *nice* when two weeks later Dean finally worked up the courage to approach him in the outdoor break area.

"Shit, yeah, Dean Fleming." They shook hands. "Jesus. How's it going?"

"Working for my dad, living the dream."

"Tell me about it."

Mark's old man also worked at Mohawk; he was probably the oldest employee on the floor, doing the same shit job as his son.

"Can I buy a quarter bag from you?"

"Of weed? Naw, I don't deal with that. Too messy, too stinky. And can you imagine dudes working this equipment stoned all the time? Naw, man. I don't want to be responsible for that."

"A heart of gold."

"Fuck that. Just watching my ass. Speaking of"—and here Mark's eyes went dark and he became that fifteen-year-old with the mustache and short temper—"you're not going to rat me out to your pops, are you?"

Dean smiled. He was afraid, but he also had something on Mark now, didn't he? Dean wasn't ten years old anymore; he had a reputation for being dangerous and maybe a little crazy, and didn't Mark know all that? "I'm just looking to get fucked up," he said. "And today's payday."

Mark relaxed and put his large fist on Dean's shoulder. Not a punch, but a gesture of camaraderie. And here was the final perk, the biggest one: a tingle in Dean's pants. But he walked it off.

At the end of his shift, Dean told his dad he'd be a minute and followed Mark out to his truck. Mark gave him ten 30 mg OxyContin pills and ten 25 mg amphetamine pills, each in separate baggies. "The Oxy'll give you a real warm float. The speed is no joke, but expect to crash after work. If this is your first time, do me a favor and try them at home. See what you can handle before coming in here all fucked up."

"Can I pay you Monday? I don't have cash on me."

"Yeah, sure," Mark said, but he wasn't happy about it.

Back in his dad's truck: "Congratulations on your first paycheck. Hold on to it until we find an apartment."

A half mile down the towpath west of the boat museum and dry docks, an old stone aqueduct crossed Chittenango Creek. At that hallowed intersection, the flat brown water of the canal was carried over the crisp rattling water of the creek. This was where Dean spent much of his free time, with a bag of weed and some books and the dog. This was where he would take the Oxy.

For the past two years, Dean had been going through a canal phase. His interest in history came from his childhood obsession with ghosts, and the ghosts that most loitered around Chittenango were those along the old Erie Canal, which passed through the village to the north. Here was a dry dock landing built in 1856; there was a two-building museum, the stones of the dry docks excavated and restored. It was a sight Dean would sometimes sit and contemplate until he could hear the hammers working the cargo boats, an easy drift into the past, a mere letting go of the moment so that the swift current of time could rush him backward. Soon he'd be sharing the thick smoky air of the canning factory with hoggees and mules, blacksmiths and steersmen and captains, who sometimes got too much drink in them and looked at a stranger the wrong way, and the shirts came off and the fists went up and some quick bets were taken to see who was the better boxer.

He'd planned to make a day of it, bringing along a six-pack of Genny, a paperback history of bare-knuckle prize fighting, and Paddy, the leash tied to Dean's belt. He set up on the towpath overlooking the creek twenty feet below, legs dangling over the edge of the aqueduct. It was a beautiful day for early April, the blue sky reflecting off the shallow water rippling under his feet. The budding leaves of the dense woods from where the creek flowed were jeweled with sun, and every now and then there was a breeze that smelled of the beginnings of spring. Dean put his face up to the sky and squinted and let the sounds of water and birds and Paddy panting in his lap take him. And they did, and that was when he knew the Oxy was working.

A jogger was crunching down the path, a female whose ponytail bounced with her stride. Dean wanted to stop her and talk to her, just to talk. He wanted her story; he wanted to tell her his. But all he could do was wave and say hi.

What was this heaven pulsing through him? This joy? There was so much beauty surrounding him; he felt full and significant and connected. He saw the water, both still and running, as that which was within him. The veins in the leaves were his veins. That bright sun that warmed his winter bones was his heart. Paddy was licking his cheeks because Dean was weeping.

He decided to move closer to the creek; the grass on the bank looked soft. He climbed over the rail and walked the stone aqueduct until it met up with the grass and then walked down, using the stone wall to steady his decline. There was his place in the sun, bent grass and oat grass, honeysuckle and clover, a reclining mattress of green, even softer than it appeared. He cracked a beer and gulped half of it, delicious and cold. He poured some into his palm for Paddy, who was accustomed to the taste of Genny Cream Ale. Down here, he could smell the rich, wet earth.

He wanted more—more joy, more beauty, more warmth, that which he'd been starved of like a prisoner is of light. He took another Oxy from his pocket and washed it down with beer.

His thoughts wandered to Mark and what he found there was no anger. In fact, he wanted Mark here with him, to talk to him about whether it feels this way to everyone and how much of this is real and if he could feel this forever. Dean lit a cigarette and thought of ways to invite Mark here. Whenever he thought of Jason and what Mark had done to him, a yellow wall of light went up, blocking the negativity. How could any of this be? A life free of all that darkness and death; he had never considered it a possibility. He hadn't thought he deserved it.

And then he wondered if it was possible to feel even *better* than this, and if that, too, was something he deserved.

The grass was sucking him in, then cradling, and then the bank was a hammock, just a light undulation. Paddy lapped at the creek. Dean chain-smoked. The warmth dissipated as the sun dipped below the trees and the shadow of the aqueduct blanketed him. He considered popping another pill, but there was the mile to walk home yet. So there he was, hugging the shoulder of the road where he could reach out and touch the cornstalks, some of that good feeling left in his fingertips.

By the time he reached his front yard, the lightning bugs were out. He hated lightning bugs.

Monday morning, back at Mohawk, Dean tried the speed. It woke him, that was for sure. Then it gave him *the focus*, and his arms and hands were doing the work without him, feeding the machine the sheets, punching them, pulling them out, and stacking them. When break came, he had to pull himself away.

"Looks like you're getting the hang of this." His dad's eyes were opaque from the dust coating his protective glasses.

Dean shrugged and moved past him, spotting Mark's broad back filing along with the others toward the exit door. The speed made Dean eager to see Mark. He butted in next to him, one of the Dozen saying, "What the fuck, asshole?"

"He's cool," Mark said. "This is Mr. Flaming's—er, Fleming's son. How's it going, Dean?"

"Can we talk?"

"Dude, you're balling. Lookit those pupils."

The Dozen examined him:

"Is this his first time?"

"How you feeling?"

"Like a fucking machine," Dean said.

Everyone laughed.

"Just try not to look your dad in the eyes."

"That won't be a problem," Dean said, then repeated to Mark: "Can we talk?"

Mark told his boys he'd meet up with them in a minute. Dean and Mark went outside, shielding their eyes from the sun. Others occupied the surrounding picnic tables, pulling sandwiches and Cokes from coolers. Dean offered Mark a cigarette, and they both took long drags.

"What's up?"

"That Oxy, holy shit."

"I know, right?"

"That shit's for real?"

"Be careful with it."

"Do you have anything stronger?"

Mark yanked at his hat, released smoke from his nose and the remainder came with his answer. "The only thing stronger is heroin."

Dean's stomach flipped at the prospect. He'd never tried heroin, but the speed made him feel he could handle anything. "Do you sell that?"

Mark scratched his beard and smiled. "I don't give a shit what you do with your life, but," he wiggled his hat, "I don't know, man. You're moving fast."

Dean now realized that he and amphetamines did not mix. His jaw was sore from clenching his teeth, and he was already on his second cigarette in two minutes. Worse, the speed was stoking his fury. He wanted to hurt Mark right there. He wanted to hold open Mark's eyelid and take the lighter to his squishy eyeball and watch it melt and run down his face and dribble into his beard and stick there like a raw, snotty egg. He noticed, too, that he was standing too close to Mark, looking at him too hard, which in any other context would be a stare-down.

But D-Mart had what Dean wanted. So Dean resorted to, "You know what I've been through, right?"

Mark stuffed his smoke out in the receptacle. "Yeah, I know."

"What do you know?" Maybe not a fair question, but the anger was difficult to contain.

"I know, okay. I know. Listen. Shit, give me another smoke."

Dean lit one for him.

"You still owe me money."

"I know, I have it."

Mark exhaled. "I don't deal H here. Do you know where I live?"

"Yeah."

"Come by this evening."

"Alright."

Mark removed his hat and swiped at his black, greasy hair. "Not that I give a shit, but before you come just think about what you're getting into."

Dean fought the urge to tell him to go fuck himself.

It took Dean twenty minutes to walk to Mark's, which was up on Falls Boulevard, in the woodsy, elevated part of town. The house, once grand in the nineteenth century, was now slumped and slouched. Dean was on the groaning front porch, careful where he rested his weight. He was on edge, despite having crunched an Oxy over an hour ago. To enter this house could be seen as betrayal. But his objective had changed since Mark had introduced him to opiates. Now there were options where there hadn't been before. There was the possibility that Dean could turn his back on his rotten past and experience a life of pretty things and pretty feelings. All he had to do was endure the treachery of befriending Jason's tormentor until he got a taste of that heaven in his guts. And then, who the hell cared?

Dean opened the storm door to knock, even though it lacked a screen. He thought of what he knew about Mark's parents, how his mother was laid up and dying of something drawn out and painful, and how his old man would have to work well beyond retirement age to pay her medical bills. Dean was here to score, but he understood the weight of grief he'd be forced to respect once he entered this house.

Mark answered the door, lifted his hat to the top of his head, what Dean read as a welcoming gesture. The house opened to a dim mudroom, crowded with coats and shoes and caps. The foreign smells of someone else's habitat were insistent; the must and musk of others' clothes and the cabinet spices and decades of cooking from the kitchen just ahead, everywhere a moldy stuffiness that felt to Dean like a haunting.

Mark walked him past the dirty kitchen, through the dining room that housed stacks of warped boxes and a table with envelopes, and into the family room, a sullen den of frayed furniture and stained carpeting and tawdry lace curtains. It took a moment to notice Mr. DeMartano sitting on the couch watching basketball, as quiet and banal as the rest of the room.

When the old man saw Dean, he snapped from his TV trance and grunted to stand.

"This is Dean Fleming," Mark offered.

Mr. DeMartano shook Dean's hand with a supplication that embarrassed Dean. It was clear that he recognized the gravity of his boss's son standing in his family room.

"Phil DeMartano. Good to meet you, son."

"Thanks," Dean said, unable to meet the man's eyes. "You, too."

"Can we get you anything? Beer? A sandwich?"

"We're going to hang out upstairs, Dad."

"Just keep the noise down so you don't wake your mother." Mr. DeMartano sank back into the couch, which coughed up dusty fibers. "Say hi to your dad for me."

"Okay." But what Dean wanted suddenly was to put his hand around his dad's throat and demand that he explain how, in good conscience, he could allow this busted old man to labor like a slave on the floor at Mohawk. Surely there had to be a desk job, something easier with better pay.

Dean followed Mark up the creaking, carpeted stairs, eager to leave Mr. DeMartano. Instead, he was met with low, dusty coughing that sounded more like a children's toy running low on batteries. Mark stopped at the first door at the top of the stairs.

"Give me a sec."

Mark eased open the door and went in. Dean heard him speak softly to his mother, sweetly. He didn't dare to peek inside. He understood too well the appearance of death, but he didn't think he could bear to see the look of dying. When she coughed again, Dean was about to go back downstairs and ditch the whole thing. But Mark emerged, closing the door behind him.

He said, "Sorry." Just like that, the dying mother was put behind them, and they continued down the narrow hallway.

At the end of it was Mark's room, dark and spacious and unexpectedly tidy. The room was set up like a studio apartment, with a microwave atop a mini-fridge, a couch, a coffee table, and a forty-inch flat screen TV mounted on the wall.

"I have plans to renovate the house," Mark said as if in apology. He unloaded himself onto the couch, nodded to a stack of home repair books on the coffee table. He smiled. "Whenever I get around to it."

"Sounds fun," Dean said without sarcasm. He sat one cushion away from Mark.

The coffee table was already meticulously set. Cotton balls, alcohol swabs, two packaged syringes, a lighter, the severed bottom of a beer can, two plastic cups half-filled with water, and a stamp-sized wax-paper package.

"You ready to do this?"

"I'm here."

Dean watched as Mark's thick, hardened fingers adjusted the sacred objects as if perfecting a collage. "I'll show you, but I'm not going to shoot you up. I don't shoot people up. I can hardly shoot myself. I actually hate needles. I used to snort, but goddamn it's not the same. I don't shoot in the arm 'cause I like to wear short sleeves, especially now spring is here. Jesus, you got some thick-ass veins on you, though. And those tattoos, maybe you can get away with it. I shoot on my thumb or feet." Mark wiggled his bare toes, ropy veins spidering the tops of his feet and around his ankles. "You want to keep a rotation going, otherwise the veins can collapse.

"I don't use spoons. I got tired eating my cereal with black spoons all the time; I felt like a junky. You can shoot and not be a junky, you know. The bottom of a beer can works better. You just want to be sure to keep everything clean."

Talking, talking, talking: an uncharacteristic nervous excitement as if he was showing a friend a new toy. But Dean was lost watching Mark play with the instruments—imagining being played.

"Use the swabs; don't share needles. I don't even like reusing needles if I can help it, but I can be a little OCD, ha ha. Always filter with the cotton. You don't want to shoot little particles in your bloodstream. The stuff I get you don't even need to cook to dissolve, but I do anyway because I like to think that it's nice and warm going in. Keep your dirty fingers out of the solution, too. I've seen infected arms, goddamn, like in that movie where the dude has to have his arm amputated. You don't want that. You'll know you hit when you pull the plunger out and see blood. If you miss, you'll get a blister. In the beginning, I had blisters all over my toes. Not a huge deal, but they can get infected. Don't worry about the air. People worry too much about air. You always get a little air in the syringe. Got it?"

Dean laughed. "Just set me up. I'll figure it out."

"I'll set you up this once," Mark said, moving his hat up and down his head. "Then you're on your own."

"A true teacher."

"Fuck that."

Mark worked quickly, tapping the white powder from its package into the concave bottom of the can, adding the water, cooking and stirring, dropping in a piece of cotton until it swelled, filling two syringes. Just watching the ritual soothed Dean.

Mark handed over a loaded syringe. "You won't need to tie off with ropes like those." Mark brought his foot up and rested it on his knee.

He fingered a thick vein that cut across his ankle bone. "Watch me first."

He stuck the vein, then pulled on the plunger just slightly. "See that?" He pointed to the trickle of blood swimming in the auburn liquid of the tube. "That means I hit. Now I can shoot the fucker home. But I'll wait for you so we can do it at the same time."

A large, swirling lollipop tattoo occupied the bulk of Dean's arm, and it just so happened that it centered like a target on the biggest vein. He aimed for that, holding his breath. The needle poked his skin.

"Right there looks good."

Dean was anxious. He didn't fear needles, but nobody really liked them.

"Just relax, bro."

He stabbed and the skin gave.

"Now pull out the plunger."

He did, and the syringe sucked up blood.

"Alright, bro. Let's get fucked up. One, two, three . . ."

It began in the stomach like a tumbling ball of white light. He thought he might throw it up at first. But then it became warm, and it grew and filled his crotch and his legs and the bottoms of his feet, up his stomach and chest and arms and fingertips. And then the light extended beyond his body, taking him with it, busting out of that old rotting death house and into the bright, boundless sun.

"Kathy wants to take you out to dinner. You and me."

"Why?"

"Just to be nice, I don't know."

There remained an unreachable corner of Dean's brain that relished this opportunity to tell his dad and the girlfriend who wanted him out of his own house to fuck themselves. But these days, with the junk in his veins, he found life friendlier, and saw the virtue in extending it to others. It was like waking from a nightmare. Or he was finally given his due, someone—or something, could it be God?—deciding he'd done his time, and now the suffering could be lifted.

"Yeah, okay."

"I've been telling her how well you're taking to work. And . . . and how your attitude has, I don't know, changed."

Dean smiled. It was amusing that his dad wasn't sure how to treat him since he'd stopped being an asshole.

They ate in the village at Kathy's request. She thought Chittenango was cute, its connection to the *Wizard of Oz* unique, and wanted to try one of its few remaining Oz-themed restaurants. This was the only thing outsiders saw in Chittenango. But the yellow-bricked sidewalks and wooden Scarecrow greeting visitors coming in from Route 5 were all but invisible to natives, save for a few community organizers. For most residents, Oz and its many fantasies were incongruous with the long winters and wounded economy. Their own modest aspirations hardly ever included rainbows.

Still, here they were, sitting in a booth at Emerald City Grill, deciding whether they should order the Yellow Brick Road Fries as an appetizer.

Kathy was young, confident, and professional, some kind of social worker or counselor; Dean never cared to know. She was attractive, perhaps, if seen through his dad's eyes. Her hair was the most striking feature, long, straight, and shiny black, like an oil slick pouring down the back of her head. She might've been Italian or Brazilian or Iranian or Native American, something that would explain that hair and those dark eyes. Dean knew that she had lived in Queens, which was evident when she spoke and how she acted, as if the world would steal something from her at any opportunity. There had to be some hidden flaw that made her attracted to his homely dad and his mouth of crooked, stained teeth. Maybe it was herpes or a deformity under her clothes, a criminal record or schizophrenia, maybe even a recovering addict. Wouldn't that be something?

"So where did you guys meet?" Dean scratched his arm under the table.

His dad looked stiff in a button-up shirt, gnawing bread and looking for the waiter for another beer.

Kathy sipped her water, eyeballed her awkward boyfriend, then said, "On the internet."

"No shit? I didn't know Dad could use a computer."

"Ha ha. Very funny."

"Are you guys going to have kids?"

"Dean, come on."

"First we have to get married. Then, yes. I would like to have children." She put her unsettling eyes on him over her glass. "What do you think about that?"

Dean liked her frankness. It reminded him of his mom. He'd been thinking about her lately, ever since he'd begun feeling good and saw the possibility of forgiveness in the world.

"Sure," Dean said. "Why the hell not?"

At this moment, that was the truth. He wasn't in a thinking mood. But before the heroin and the pills, he'd thought a lot about his dad starting a new family. It was the worst offense imaginable. A family to his dad was like a car: if one breaks down, he goes and buys another. He didn't waste any time shopping around, either. That was what had sent his mom away. Of course, Dean had had a lot to do with her leaving, too.

"You could have brothers and sisters again," Kathy said. The *again* stung the table. Dean's smile was on pause; his dad quit chewing. Kathy didn't register or care. "We would love to have you around," she continued. "Isn't that right, Karl?"

His dad swallowed before he was ready. He tipped the Bud Light, but it was empty. He cleared his throat. "Yes. You know, if you keep on this track, then, you know."

Like a shadow hand reaching into his brain and grabbing hold, Dean felt himself dragged into thought. He'd been digging a fork tine into his fingernail, and now he could feel it. He said he had to pee and got up to find the bathroom, nooked away in a dark corner near the kitchen. He didn't have his works with him, so he scooped some powder with the corner of his driver's license and sucked it up his nose. That shadow hand dissipated into pixels of light.

"Kathy," Dean said when he returned to the table, "since you're going to be living here, you ought to know something."

Kathy and Karl both inched closer, appearing anxious.

"People here will tell you that Chittenango means water running north," Dean said in a conspiratorial tone. "But it doesn't."

"So . . . ," Kathy played along. "What does it mean?"

Dean smiled and leaned back in his chair. "That's for you to find out."

They were both nodding off on the couch, watching but not watching basketball on the TV. It was the NCAA tournament, an important game, even though Syracuse wasn't playing. The motion on the screen was slow, as if the players were musical notes bouncing along the bright yellow court, lofty and airy like a hay field in autumn.

After a time, Mark lit a cigarette, then Dean did, too. The smoke and music mingled.

"Talk to me, Dean."

"What?"

"Tell me something."

"Like what?" Dean asked, his head rolling to the left to meet Mark, whose head had rolled to the right.

"Just anything, bro. Just anything."

Dean glanced lazily at Mark's big, work-bruised hands.

"Okay. Well. Okay. Have you ever heard of Paddy Ryan?"

"Tell me about Paddy motherfuckin' Ryan."

"Okay. He was a huge fucker, a bare-knuckle fighter from Troy. They called him Trojan Giant. He had a saloon on the Erie Canal and would beat the shit out of the mean drunks who talked big. So they called him King of the Erie Canal, too. People started talking about how much of a badass he was, and so some trainer recruited him to fight official."

"Tell me more, Dean."

Dean laughed.

"Seriously, man. I want to learn."

"You know how the Irish came over here for work? It was a potato famine going on over there, and so they came here and it was most of them Irish who dug the canal. Course you know them Irish like to drink, and they like to fight when they're drunk. Well, after a day of digging, they went to the saloons and tied one on and fought bare-knuckle like they did back home."

"The fighting Irish. Tell me more."

"Paddy Ryan won a bunch of fights from 1877, I think, to 1880. Then in May of 1880, I think, he fought an English dude called Joe Goss, who was the heavyweight champ. Aw, man, do you know how long they fought?"

"Naw, man."

"These dudes are pounding on each other without any protection. According to the London Prize Rules, they could wrestle, too."

"How long did they fight, Dean?"

"Eighty-seven fucking rounds."

"Fuck you."

"Ninety minutes of grappling and pounding the shit out of each other. Ninety minutes."

Mark was silent and looking at nothing.

Then Dean said, "What kind of will does it take to keep someone fighting that long?"

"Will. Is that what you call it?"

"And then I think about Joe Goss, who fought for that long and lost."

"I got to believe there's no loser in a fight like that."

"Maybe."

They both stared at that same nothing spot for a while.

Mark said, "Tell me more. I like to hear you talk."

"I can't think of anything right now."

"Hey Dean."

"Yeah."

"I'm sorry."

Something hot and thin sliced through Dean's stomach. "What?"

"For your brother. I'm real sorry about it. I felt like such shit when I heard what happened to you guys. I remember thinking the police would come and arrest me. I've been saying sorry to you guys in my prayers for a long time. But it don't mean shit unless you say it to the person who needs to hear it, right? So I'm real, real sorry, man. I mean it."

Mark put his arm around Dean and pulled him in for a strong hug that made Dean feel like a boy. It was enough. Such a simple apology, so easily said. Everything now so easy and simple.

According to the logic of the supernatural, Jason had owed Dean a visit for a while now. As children, the brothers had grown up with ghosts, with the frightening awareness that they swirled about their everyday lives and the boys had to wade through them as if moving through a crowd. In the basement ghosts, in the bathroom ghosts, under beds ghosts and, watching as they slept, the ghosts that'll get you if you're not sleeping.

But their fear was complicated, since they also tried summoning these spirits that they so feared. They wanted an experience, and since they had each other, they felt they could brave whatever came at them. On the floor of their shared bedroom, with one of Mom's bathroom candles, a Ouija board borrowed from a friend, each promising the other he wasn't pushing the pie around and around, landing so urgently on letters forming frightening names: Bloody Mary, Beelzebub, Lucifer. When asked where these demons were right now, the boys' hands jerked from the pie and they leapt into bed and under the covers before the answer completed: *Inside y—*

So in the days and weeks after Jason's death, Dean waited for his brother's inevitable return. Maybe he would come in the form of smoke at the foot of Dean's bed, or that spiderweb tickle on his neck while Dean brushed his teeth, or the banging of walls, the flinging of chairs. Even if he returned to terrorize Dean for not protecting him, appearing in a dark corner of the basement staring with TV-static eyes, at least he'd be there with him, reassuring Dean that Jason was not nothing.

But there was nothing. No amount of summoning or pleading or weeping or shouting brought him back. His brother was absolutely stricken from existence.

They were both nodding off on the couch. Something was on the TV, the main menu of a DVD with quiet sounds like snow falling in the woods. Or was it the mother's raspy coughs penetrating through the door? No, there was no death in here.

After a time, Mark lit a cigarette, then Dean did, too. Mark pulled on the crotch of his mesh shorts and smiled.

"Dude," he said. "Do you get a boner when you shoot?"

A thrill danced inside Dean. "Yeah," he lied.

"I get the hugest boner when the junk is good."

"Me, too."

"We should get some hookers up in here."

"By the time they got here . . ."

"How great would it be to just snap your fingers and have some pussy riding your dick?"

"Yeah."

"Do you know anyone we could invite over here?"

"Naw."

"Remember April Callahan? I used to call her and she'd come over and suck my dick and then leave. I think she's sucked every dick in Chittenango. She got married a couple years ago. Maybe she'll still come over."

Dean reached over to Mark's side of the coffee table for his lighter. He shot a peek at Mark's crotch, but his shorts were too bunched up to notice anything. When he sat back on the couch, he returned a bit closer to Mark so that if he raised his arm to scratch the back of his neck, like he did now, his elbow would touch Mark's shoulder, which it did.

And that was all it did.

At the aqueduct, thinking about *that kid*. Brett had taught Dean that violence and lust are entangled, a strange and wonderful braid. Years and years of going ignored, of testing God and fate and getting no reaction, Brett was finally there to acknowledge him. All Dean had to do was deform Brett's face with that egg. On a different bank of the creek, both of them teenagers, both of them angry at a world that wanted nothing to do with them, though what caused Brett's angst Dean couldn't name, didn't care to at that dark time. All Dean knew was that he wanted to damage everything he saw. Take this world that wanted nothing to do with him and reshape it with a blunt hammer so that it looked like how he saw it every day. That meant crushing someone's face. That meant setting things on fire. That meant pissing in the gas tanks of cars parked at St. Patrick's during ten o'clock mass. And that meant, early on, secreting away any information about his abductor out of a loyalty to her he still didn't understand—a loyalty and respect that replaced what he'd once had for his mother, whom he instead began treating in vile ways that should have struck him dead on the spot. If there was a God, he wouldn't have stood by and watched as Dean tried to climb on his mother.

But there were never consequences. Of course there weren't. Consequences required justice, and there was none. No rules, no morality. Just nothing. Always nothing.

Until Brett, who either awoke something in Dean or planted it in him. On the bank of the creek, yes, in the wet snow, waking to Brett's hot dick in Dean's pants, Brett's tongue in Dean's mouth, the fire raging through him as he pretended to be unconscious to let Brett do all he wanted to do—and hopefully he was in a doing mood. If he didn't open his eyes, didn't move, he couldn't be accused of anything. Not faggot or queer or fairy, all names he leveled on others as the worst thing you could be. But Dean wasn't yet thinking of what to call it, because he was busy feeling discovered. Feeling a part of life's prettiness, that silky skin he hadn't been allowed to see in so long, and never like this. Then feeling what Brett had left gooped in his pubic hair, then tasting it to emblazon this moment in memory, to secure it so he could easily find it again.

But like Jason, Brett had abandoned him. They never again shared that mysterious act, not even close. Brett became interested in a girl, and now Brett was gone to college, gone maybe for good because why the hell would he come back here? The only memento left behind was the dog.

Nodding off on the couch. Spring thunderstorm, dark sky, dark house but for the light from the TV. Rain pelted the roof; Dean felt wet.

They lit cigarettes, heads rolled to meet each other's glassy eyes.

"Wanna hear about John L. Sullivan?"

"You know I do."

This had been rehearsed. Dean displayed the book he'd stolen from the library. He opened it to the page he'd bookmarked earlier. He teased Mark with a photograph on the page so he'd sit closer. He did, and they sat hip to hip.

"This is John L. Sullivan, the man who beat Paddy Ryan."

"Lookit that dude."

The man in the photo had perfectly parted hair and a large, twisty mustache, and posed with his fists in front of him, fighting Irish style.

"Sullivan was more badass than Paddy Ryan. He was American-born, from Boston. At the age of seventeen he was challenging every man in every Boston bar to a fight and winning. When he was nineteen, he started getting into official matches. He fought for over an hour, beating some dude called 'The Bull's Head of Terror.'"

"Goddamn."

Mark's shoulder pressed against Dean's as he continued to gaze at the photo. His breathing was slow and smooth. Dean could feel it on his neck. Dean looked past the book to Mark's shorts, where this time, his erection was unmistakable through the mesh.

"In one of his fights, Sullivan showed up to the ring drunk. He even drank whiskey and tea between rounds. His opponent, Kilrain, I think, Jake Kilrain, was beating him up pretty good. And in the forty-fourth round, Sullivan leaned over the ring and puked."

Mark laughed.

"I know. But that turned things around, cleared him up good. Sullivan won that fight in seventy-five rounds when Kilrain became too exhausted to keep on."

Dean let his hand holding the book fall, landing on Mark's lap. The back of his wrist was on top of Mark's dick. Mark said nothing. Though his heart hammered, Dean was strangely calm. He felt like an engine thumping steam while coasting down a glass-smooth canal.

"When Sullivan beat Paddy Ryan, he became the last bare-knuckle champion." Dean rolled his wrist gently back and forth. "A few years later, fighters started wearing gloves. Even under the new rules, Sullivan still kicked ass. Then he was the first boxing champ."

"Badass," Mark said into his eyelids, wherever he was. "Tell me more."

Dean turned his hand so that he now held the thick head of Mark's dick. He ran his palm down to its base, then back up, *talking talking talking* about whatever facts came to his mind, all his reading and studying, all those Irish fighters, all those canal kings, culminating in this moment, talking until he couldn't talk anymore, the words made into all that flesh, and Mark's big hand on the back of his head, then both hands, and the rain pounding the house and everything wet.

Sunlight beat through his drawn blinds. Something wasn't right but it was too early to know. The clock said nine a.m. It wasn't Saturday or Sunday. Every day for the past month his dad had woken him for work.

Dean stumbled out into the kitchen before his morning taste. In the center of the kitchen table, he found a note placed on top of his shave bag. *Get your ass out of the house. Don't be here when I get home.*

"Fuck."

Then a car's engine, and in the driveway, a black, shiny Jetta. Kathy emerged, heels clapping as she charged toward the front door. His head thrummed and he sat at the table and rubbed his temples.

"You stupid shit," she announced, stomping into the house and into the kitchen.

He didn't look at her. Kept his head down and took the lashing.

"Your dad was trying to help you. He was actually proud of you. And you've gone and broke his heart. Look at me when I'm talking to you."

He didn't. He studied the way the wood rippled in the old table.

"So this is where you keep your junk, is it?" She snatched his bag. "Oh, you'll look at me now."

"Put that down."

"I deal with shits like you all the time. Deadbeat junkies who throw away their entire lives. You know where they end up?"

"Put that down."

"In a gutter, dead."

The chair suddenly crashed and the table lifted and slammed back down and his neck broiled and he shouted, "Put that down, you bitch, or I swear to God."

"Don't you dare—"

"I swear to God!" He flipped the table on its side and raised his fist at her and those so-dark eyes of hers flooded with light so they became plain old brown. He wanted to hit her. Or he wanted to hit and ruin in general, that old reliable feeling of watching things fall apart. All that ugliness was still just below his skin.

She dropped the bag and moved toward the front door. In the safety of its threshold, the daylight on her back, she shouted, "Don't come back here, Dean. Don't ever come back here."

He snatched up the bag and headed to his room. His fingers shook trying to get the powder out of its package. His eyes watered as he dissolved it in the cap of a water bottle. The veins were always easy to come by. He stuck the big, bruised one in the crook of his arm, and by the time the drug mingled with his blood, the tears spilling down his face were those of joy.

The grass behind the aqueduct wall was rain slick. The creek ran heavier, a frothy rush more than the usual murmur. Dean nodded off on the bank as Paddy barked at birds. Duffel bag stuffed with clothes, books, a blanket, a bag of pretzels, and maybe three days' worth of H if he was careful. This would be their home, unless Mark invited him to live with him. Dean smiled thinking about it, renovating the house while Mark was at work, getting high together in the evenings. Living the rebel life, a secret relationship in a small town. Why couldn't it be this way?

He woke to his thigh buzzing. The sky was deep blue and the trees were black. He scratched his thigh and it was hard because it was his phone. A series of texts from Mark. It was the first time he'd heard from him since the previous evening.

U said u wouldnt rat
Ur dad searched are lockers for drugs
Bunch got fired cause of u
Not me but friends
U come back to work I kill u

It was exhausting to think about trying to defend himself through text. He flopped the phone to the grass. He called Paddy, who didn't know its name, but knew when it was being called. Dean hugged its wet body to his chest, and it responded by lapping his cheek. "I guess I got my fight," Dean said, and then he nodded off again.

He woke, though he was never really asleep. Paddy was nestled into Dean's arm, breathing deeply. The woods were alive with creature noise, some sounding very close. The sky was muddled with clouds, allowing no moon or stars to see by so that everything before him, even the creek only a few yards away, was muted in pitch. He was afraid. He took out his cell, squinted at its light. It was two a.m. He saw again the texts from Mark.

All that he had tried like hell to bury and run from, he was now digging up and sitting on in an attempt to get ready for a fight. Now that he had found a way to forget, and forgive, and even to love, he was forced to ditch it for the old angry bastard who liked to wreck and ruin. The problem was, it had been six hours since his last hit, and Dean could feel the call of the needle. But once that was in him, everything became warm, gooey sunshine. Not the fighter's mentality.

He tried to put it out of his head. He crunched some pretzels. He wrapped himself in the blanket and read by the light of his phone. He tried thinking about fighting Mark, sitting atop of him and pounding. But those scenarios kept slipping into the beginnings of something sexual, a hot wrestling fuck peppered with punches. When he felt the stiffness in his pants, he smacked his skull.

By two thirty, a fierce shiver overtook him and he felt the need to shit or puke. Paddy barked at his groans. Maybe he could take a small bump to settle the pains, and then pop speed to get him jacked up. That should get him to three thirty, when the plan was to walk back home and steal his dad's truck and drive to Mohawk and then see what his fists could do.

A floodlight suddenly blasted the path overhead. Dean grabbed up Paddy and hugged the wall of the aqueduct until it passed. Then he vomited pretzels and bile. Fuck this night.

Using his house key, he scooped a small bit of powder and sucked it up his nose. He quickly stuffed the rest away before doing more. From his duffel bag he found the speed and swallowed one. He cupped water from the creek to get it down. It tasted good, cold and fresh. He had another drink. He fell to his knees and plunged his face into the water. Then farther down, so his ears were submerged, and it felt he was filled up and part of the creek. He came up gasping and changed. His body didn't feel right, like the drugs were fighting for his attention. He was drowsy and warm, but the muscles in his jaw and arms and legs were tense. One drug brought the sun and the other made it sizzle.

Body buzzing, he pulled out his phone and texted Mark. *Meet you in the parking lot.*

"What do you mean you're not going to fight him?"

"Lookit'm. It'd be like beating on a retard," Mark said.

"Fuck that, after ratting us all out?"

The lamplight swirled like a spotlight finding its mark. Dean scratched his arm where only twenty minutes ago he'd shot up, the calling of a fix he couldn't ignore any longer. Paddy yapped from the truck behind him. There was no desperation, but Dean understood that this was his time to do *something*, before he lost his audience, before he was beat down, before he gave in to the high and melted into the cold asphalt.

"I forgive you!" It was his own voice, though it sounded as though it came from a recording of him from some forgotten time in history, when the technology was new and crude.

"The fuck did you say?"

"I forgive all your transgressions," he said, laughing.

"Motherfucker."

"Jack him up!"

"I swear to God, D-Mart. I swear to fucking God if you don't."

The Dozen entered the ring, shaking with hate. Mark was in the middle, commanding his boys with an upheld hand and eying Dean from under the shadow of his hat.

"I can't hold'm off," Mark told Dean. "You understand that, don't you?"

Dean put up his dukes John L. Sullivan style. He'd come to fight, goddammit. When asked from that future place where someday he will be judged, he'll be able to say he fought. He said, "Bring it, pussies. Ha ha."

They rushed him. There he was, watching again. Watching the dirty tread of so many boots, the gum and pebbles and caked dirt of the few places they'd been. Watching the knuckles, some bony, some plump, some hairy, all singularly bloodied. Watching the faces, the variations of teeth and mouths and lips and tongues and what those all do in combination when contorted into exertion. Watching, and doing nothing.

And then the movie changed. The faces and knuckles and boots were disappearing, revealing more of the sky. A hat fluttered down from above, landing on Dean's chest. It belonged to Mark, who had now turned on his Dozen. At his canted angle, he saw Mark recover from a punch: his hand on the ground keeping him from falling. Half of his Dozen circled him, the other half stunned and bleeding. Mark righted, got his weight on his back leg, brought up those hulking fists, and spit out a tooth. Dean watched its slow, bloody trajectory, its bounce, and when it settled, the next round had begun.

They charged him, and Mark crunched the nearest face, the nose and cheekbone caving. He took a hit on his ear and in his ribs but then swung the blade of his elbow, slicing open an eyebrow that sprayed the lot of them. The growling he did, goddamn. Two more remained. They moved around him cautiously, not wanting to be there but way too late to back off.

"Come on, motherfuckers."

Mark was shiny with blood. His beard and hair made him look wild. The light in the sky was taking over the dark. The lamp was flickering, as if straining to stay on to see what happened. The one jumped Mark from behind, getting him in a choke; while Mark's hands went to his neck, the other shot his boot into Mark's groin. The sound of him roaring shook Dean's ribs, the first real sensation of pain that morning. Mark fell to his knees, the choker trying to get under his chin, and if he did, it would be over. The one in front took advantage and hit Mark in the face. His eye instantly swelled. He took another punch on the other side of his face. This one landed too high on the head, causing the puncher to grab his wrist in pain. From his knees, Mark swung, landing a violent blow in the soft spot of his friend's kidney. This small victory seemed to rile Mark. It was as though he'd been shot up with a sudden dose of adrenaline. He hollered and stood one leg at a time, bringing the choker up with him. He swung around so fast, using the choker's momentum to bring him around, where Mark hugged his waist and detached him from his neck, and then brought the body down hard over his knee. The last of the Dozen folded disgustingly, bounced off Mark's knee, and fell in a heap that looked like death.

"You motherfuckers!" Mark turned, leveling this curse on each of them, spitting and maybe even crying.

And then he turned to Dean. He bent to get his hat, shoved it down on his head. Dean felt like a crime scene the way Mark was looking him over.

"Dean," Mark said, slapping Dean's cheek, then snapping his fingers in front of his eyes.

"Yeah?"

"You okay?"

"Yeah." Then he wondered if he was.

"You're an asshole." Mark sat on the ground beside him. He winced, put his hand to his crotch and grunted.

"I wanted to fight you."

Mark looked at him and shook his head. "I should've never sold that shit to you."

"You're John motherfuckin' Sullivan."

"Shut the fuck up."

"King of the Canal."

Mark sighed. The bodies laid out were writhing and groaning. Beyond the corner of the factory, cars and trucks were filing into the parking lot. He said, "I'm fucked for this."

"I didn't tell my dad nothing." Pain was beginning to call to him from far below, just an echo, really, but a reminder of what was waiting to greet him. He said, "Sorry," feeling the weight of each letter on his tongue as if they were little plastic pieces in his mouth.

Mark hit Dean on the arm and said, "C'mon, get up."

"Naw, man. Just leave me here."

"Get the fuck up." Mark stood, then grabbed Dean by the arms and yanked him. The parking lot swirled and didn't immediately settle. Mark held him up, more or less dragged him.

"Where we going?"

"I'm driving us out of here."

"I need my dog."

Mark sighed. He swiveled them around and headed to the truck. Paddy's tail flapped at the sight of them. Mark opened the door. "Cute dog."

"I need my bag, too."

Mark reached across the driver seat to get the bag. He handed it to Dean, who worked it over his shoulder. Mark held the dog like a football and, while hugging Dean, kicked the truck door closed. They then continued across the ring and the cursing Dozen to Mark's truck.

"Are we going to your house?"

"Hell no. I'm taking you home. I don't want to see your face again."

"I can't go home. My dad kicked me out."

"Jesus Christ." Mark got him into his truck and slammed the door. He walked around and got into the driver's seat. "Then I'll take you to the hospital. And then I hope you get the hell out of Chittenango. You should have a long fucking time ago."

He turned the ignition and put the truck in drive.

"What about my dog?"

"I'll hold on to your fucking dog."

Paddy stayed on Mark's lap as they drove out of the parking lot, past the stream of cars coming in.

"He likes you," Dean said smiling.

"Fantastic."

Dean kept looking at Mark and smiling.

"What?"

"John motherfuckin' Sullivan."

"Dude, shut up." Still, Mark couldn't help but laugh.

A MOTHER'S MANIFESTO

"Don't you just wish you finished me off when you had the chance? Don't you just wish you killed me?"

—Seung-Hui Cho, Virginia Tech shooter

Spring, 2007

WHEN IT HAPPENED, SHE was sure Dean had done it. Early reports had over twenty students and faculty gunned down on a college campus. The unidentified shooter killed two in a dormitory, then crossed campus looking for more. From the inside of an engineering building, he chained the doors, then opened fire on the classrooms. Students and professors barricaded themselves in rooms and offices, heard the gunshots go on for twenty minutes, heard screams, heard the shooter laugh between rounds. Then he turned the gun on himself.

Since leaving Chittenango almost ten years ago, Rene Fleming Hayes had been following local and national reports of rapes, molestations, Satanic sacrifices of animals or young women, and mass shootings. Anything sick and twisted. Nearly every morning, she searched the Internet, knowing one day she'd find Dean in one of these articles, hoping for it to happen to get it over with while praying that it wouldn't. So when the reports came of the shooting at Virginia Tech, she sat in her administrator's office at Erie Community College refreshing the news page, waiting for the shooter's name.

"You hear about the shooting?" Gloria, the work study student, wheeled her chair into Rene's cubicle. She was a big, beautiful Puerto Rican who wore low-cut blouses and short skirts, despite her size. She was also Rene's only friend.

Chair to chair, Rene put her head on Gloria's shoulder, smelled the coconut shampoo in her still-damp hair. "Seriously messed up shit."

"You said it, Rene." Diane Baker leaned onto the dividing wall, pulling her scarf across her chin. "Just awful."

Diane was their boss, dean of the Arts and Sciences Department. She was in her sixties, tall and stout and square-jawed. She wore no makeup or jewelry, nor any product in her flat, sandy hair, but compensated with colorful silk scarves. Every day, a different scarf. Today it was a black-and-yellow tiger print.

Rene asked, "Do they know who did it?"

Gloria was about to speak, but Diane interrupted. "They're not saying. But he shot himself. They always shoot themselves. I don't understand why they don't shoot themselves first."

Rene looked at the image on the computer screen of two female students crying and hugging each other, their everyday lives irreparably wounded. She closed the page. "Because they're sick shits."

"Sick shits! You have such a way with words, Rene." Diane's eyes softened again. "I always want to know where these shooters' mothers are. It seems like they just need some affection."

She stared at Diane longer than was appropriate. This coming from a woman who never married and had no children. Unless she considered Rene and Gloria her children, which was a strong possibility. Rene assumed that Diane had hired her out of some vague liberal guilt. Rene wasn't college educated, had come from working-class people, and cursed more often than she should have. Despite how slow Rene was to learn the computers and how many projects she messed up, Diane was always patient and kind. Maybe she could put a sentence together in a way Diane liked, but Rene would have fired herself long ago.

"I think we should make some sort of announcement about all this to send to our faculty. Could you draft an email for me? I don't know, something about keeping our eyes and hearts open. Maybe use that phrase. You have such a nice way with words. Thanks, Rene."

As you all are aware, Monday morning brought tragic news of a shooting on the campus of Virginia Tech. While hundreds of miles away, this horrendous act affects us all. On behalf of the Arts and Sciences Department, I would like to express my utter sadness. While the loss of life has not happened here at ECC, it easily could have. The victims could have been our sons and daughters—could have been you or me. We've all had to huddle under desks, barricade ourselves in closets and classrooms, begging to be spared. We've all encountered those who want to ruin as many lives as possible. And some of us even know the shooters, casually or intimately. He bags our groceries or sits at our dinner table; he makes our lattes or calls on Mother's Day and you don't speak, but maybe sometimes you let him slur some version of a greeting before hanging up on him and feeling so gross that he came from you, that he is part of you. And maybe you're most disgusted, repulsed, that you gave up on him. You tried, but did you try hard enough?

I tried on motherhood, but it rejected me. If I tried any harder, I wouldn't have survived. Sometimes I have my doubts that I did. I am a divorcée; my youngest was abducted and murdered; the other, the Shit who lived, went on to molest and psychologically torture me. I am afraid of him. I am afraid of what he will do, not to me—because he's already ruined me—but to others. Call me what you will, but I know that it would have been better had the Shit never been born. I can already hear you clucking your tongues, arguing that a good mother should stick by her son no matter how sick he is, especially if he was kidnapped as a child and his little brother was killed. Believe me, I endured this thinking for years. Until I learned to let go of this burden of being a "good mother." I have stopped blaming myself. No, that's not it. I have grown exhausted with blaming myself. I'm hungover with it. So a few years ago, I made the decision to leave the Shit back in Chittenango. I don't see it now as much of a choice; it was either stay and rot, or leave and live. Blame me if you will, but I am no martyr. I am not in the business of sainthood.

The day after the shooting, Rene woke to find Dean sleeping on her couch. He had found her. He'd dug around in the poison muck that was his heart and found the unbreakable thread that binds mother and son. Either that or her ex-husband had told him where she lived so he could get Dean out of his hair.

As soon as she discovered him passed out in her apartment, Rene got the .45 down from the shoe box in the closet. She'd purchased the gun when she first moved here, never having lived in a city or by herself, for that matter. Now, she made sure it was loaded. She then leveled the gun on Dean.

She had long abandoned the useless exercise of thinking about why he turned out the way he did. What was even more liberating was when she stopped thinking of him as her son. That way, she could see him for who he was: a twenty-five-year-old shit of a man who was capable of the kind of evil that had taken place in Virginia.

Early on, she'd done what she could to save him. She gave him attention and affection, took him to church every day for a year. He saw as many therapists as she and Karl could afford, and many they couldn't. And all the while, she had endured being groped and masturbated on by him, by her son. She could still feel that scalding hot prick poking her thigh. Some nights she'd climb into her bed to find a pool of his semen on her pillow. She had put up with this for years, because, she'd thought, that's what a mother should do. He needed positive attention; he needed not to be judged or scolded, but talked to, openly and frankly. She'd bought him a stack of *Hustlers*, plopped them on his bed, and told him any jerking off he planned on doing in the future would be to these magazines, on these magazines if he wanted, and in this bedroom. If he got bored of these then she'd get him something else. Redheads, black ladies, bondage, or men—she'd get him whatever he wanted as long as he left her the hell out of his sick fantasies.

She didn't kill the Shit. She thought about it, squeezed the .45 until the crosshatch grip dug into her palm. Watching as he slept on the couch.

Then she stuck the gun in the waistband of her pajamas and shouted at him to wake up.

His green eyes popped open directly. Those creepy eyes, the ones that saw in the conventional way, but not what most saw.

He sat up like a homeless man might from a park bench, slow and painfully. His face was busted, yellowed with bruises and crusted with scabs. His long, thin arms were crowded with tattoos: skulls and fire, crows and crosses, a rebel flag and "Mom" inside a bleeding heart. He was about to say something polite, Rene could see it. He got a soft look sometimes, sifting through the ashy wasteland that was his heart for goodness. That was the look that had kept her believing in him for too long.

"Get the fuck out."

He expected this. He rubbed the brown stubble of his shaved head. His hands, even his fingers, were tattooed. The fingernails were bruised purple, maybe a couple were missing. He stood, up and up, so long and tall, so gross. He stepped into his battered brown sneakers and slung the duffel bag over his shoulder.

"Just . . ." She crossed her arms on top of her head and growled, "Just wait." She huffed and stomped into the adjoining kitchen, slamming through the refrigerator and cupboards. She tried not to get too angry at herself for this weakness. She slapped mayonnaise and mustard on four slices of bread. Pounded the bread with bologna that she found in the back of the fridge. Tore the processed cheese from its plastic. Cut the sandwiches on a diagonal, how he liked. There was a bruised apple in the crisper, a can of Coke Zero in the door, and an unopened box of Wheat Thins in the cupboard. She jammed the food in a plastic grocery bag and shoved the bag into his chest.

"That's all you'll get," she said, and was about to tell him to go. Then she noticed his arms. Hidden in the darkened maze of tattoos on the insides of both were numerous punctures, as though he'd reached into a hive of African wasps.

The Shit gave her his saddest look.

The next day, Rene sat at her desk, fingers poised on the keyboard, pretending to be in deep thought. She waited in that position for almost an hour, until Diane finally emerged from her office, tussling her hair for the lift it would never have.

"How's that email coming along?"

She exhaled dramatically. "It's difficult, Diane."

"I was hoping to send something out by this morning. Get a jump on President Spiegle."

"I'll try."

"Please include a note to our instructors to contact me right away if they are suspicious of their students' behavior. Phrase it however you want, but make it clear that we're taking this seriously."

"I already have that in my notes."

When Diane was gone, Gloria wheeled her chair into Rene's cubicle. Gloria was a junior, the first in her family of eight to attend college. When she came to the office in September of 2005, Rene had been tasked with training her; by October of the same year, she was going to Gloria with questions about how to sort a spreadsheet and how to convert a Word file into a PDF.

"Raynay, why don't you tell her you can't do it?"

"I've been writing something, it's just not what she's looking for."

"Say the word, and I'll do it for you." She put her hand on Rene's. Gloria's fake nails glittered, one of them pierced with a tiny, dangly ring. Rene toyed with it absently.

"How long do I have to sit here before you tell me what's going on?"

We ask that you are vigilant. If you notice any suspicious behavior from your students, either in the classroom or in their written assignments, please contact my office and Student Services right away. Suspicious behavior can take many forms:

Poor impulse control

Sudden changes in hygiene

Lethargy

Bones poking through scaly skin

Blackened fingernails and yellowed eyes

Sunken, hollow face

Regardless, I let him stay. Let him put his body on my couch, his hands in my fridge, his piss in my pot. He uses my toothpaste, my bathtub, my towels, watches my TV, plays on my computer. We don't speak to each other. I don't stay long in the same room as him. I absolutely won't fix him any more meals. He is like a ghost I tolerate but never acknowledge.

Because I want to give him a place to die.

As his mother, this I can do in good conscience: encourage his drug use, hold his hand as he slips into a coma that he will never return from.

The heroin was his choice. I didn't push that on him. He showed up at my apartment with the track marks in his arm, remember? It is a choice—using—that I respect, so long as he understands he is killing himself, and I believe he does understand. He has a mirror; he can see the state he is in. So maybe he came to me, to his mother, to waste away. I can love him for this. But I can't show him tenderness, otherwise he might get the wrong idea and stick around.

But there is a big problem: he is out of heroin. He showed me, without any embarrassment, what he had left, a small bit of dust that filled the corner of a plastic bag. My role now, as I understood it, is to be his supplier. And to provide him with a couch to die on.

A plate of diced potatoes, an omelet with bacon and cheese, a pool of ketchup. Gloria aimed a forkful into her mouth, careful not to smudge her lipstick. Rene pushed the gray mound of tuna salad into the lettuce leaf and waited for the waitress to finish refilling her coffee. They'd been talking about Dean; Gloria was the only person in western New York who knew about him. When the waitress had moved on, Rene leaned over the plate.

"Do you know where I can buy . . . Jesus I can't believe I'm saying this . . . heroin?"

Ketchup dripped from Gloria's suspended fork. "For real?"

"Now, I'm not assuming you know just because you're—"

"'Cause I live in the 'hood?"

"I have no idea where to even begin looking."

Gloria leaned forward, her breasts bulging on the tabletop. Rene admired the way she displayed her thick thighs and massive breasts, the gaudy gold chains and crucifixes buried in her cleavage. "Raynay, what kind of shit you into?"

"The Shit shit, that's what kind."

"Let him get his own junk," she said, tucking food inside her cheek. "Don't let him use you like that. You want me to come over and toss his skinny ass out?"

"It's not his idea. It's—" She looked around the busy diner filled with professors and administrators, people she had to smile at and say hello to every single day. She let the breath out, but the sentence failed. She didn't know how to say it out loud.

Gloria sat back in the booth, gave Rene that sideways glance. "You smart bitch," she said. They had talked plenty about Dean in the past at this very table, but that she guessed Rene's intentions so quickly was disturbing. Was this something others did, push drugs on someone they were trying to ruin?

Gloria stabbed at the potatoes and with a mouthful said, "I might know where you can get some."

Let me ask you this: if you had the opportunity to kill someone who fit the profile of a murderer, wouldn't you at least think about it?

We now know the identity of the Virginia Tech shooter. I've been researching this young man—this Seung-Hui Cho from South Korea. He is only a few years younger than the Shit. He was a student, an outcast who despised his peers, who never made eye contact with them, never responded when they spoke to him. There were warning signs; there always are. He stalked female students, wrote violent plays and poetry that scared his professor. He was even hospitalized for mental illness. And you've seen the photos by now: his shaved head, backwards hat, military vest, guns drawn as though posing for a movie poster. But do you know of his manifesto? Have you read it?

It's mostly vulgar threats, provocative religious prophecies, accusations thrown at the rich, and other vague warnings. But his anger is pure, beautiful in its honesty. He's about to orchestrate his suicide, and there is no remorse, no indecision. He believes he's been wronged, his soul "raped" by us "descendants of Satan." On the one hand it's laughable in the way teenage angst is, and on the other hand, the one behind my back, it's convincing.

Ernesto was Gloria's younger brother's high school friend. A year ago, she'd smacked him around him when she found out he was selling junk to her brother. The two still hung out, but the permanent ringing in Ernesto's right ear kept him from pushing on her family.

Rene's heart was thumping against her temples as she and Gloria sat in Rene's Civic outside a high-rise, waiting for Ernesto to come down. Rene was still in her work clothes—of all days to wear a skirt and heels, but then, what does one wear to buy heroin?

Gloria's fingernails clicking on her cell made Rene anxious.

"When do I give him the money?"

"When he gives you the drugs," Gloria said to her phone.

Rene had the folded twenties sweating under her leg for quick access. She'd taken two hundred out of the ATM; the cable bill would have to go unpaid this month. She had no idea how much heroin would cost. She only knew that she didn't want to have to do this again, a forty-four-year-old woman purchasing drugs from a high school kid.

Suddenly, a boy was getting into the back seat, smiling and spouting Spanish to Gloria and smelling like cigarettes and baked chicken. He had a soft mustache and chin hair, hardly a shadow. A Bills hat was jammed low on his brow so Rene couldn't make out his eyes. But he filled the car with bouncing, youthful energy, the kind specific to boys. She found it familiar and comfortable. She turned in the seat so she could face him, knowing she'd find a smart-ass and happy for it.

"You want to buy some H, lady?" Ernesto said, grinning, holding in a laugh.

"Have some fucking respect." Gloria put her thick arm behind Rene's seat, promising to use it. Ernesto cowered but obviously enjoyed her attention.

"What do you have for me, Ernesto?" Rene said.

He spit out a laugh, then covered his mouth when Gloria flexed her arm. "I don't got shit on me."

Gloria shouted at him in Spanish. Rene tapped her knee, and Gloria relaxed.

"We're not fucking around here," Rene told him with a smile. "I have two hundred cash. Either I buy from you or from someone else."

"She got three hundred," Gloria said, flashing bills.

"Gloria."

"Three hundred," she repeated.

Ernesto pulled his hat up and down as if scratching his forehead. "I didn't know how much to bring is what I mean. Three hundred dollars?"

Rene showed him the money, separating the bills with her thumb. She was impressed with herself for pulling this off.

"Okay," he said. "I'll be right back."

He was getting out of the car, when Rene reached into the back seat and tugged him by the shirt. "Ernesto," she said. "Don't fuck me over. I want the shit that'll get a horse high."

"Yes, ma'am."

Rene laid out the little bags on the coffee table in front of the Shit. There were nearly thirty wax-paper sleeves folded into tiny squares. Each was stamped with a blue basketball player dunking, and underneath, the word MELO. Ernesto had said, "That's Carmelo Anthony fire right there." She didn't know what he meant, but it sounded potent.

The Shit didn't even acknowledge her. His moist fingers were tearing open a sleeve. He'd been sweating on the couch, so much that she thought he'd just returned from a jog. He was going through his duffel, his shave kit, whimpering, shaking. He couldn't unzip his tool bag and he was screaming at the ceiling. She had no other choice but to help get the drugs in him. It was as though he was testing her, wanting to know how serious she was about her intentions. *You really want to kill me, you're gonna have to get your hands dirty.*

He guided Rene through the process, his face on her shoulder as she readied the items at his frantic commands. She angled a drinking glass to make a pool of water. She put the needle inside, and used her teeth to pull the plunger. Syringe filled, she turned and found Dean holding the concave bottom of a Coke Zero can. He filled it with the snowy drug, losing some to his tremors. She grabbed the can from him before he spilled any more. He took the syringe and removed the plunger and used it to stir the mixture. It dissolved into what looked like a puddle of whiskey. As she held the can, he tore a bit of cotton and rolled it into a pebble, then dropped it in the solution. It instantly blossomed, a moment of strange beauty. He inserted the needle into the blossom and slowly filled the syringe. He unbent his left arm and smacked the skin a couple times while opening and closing his fist. In the bend of his arm was a tattoo of a lollipop, the big, swirling Munchkin kind. A fat vein ran through its center, which was already pocked with small scabs. He was trying to steady the needle enough to stab the vein, but his hands betrayed him. He sobbed, snot dripping from his nose. Rene didn't take the syringe from him, but she steadied it against his arm and aimed it for the center of the lollipop. The needle was touching his skin, the vein swelling, yearning. Their heads were pressed together, vying for the best angle. Her eyes were watering with concentration as she dragged the needle down one follicle. He kept sniffling, sniffling in her ear. Her vision blurred as if in self-defense—her eyes' pact with her brain saying, *We will not take this in, we will spare you this memory.* She guided the needle as Dean kept his thumb on the plunger. The skin gave like a trampoline weighted by a brick, but it didn't break. She pushed harder, fingers slimy. The skin broke. Her stomach flung up into her chest. He began to inject. Then he made a sound like he'd been stung and jerked the needle out. He screamed that she'd missed. A blister was forming, bubbling up angrily next to his vein, the lollipop a deformed bulge.

She wasn't about to back off; she'd stab him over and over if that was what it took.

His face was creamed with snot and tears. Sensing danger, the vein retreated. But it couldn't hide completely, and again Rene got the needle in position. She wasn't breathing, fearing even the act of inflating her lungs would tremble her fingers. She pushed. This time the skin pierced quicker. She gave the syringe over to the Shit, who'd come alive some. All of her insides were on pause as she watched him, waited for his reaction. Instead of pushing the plunger in, he pulled it slowly out. A smoky trickle of blood mixed into the amber within the tube. He nodded, a good sign. He then plunged the heroin into his body. He let out a quivering call as though he'd been allowed to piss after holding it in for a long car trip. Then his head fell on her shoulder and his breathing was slow, so slow. She tugged her arm out and put it around him. Pulled him close, feeling sleepy, feeling settled. Feeling they were both losing themselves to darkness.

"I was thinking last night that you could help me put together a mental health–themed newsletter." Today Diane's scarf was deep blue with white seagulls. "I'll ask Gloria to gather up phone numbers of psychological services and hotlines. What do you think?"

Diane had informed Rene yesterday on her way out that she'd written and sent the email. Rene could tell that she was disappointed in her, which was worse than anger. She recognized it immediately as a mother's tactic, one Rene had used many times when the boys were young. It elicited guilt, internal brooding, rather than outbursts. That Diane was using it on her, for this, and now of all times, seemed calculated—and unfair. But those too were a mother's tactics.

"Sounds like a good idea."

Diane pulled the scarf back and forth across her chin, choosing her words. "Does this sound like something you can manage?"

The word *manage* opened the door to discussing feelings. Fright flashed through Rene's chest as she considered, briefly, telling her the truth. Diane would pity her, no doubt. She'd probably get excited to be involved in a real drug problem, the kind she watched on TV. She'd maybe even be able to help. While Diane wasn't a mother, she definitely had mothering in her. The gifts in glittery bags she'd give to her and

Gloria for their birthdays, or the ibuprofen on their desks when they'd complain of headaches, or even the completely appropriate scolding when they were gabbing too much and getting nothing done. But Rene thought better of telling her. Diane would get too involved. And she almost definitely wouldn't understand the tactic Rene was using with Dean.

"Yes. I can handle it."

"Oh good."

Be proactive. Encourage your students to take advantage of campus resources at the earliest signs of emotional health issues. Don't ignore the signs. Signs are important.

The Shit is leaving signs all over my coffee table: those little MELO bags, a few still left; leaking syringes; bottoms of Coke cans; and the dried corpses of cotton blossoms. He'd set up an iPod on a portable, battery-operated speaker that rattled with walls of noise. And he is reading. A stack of library books that he most likely stole, all of them histories of the Erie Canal. Skull against my Target throw pillow, eyeballs with a Vaseline sheen, a slow smile for me whenever I get up in the morning or come home in the evening. He resembles a concentration camper: a body taken beyond its limits. But how long will this take? Because I have my own limits; I can feel myself nearing them.

The clearest sign is the blister I birthed. It has torn and spread like oil slick—the Shit probably scratched it in his sleep or shot up too close to it, who knows. It now resembles a gunshot wound, dark around the edges, pink in the middle, hours away from infection. The mother in me wants to rinse it, swab it with peroxide, slather it with Neosporin, and then watch the healing begin. Sure, I want him to rot, just not this goddamn slowly.

Those are the limits. I need to come out of the other end of this sane. Pushing my son down the slope toward death will leave an indelible scar of my own. I've anticipated this. I am afraid, however, that this could be uglier and messier than I'd imagined, and if it takes months, even weeks, where each day I return to new forms of the grotesque lumped on my couch, then I too will be ruined.

The problem, I guess, is that the Shit is too knowledgeable about doses and potency to misuse. I've begun researching junkies on the internet. In most cases, overdose happens to those who don't know what they're doing. I've read of some users who kept up the habit for years, even decades. What if he is capable of this? It will be the cruelest irony if he is lousy at every facet of life except for how to responsibly shoot heroin.

So yes, if you're looking for doubt, if that makes you feel comfortable, that a mother is having doubts about ridding the planet of her only son, then yes, after only two days, I am having doubts.

"Whatever happened to that newsletter, Rene?"

Black, tan, gold and red, horse shoes and stirrups and Texas roses. Her gaudiest, most passive-aggressive scarf.

"I'm so sorry, Diane. The end of the semester happened." It had been three days since Diane floated the newsletter idea, though Rene knew almost instantly that she couldn't do it. The notion of trying to comfort others, an entire department of faculty and students, felt exhausting and pointless. In her weaker moments, she wanted all of them to know about her plight, to pity her. To write something that would help *her*. "I've been busy with commencement. But I'm still working on it."

Gloria leaned into Rene's cubicle. "I got the numbers you wanted," she said to Diane. "We could still put something together."

"I think it's too late for that, don't you?" Diane said this to Rene, her way of telling Gloria to butt out.

Rene tried not to concede too eagerly, but she desperately wanted Diane to drop the idea.

"But what about an address at commencement?" Diane's eyes lit up. "Ooh, Rene, that would be perfect! I'm slated to speak and I wasn't sure what to say. But this. Yes, this would work. It could be about going forward with compassion, about honoring those fallen by loving someone you've never met. You have such a way with words, I know you could make it beautiful. What do you think?"

"That's a great idea." Rene pretended to take a note about it in her day planner.

"You have more than a week. That's enough time, don't you think?"

She forced a smile while doodling lines in the notepad. "Plenty."

"Listen, Rene." Diane leaned in, chin tucked under the scarf. "Are you going to take your vacation this summer? Because I think it would be a good idea, just to clear your head a little. This semester's been difficult for everyone."

Summer, what faraway place was that? It suddenly seemed like an exotic city in one of those fantasy novels where one has to traverse mountains, caves, and ancient woods to get to it.

"I think I will, Diane."

"You know, if you ever need anyone to talk to . . ."

"I appreciate that."

Every day, more information about Cho was released to the public starving to understand him. Tonight it was the homemade videos he'd mailed to the news channels just before the rampage. His young face, his round head and short black hair, the eyes and dark skin of a foreigner. He swore softly to the camera, angry at being pushed to violence.

It was a rare moment when Rene and the Shit were in the same room for an extended period of time. One evening she was microwaving herself dinner and heard Brian Williams on the TV. She came into the room and sat on the arm of the couch as the nightly news continued to cover the aftermath. She turned up the volume. Then she looked to the Shit, wondering how he would react, whether he'd make some comment about Cho being a misunderstood hero, whether he'd mock the victims. Something to bolster her case against him. But he just sat slumped and nodding, the images meaning no more to him than a commercial for super-absorbent toilet paper.

Of course she wouldn't get a clear response. Nothing was clear in this mess, a mess she was finally seeing as something she'd created.

But then, the next morning when she went into the kitchen to brew coffee, the Shit and his tattered duffel were gone.

When Rene didn't show up to work that day, Gloria stopped by with two sacks of greasy food from Wendy's. They ate the burgers and fries at the table in the tiny kitchen, the TV on to *Judge Judy* in the other room. Gloria talked but didn't talk about him. Maybe it was Rene's swollen eyelids, but Gloria understood it wasn't what she needed.

What she needed. Rene couldn't say what that was anymore.

They finished gorging themselves and needed to lounge. The couch was not an option. No amount of Scotchgard could prevent against the Shit's grime or memory. So they went into the bedroom. They lay on the bed hugging pillows like teenagers while watching trashy television. Then Rene didn't want the pillow. She sunk into Gloria, put her arm around her abundance. Rene's face nestled into her neck, soft and floral. Gloria wrapped her up with both arms. Her lips on Rene's forehead, not so much kissing as just being there.

What she needed.

As you go out into the world, never underestimate the power of love and compassion. Be fearless in your own pursuits, but don't do so at the expense of others. And remember, always, to show yourself love and compassion, too.

At the end of the day, you are the one who has to live with yourself; you are the one with whom you'll spend the most time.

I don't trust myself alone, so I'm back at work. The Shit's been gone for forty-eight hours now, and I keep refreshing the Buffalo News *website for reports of a body found. The police won't come here if they find him dead. I don't know what address is printed on his driver's license, but it's not mine, and it's been years since we shared the same last name. I feel on the brink of lightness, of being unburdened, but I need confirmation that he is dead. Perhaps it's a feeling of elation. At times of weakness, when I allow myself to believe he is gone for good, I sense guilt waiting, like an ugly storm cloud just beyond the tree line. The lightness, I think, is the freedom to succumb to the guilt. A resolution. If he is dead, I can finally experience what I've been denied for so long: reliable, predictable guilt, and not this murderous rage that flares and swells and seeps and sneaks.*

But there are also flashes of fear where I imagine him wandering into an elementary school or playground, and in his desperate state of withdrawal, terrorizing children. Terror is the best case scenario. The worst case is what sprung me from my desk yesterday. I ran every red light to get home, where I dashed into the closet and yanked down the shoe box to thankfully find the .45 was still there. How stupid of me to keep it so close to him. I felt like all my common sense was becoming sand, slipping through my fingertips as I tried to keep it intact.

I sat on the floor and cried for a while until my eyelids puffed and burned. When I was finished, I realized the gun had been in my hand the entire time. My cheek was indented with the handle's crosshatch.

Diane held out a glittery gift bag fluffed with tissue paper.

"What's this?"

"To say thank you for your hard work this year."

"Diane."

"You earned it."

Her office was ornamented with tribal themes and nature scenes, sunlight spearing through trees, wooden figurines dancing on her desk, unlit candles smelling of pine and mint and smoky earth. These competed with paper stacks and piles of books. There were three chairs other than the one behind her desk, all of which were cluttered with files and notebooks and reusable grocery bags bulging with who knows what. So Rene had to stand while opening the gift, as though on a stage.

A scarf.

"A scarf."

She pulled it out for her audience, held it so she could see its full design. Abstract butterflies made of green and pink triangles on a deep indigo sky. It was strangely weightless, like something patterned on air. Its silk so delicate between her fingers, it seemed she was pinching a swath of lotion.

"Put it on."

Please, no.

"How do I wear it?"

Diane came around her desk to help. Rene watched her pursed lips as Diane arranged it around her neck.

"How does it feel?"

It felt better than her. More beautiful than anything she deserved.

"Nice."

"It looks wonderful on you."

Rene couldn't breathe.

The Shit returned.

It was just before midnight, and she was up vacuuming. It helped her feel in control, to clean. When she pushed the vacuum into the family room, she saw him standing in the soft light of the lampshade.

Strangely, he hadn't frightened her. It was like the room had reclaimed him as its own, as part of the furniture, a fixture.

His arm was wet and black inside the elbow. It leaked a dark, angry ooze. He was pale, blue in the eyes and cheekbones.

What will kept him alive? she wondered. How easily some people die, how quickly it happens. But leave it to him to load up his veins with heroin, to have some awful infection turning his blood to pitch, and to be a despicable human at that, and there he was in her family room, still standing, speaking.

"I need to go to a hospital." He raised his infected arm as if evidence was needed.

"No," she said defiantly.

The surprise on his face said this whole thing had been a big misunderstanding. This entire time, he must have thought she was trying to help him. She'd given him too much credit.

So she asked, "Why?"

"My arm."

"I have eyes. I'm asking you why you want it fixed. Is it just your arm, or are you hoping to get clean, too?"

"Paul said it might need to be amputated."

"Paul? That's what Paul said? Is that what he said, while you were sucking him off?"

"What?" His ashen cheeks turned red. "I don't . . . do that."

"Of course you don't." She was laughing. She was throttling the vacuum and laughing.

She didn't know why she accused him of this, other than she was furious and wanted to hurt him. In her brain was some hazy depiction of a young, homeless man desperate for drugs, forced to give head for money.

Then he said it. The thing she feared most, the thing she didn't know she feared most until he said it, and when he did, Rene realized she'd been fearing it not just because she'd been wanting it so badly for so long, but that, when he said it, she'd be forced to consider it and she didn't want to do that; it was unfair, after all he'd done, to make her consider that.

"Mom, I'm sorry." The Shit even made himself small and sincere.

Rene swung the vacuum like a baseball bat, smashing the walls and TV and lamp, whatever was near to smash. Undoing the air where his words tried to exist. She gave up the vacuum and grabbed his arm just above the infection. She squeezed and yanked so his face was in hers, and she growled into that sick face.

He took the punishment and that too was an insult. That too, because he was a boy again. Passive, accepting more than what he deserved. It used to drive Karl crazy, but it was what made her favor him over his brother—his tenderness, his need for her when he was nervous, and he was always nervous. Loud noises, bees, very old people, the ocean, cemeteries, and dark rooms—so many occasions to run to his mama. But that boy was dead. This one was just a shit of a man. Just a black-blooded, poisonous man. And she was pounding his chest calling him *poison, poison* until he fell onto the couch, eyes rolling back until he'd blink them straight. Rolling back and blinking straight.

That will to live. That was how he'd survived when his brother couldn't. Why? What was he holding out for? Not this.

Then he passed out. Sprawled stupidly on Rene's couch, head buried in the Target pillow, looking like he'd been shot. Of course, he wasn't dead. Maybe if she left him there for long enough, twelve hours, twenty-four, the infection would take him. Maybe.

Rene suddenly collapsed onto the carpet beside the Shit. She was crying, or trying to. The tears poured out, but her face, her whole being, was too tired for any of the other motions. Her head tipped forward, butting up against the Shit's ribs. When she opened her eyes, she was looking into the hole. The winking puddle of tar. She jerked away, sat up, gagging. But then she returned to it. *You deserve this shit* sang in her head. She put her forehead into his wound, rolled her face around in it. The fetid odor, the oily sound, the dampness on her cheeks, her lips. *Ugly, ugly bitch*, she told herself.

By the time she got home from the hospital, it was six in the morning. She didn't stay long enough to get his condition, but he'd be fine. It was something she just knew.

The sky out the bathroom window was just distinguishing itself from the trees. She showered and put on her makeup and did her hair. As she was going through the closet to pick out an outfit for work, she took the .45 down from the shelf, just to hold something of substance, something real. Suddenly, there was a colossal pressure on her shoulders that sent her to the floor. Had she exploded into tears and screams of agony, it might have provided some relief. Instead, she was weighed down, pressed into the carpet by a merciless hand. She managed to crawl to the bed and drag herself up to it. There, the glittery bag containing Diane's gift. She wrapped her sagging, naked body in the butterfly scarf and shivered in the silk.

She thought suddenly of Diane, delivering a commencement address that she'd have to write herself. Rene could see Diane standing at the podium, her face and shoulders awash in sun, her sandy hair catching a breeze, maybe a bright, rebellious scarf over the black robe. Had she confessed her problems to Diane, she'd surely have pitied Rene. Maybe she'd have invited her out to her house on weekends where they'd have gone for long walks on a nature trail and she'd have talked about quieting the voices, finding your center, aligning the spirit with that of nature—whatever the spiritual trends were. Rene would have been her project. It would have been nice to be someone's project.

She wished she'd met Diane twenty years ago, when it would have helped.

She put the feather pillow over her head and pressed the .45 into it. She steadied her breathing by counting to ten.

An inhale–exhale for each number.

A confetti of feathers.

If he gets his hands on another gun and goes on to shoot up a college campus or movie theater or elementary school, then I'm to blame. You always blame the mother anyway. If he turns himself around, somehow, by some fucking miracle—like if the universe suddenly becomes the kind of place that allows for miracles, then so be it. I don't want the credit, and I sure as hell don't want to know. If miracles start landing on people like him, I don't want to know.

OVERTIME

"I knew we would be tired; I thought it would be very difficult to come back from that night."

—Jim Boeheim, head coach, Syracuse Orange

Winter, 2009

———◆———

PHIL DEMARTANO AND HIS son, Mark, scraped at the windshield as the truck warmed. The shrillness of plastic on ice invaded the quiet neighborhood. Phil had never gotten used to the profound loneliness of four thirty in the morning; he imagined everyone else in the world sleeping and then waking with the sun. Having Mark with him helped, especially since his wife, Sue, had passed last year.

Phil was still squeezing sleep from his eyes as they drove out of Chittenango, onto the thruway toward Syracuse. Mark, however, was fidgety and alert. Phil figured it had to do with the pills Mark and the other young guys at the factory took to endure the long hours. Phil considered Mark a man now, bearded and hardened, unrecognizable from his childhood, so he let him alone about the pills, and everything else.

"Still can't believe we're going to the game tonight," Mark said, digging his fingers into the scruff of his beard. "Syracuse usually plays well in the tournament."

"They'll blow it. They always do." Phil noted his cynicism but was too tired to add something upbeat.

"At least we can watch them blow it courtside," Mark said. "Uncle Sal's got to have good seats."

Phil's brother-in-law Sal was a successful lawyer in Syracuse and a good guy, despite his opinions on how to finance Sue's medical bills. Yesterday, Sal had called Phil and told him he couldn't make the Big East tournament game and offered them the tickets.

"Listen," Phil said. "Try not to tell anyone at work that we're going. If Fleming gets wind of it, we could be in trouble."

Mark breathed deeply through his nose at mention of Fleming, their manager. "What," he seethed. "So now we can't do shit on our own time without that motherfucker getting involved?"

Mark got angry at the smallest things lately. Or maybe it was longer than lately.

"Look," Phil said steadily, lest he rile his son. "The drive to Manhattan is four hours from here, and the game'll probably end at midnight. We'll have to haul ass to get back in time. But the last thing we need is Fleming knowing we've been up the whole night before our shift."

Mark didn't say anything else until the downtown Syracuse skyline soon came into view, half-lit and dreamy against the purple sky.

"You think Paddy'll be okay on his own for that long?"

Phil fought the urge to say, *Who cares?* He hated the stupid dog Mark had brought home a couple years ago. It was more like an overgrown rat that left turds on the kitchen floor. The thing had brought some pleasure to Sue in the last years of her life, lying at her feet in bed, but now Phil couldn't give two shits about it.

"He'll be fine."

Salt-rusted trucks and screechy rattling cars filed into the parking lot at Mohawk for the five a.m. shift. Many employees traveled from as far west as Rochester or as far east as Albany. No one dared be late, not with Mohawk looking for more people to lay off. A wave of a hundred had already gotten the ax just before Christmas.

Mark saw some of the younger guys at the plant entrance and went off to join them. Phil's son was well-liked, despite some trouble he had gotten into a few years ago, a fight in this very parking lot with these very friends over God knew what. But they must've gotten over it, in that stupid way that an ass kicking can renew men's respect for each other.

Phil heard these guys call him D-Mart. It was the same nickname the boys on Mark's high school basketball team had given him. Every time he heard it, Phil thought of watching Mark play. He'd been good, maybe the second-best player on the team. He was strong and quick and a good three-point shooter. Phil took special pride in what Mark's coach had said about him: Mark was the hardest working player on the team.

Luke and Grant, old dogs who'd been there as long as Phil, caught up with him, carrying similar coolers. They hardly acknowledged each other, but their tired bodies gathered together, and they proceeded in a soulful cadence.

Luke turned to glare at the young guys hollering and cussing; he grumbled and spit. Phil knew Luke held his tongue only because Phil was around.

To show his loyalty, Phil said, "Pricks."

"Especially that DeMartano asshole," said Grant, laughing.

"Ah, Mark's a good kid," Luke added. "It's those other punks, all jacked up on speed or whatever it is makes'm work like lightning."

"I think it's called youth," said Grant.

"My ass."

The line of men and women punched in, and soon the factory hummed and clattered. Phil assumed his position between Luke and Grant, and then his body took over, feeding sheets of aluminum into the machine, yanking the lever to punch the sheet, pulling out the tray, and pushing it down the line. These were the motions his muscles enacted; Phil himself wasn't needed. He often joked to Luke and Grant that if he was knocked in the head and suffered brain damage, they could just wheel his old ass up to this machine and his body would know what to do.

This morning, Mr. Fleming, the floor manager, made his rounds more regularly. It took effort to hate Fleming. His two sons had been abducted about fifteen years ago, and only one survived. That one, Dean, was a fuckup who had even worked here at Mohawk for a few months until Fleming was forced to fire him. If he could fire his own son, he'd lose no sleep laying off any of these other sorry bastards, Phil included.

"You and Fleming got a date tonight?" Grant asked Phil.

Grant confirmed Phil's suspicion: Fleming kept making eye contact with him.

"Hell if I know."

Nothing more was said, for what Phil feared had to be obvious to the guys; they'd fear Fleming too if he kept eying them. Phil focused on the work to keep from agonizing.

The lunch break arrived, and everyone shuffled into the cafeteria. The old guys twisted the cricks out of their backs and necks. Phil passed Fleming's office, and Fleming leaned his long body out the door.

"Hey, Phil," he said, his Adam's apple bouncing under his small chin. "Can I talk to you a minute?"

Phil's palms became slick with sweat, and he tightened his grip on the cooler. He nodded and squeezed past Fleming. Phil hadn't been in Fleming's cluttered, closet-sized office in a year. It was then that he'd asked for a week off so that he and Mark could attend to Sue's death. Later he'd asked if they could work overtime to pay the hospital bills that their insurance didn't cover. Fleming had said yes to the former instantly—the company had even sent flowers to the house. Fleming had dragged his feet on the latter but eventually, and grudgingly, gave them both another shift.

"This'll just be a minute," Fleming said. He picked up a paper clip and tapped it end-over-end on the desk. "Want to talk to you about your son. We did a random locker search this morning, and no surprise, found some interesting stuff. Interesting, to say the least. A lot of jack-off magazines, for one. Who the hell's jacking off at work? Why not do your business at home? Disgusting."

Phil instantly recalled the drug bust that had gone down here a while ago, and his temples began to throb. He wanted to reach across the desk and rap Fleming's bulbous Adam's apple for dragging out the inevitable. Phil asked, "What'd you find in Mark's locker?"

"Four bottles of speed and some cocaine. He's not the only one, either. The others I'm going to talk to the end of the day, tell them not to let the door hit'm in the ass the way out."

Phil looked down at his lap, the worn threads of his jeans.

"I'd can Mark, too, if not for you and your . . . situation. You guys need this job, and I guess I don't have the heart to deprive you."

"What do you want me to do?"

"I can talk to him if you don't want to. I'll haul him in here and read'm the riot act. Tell him get his nose clean and his locker. I just thought . . ." Fleming sat back, pinching the paper clip into his thumbnail. "You're his father; you know how to get through to him."

Get through to him.

"Yeah, no, I'll do that." Phil sat up in the plastic chair. "I can do that."

"Make sure you tell'm if I catch him again—if I even suspect him . . ."

"I will."

Phil ate his lunch alone on a picnic bench outside, preferring the iron-cold weather to facing his friends. He sure as shit wasn't going to tell them the truth, nor was he much of a liar. When Luke and Grant returned from lunch, Phil told them that Fleming had wanted to discuss scheduling and said nothing more for the rest of the shift. He was busy thinking about how he'd bring this up with Mark. If he would.

The first shift ended at one o'clock. Grant and Luke, and most everyone else, left as the second shifters replaced them. Phil remained at the same station, and as part of their overtime agreement, Mark worked alongside Phil. Phil typically enjoyed working with Mark, even if he was careless. Today, however, Fleming came by more often, hovering behind their backs and scribbling into his clipboard. The moments alone with Mark were equally torturous, as Phil continuously searched himself for the courage to say something. He missed a good opportunity when Mark reached in too eagerly for the aluminum sheet as the machine was about to thrust, and Phil had to pull his hand away. "What's gotten into you, lately?" he could have easily asked. But he didn't. Mark was probably just distracted by the basketball game. He kept smiling at Phil, his eyes sparkling with excitement.

At five p.m., Mark and Phil punched out. Mark sprinted into the parking lot, then ran back to Phil and jumped all over him like a kid. Phil squealed the tires out of the lot. He filled up the tank on the way out of town and picked up a six-pack of Genny and a box of Ring Dings. They listened to the pregame coverage on the radio, drank beer—Phil limited himself to two—and made their way down the thruway to New York City.

The long drive muted their excitement. Negotiating city traffic, finding parking, and paying for it—twice the cost of a fish basket and pitcher at the Ten Pin—ruined Phil's mood. The cold energy of the city, however, rejuvenated them. Phil had been to New York years ago, but this was Mark's first time. Both he and his son kept their hands jammed in their pockets and chests puffed to ward off pickpockets preying on tourists. Phil, though, couldn't contain his wonder as they neared the looming, blue-lit Garden. He drifted wide-eyed through the bright, expansive lobby toward the arena. The swarming din of the crowd thundered in Phil's chest as he held out his ticket at the gate.

Mark thumbed at the concession and shouted that he'd get some beers and hot dogs, so Phil wandered in to get a peek at the game. Phil was surprised to find that Syracuse—ranked eighth in the country— was beating the third-ranked UConn by two. He stood between the balustrades at the top of the stairs and gazed at the crowd, a dizzying collage of faces and colors and movement. The basketball court glimmered bright yellow. The players' sneakers squeaked the polished wood; the ball thumped like drumbeat. Phil looked at the massive jumbotron suspended over the players. It was nearly the size of the entire court, and a sudden fear struck him that it could fall and crush everyone underneath.

Mark arrived with a tray of beers and hot dogs. They hurried along the vacant outer corridor and found their section. Mark was excited that they didn't have to go up any levels. "Shit, we might have good seats," he said. Sure enough, they walked *down* the steps into the crowd, Mark leading the way, stepping faster the closer they got to the court. At their row, some ten yards from the action, Mark looked up at Phil and mouthed, *Holy shit!* Phil laughed and shook his head. They apologized as they shuffled past the others seated in their row and sat in their seats—not aluminum benches, but actual chairs.

"This is amazing," Mark said, chomping his hot dog.

Syracuse scored a basket and a third of the stadium roared. Most of the fans seated in their section were wealthy business types: men with crisp haircuts and mohair blazers with clean, dark jeans. The women dressed like models or actresses. Maybe they were. Phil felt eyes on his grimy Carhartt jacket and boots—they probably thought he and Mark were taking other people's seats. Mark shouted at the refs, a bit louder than anyone else. Phil handed Mark his beer and hot dog as he took off his jacket and stuffed it under the chair; Mark did the same. Phil nodded hello to a young, black Wall Street type, wearing suit pants and a white, collared shirt with the sleeves rolled to the elbows. He gave Phil a curt nod, then continued texting on his phone. Phil bit into his soggy hot dog, sipped his watery beer, and focused on the court.

The Orange scored another bucket, and Phil and Mark cheered. Phil was awash with a familiar anxiety. Lifelong SU fans faced years of disappointment and stress. Sure, Syracuse won games. They were often highly ranked, and sometimes, though rarely, ranked best in the country. Still, Phil recalled the countless times he'd sat on the sofa with Mark, watching SU blow a lead and lose at the last second. Phil would be crushed for the rest of the night, and not even Sue—who thought sports was pure nonsense—could console him.

SU basketball was one of the few joys for most Central New Yorkers. It got you through the bitter, relentless winters and helped to distract from the scarcity of good jobs. You knew when the Orange were playing, if they were on national television, if they were at home. Sometimes you'd shell out a few extra bucks to watch them in the Carrier Dome, braving the biting cold as you trotted through the Syracuse campus. And you remembered 2003, when Carmelo Anthony took the Orange to the national championship and won. That young freshman couldn't have known whom he had carried on his shoulders, how high he had lifted Phil and Mark. The elation of a desperate city, the pride of those surrounding, forgotten villages. How quickly it had ended, though. When Anthony left for the NBA, the Orange went back to their frustrating play: losing the easy games, blowing the big ones, but winning enough to get to the NCAA tournament—and then getting knocked off in the first or second round. This was around the time Phil and Mark needed the wins, when they found out Sue was sick and would continue to be for years. She fought as hard as she could, and still she lost.

Phil had since learned a lesson, though it took him long enough: he'd go into a big game expecting his team to lose and trying not to care.

Mark smacked Phil's arm, pulling him back into the action. He pointed to Syracuse's small point guard dribbling the ball up the court.

"Watch Flynn," Mark told Phil. "I bet he's going to take it to the hole."

Johnny Flynn advanced the ball casually until he neared his defender. He then lowered his shoulders and dribbled so low to the floor the ball hardly bounced. Phil watched him closely. He knew Flynn was capable of it, but sitting so close to the court, he had never appreciated just how small he was, especially compared to UConn's seven-foot-three giant of a center. Everyone on the Huskies was the epitome of agility, strength, or size. They might trail by a few points early in the game, but they would out muscle and out play a scrappy team like Syracuse. Still, there was Flynn, dribbling before his defender, head up, searching for his opportunity.

"Here it comes," said Mark.

Flynn pushed the ball past his man and darted into the paint. UConn's giant was waiting. Flynn threw his body into the big man, stunning him, making space to score. The collision sent Flynn crashing to the hardwood. The crowd went quiet. He scrambled to his feet, smiling.

The Syracuse fans erupted.

Mark called at Phil, "I told you!"

Phil swelled with pride that this smaller man would so fearlessly challenge someone so much larger, and best him.

Flynn played as Mark had in high school, going as fast and hard as possible until the whistle blew. He had been a favorite of his teammates and the fans, who'd chant "D-Mart! D-Mart!" whenever Mark threw himself on the floor for a loose ball. At the end of one particular game, Mark was so exhausted his teammates had to carry him off the court. Even when the bleachers were cleared, Phil had to help his son off the bench, out of the gym, and into the truck. Halfway home, Mark's first words had been, "Who won?" Phil hadn't had the heart to tell him it was the other team.

Mark had dreams of playing for SU, just like all the other Chittenango boys with basketball hoops in their driveways. But Mark didn't have the grades or talent, not to mention the money, for a university like Syracuse.

Now, as Phil suspected, UConn fought back to take the lead. Syracuse's head coach, Jim Boeheim, tossed his squeeze bottle under his chair and stood to yell at his guys. He raised his hands and lifted his eyebrows to crinkle his large forehead, as if that were enough for his team to understand his disappointment. Halftime came quickly, and the Huskies were beating Syracuse 37–34.

"They're hanging in there." Mark stood and stretched his arms over his head.

"We'll see." Phil stood with him.

They watched as people walked up the stairs to the bathroom or concession stands. Mark pointed out a young, attractive blonde approaching. He shook his head when she walked past and blew out his lips. He watched the crowd and pantomimed shooting a basketball—dribbling and pulling up for a jump shot. Phil hadn't seen his son lit up this way in a long time, and it wasn't the pills. The two of them didn't get out much Sundays; they went to mass in the morning, then hung out the rest of the day, sneaking catnaps while watching TV. Occasionally Mark went out with friends, but he didn't have a girlfriend, as far as Phil knew.

As they stood watching college girls in tight shirts, Phil's heart pounded. Here was another perfect moment. Phil said suddenly, "Look." His tone was harsher than he intended, causing Mark to freeze. The smile on his face slacked, gone to his scraggly beard.

"What's wrong?"

Phil hoped Mark could handle the pills, that they were just a phase. Mark was an adult now; he didn't need his daddy lecturing him. "Got to use the boy's room," Phil said quickly. "I'll get more beer."

On the way to the bathroom, Phil stopped at a vendor selling souvenirs and studied the Syracuse shirts. They were expensive, but the one Mark wore had to be ten years old. Phil thumbed the cash in his wallet, then left and stood in line for the urinal. He stood in another line to buy beers and popcorn and then stopped again at the booth.

"I'll take a T-shirt. Large." He wanted Mark to have something new. It had been too long since he'd bought him anything.

He balanced everything on his way back and gave Mark the shirt.

"Hey, thanks Dad." Mark held it up. On the back it said *Anthony* in white, with the number fifteen on the front and back. "Alright, Carmelo."

Mark took off his hat and shirt, flashing his hairy stomach and ribs at everyone, and put on the new one. He looked down at himself, pleased. He sniffed the fabric and smiled. Phil laughed and sipped his beer.

The players were back on the floor. A horn sounded the beginning of the second half. It started well for Syracuse. Their two big-men— Jackson and Onuaku—scored layups, then UConn pulled ahead by six points. It went back and forth, Syracuse always behind, until little Johnny Flynn got the fire in him. Phil could see it happening and it tickled him.

Flynn dared take the ball to the hoop, dense with towering defenders. Instead of shooting, however, he passed it outside to Syracuse's best three-point shooter, Andy Rautins, who sunk a beautifully arching shot. Suddenly, the Orange were ahead 54–51. The Syracuse fans in the stadium, and those neutral spectators won over by the underdogs, exploded in frenzied cheers. Mark gave Phil an awkward, enthusiastic high-five; even the Wall Streeter slapped Phil's hand.

Phil felt the fluttering charge of victory. He should have known better.

UConn quieted the fans with a three-pointer. The two relentless teams exchanged points for the remaining seven minutes. With 1.1 seconds left in the game, the score was tied.

Phil looked at his watch. It was a little after eleven thirty. To get back in time for work, they had to leave by midnight. If the game went into overtime, a five-minute period, which in basketball time meant closer to fifteen, they'd be cutting it close.

Syracuse in-bounded the ball from the far end of the court, a hurling, desperate pass. Devendorf, Syracuse's other guard, snatched it up with .3 seconds left, and heaved an off-balanced shot. Phil felt

186 of KEVIN CATALANO

his heart suspend interminably in the air with the ball. It came down through the hoop. The stadium roared, and the Syracuse players on the bench swarmed the court. Phil leapt off the ground and hollered. He felt silly for this public display of joy, but he couldn't help it.

"Wait a minute," the guy next to Phil said. The refs were waving their arms. All eyes were on the jumbotron replay. The ball was just on the fingertips when time expired. Phil's heart sank as the scoreboard removed the points. The game was still tied at seventy one.

"Overtime," Wall Street said.

"Fuck," Mark yelled, still smiling from the excitement.

Phil realized he had picked up his jacket, ready to leave. He put it back, lingering near the littered floor for a moment. Pain fired through his hamstrings and pulsed in his knees, reminding him of the factory. When he came up, he checked his watch. It was quarter to midnight.

"Typical Syracuse basketball," Wall Street said to Phil.

"That's what I keep telling my son." Phil took off his hat. "I used to have a full head of hair before I started watching them play."

Mark leaned over. "Game's not over, fellas."

"See what I mean?" Phil said to Wall Street. "Always the optimist, this one."

Phil, however, was hiding his disappointment—not with the team but himself. He was a fool to think this would end in any way other than a loss. This wasn't about Syracuse. Loss was part of his blood. It was what everyone must have said about his family behind his back: the DeMartanos were cursed. They'd had a good life once, before Sue died, before Mark began working with his old man, before they were in so much debt that it sickened Phil to consider the sum. To root for a win, to hold out for one, was pointless.

The players came back onto the floor.

Mark called out, "Come on SU!"

UConn took the lead. Syracuse trailed but fought hard to keep the score close. The time went by quickly, both teams taking turns scoring until, with fourteen seconds left, Syracuse was down two. Johnny Flynn had the ball. Boeheim was standing, arms crossed, leaning ever-so-slightly to the left. Mark was biting the rim of his hat. Phil chewed the inside corner of his mouth, trying to convince himself he didn't care. Flynn drove the ball inside. Just as the opponents swarmed him, he snuck the ball to an open man who slammed it hard, tying the game. UConn failed to score on their next possession, and time ran out.

"Another overtime!" Mark grabbed Phil's shirt and laughed.

It was midnight. The hot dogs in Phil's stomach roiled when he thought about getting on the road. He did the math again in hopes of finding more time: four and a half hours to get back, leaving at twelve fifteen. He could speed. There'd be no traffic that late. They could just go straight to Mohawk, without stopping home to shower or change. Mark was chanting "Let's go Orange!" with the crowd. The horn sounding the second overtime made up Phil's mind.

Phil watched the game, wishing someone would win. It didn't matter who. He just wanted it to end so they could leave. UConn was up two, and Phil now silently pleaded for them to stay ahead. It was a familiar betrayal, so much that he hardly registered it. Syracuse was not backing down. UConn kept scoring; Syracuse kept tying. The final seconds ticked off the clock, UConn heaved up a wild shot and missed. The score was still tied. A third overtime.

"I can't believe this," Wall Street said, but Phil didn't respond. It was twelve fifteen and they had to go. Phil looked at his watch until Mark noticed.

"Oh shit, what time is it?"

"I think we need to hit the road."

"Yeah, absolutely," Mark said, grabbing for his jacket, eyes sobered with concern. "Where you guys going?" said Wall Street.

"We got to get back to Syracuse for work in the morning." Phil hated his words and hated Wall Street for making him say them.

They climbed the steps, and Phil noticed everyone eying them, incredulous. He focused on Mark, who was leaning heavily on the dividing rail. Mark looked over his shoulder at the court every few steps. Phil's chest tightened. He became furious and sad. He'd never, not once, felt sorry for himself. He'd resigned himself to misfortune, but maybe he'd resigned Mark to it, too.

Phil had gotten Mark the job at the factory right out of high school, so he could pay his own way through college. He wanted to teach him discipline and responsibility. Sue was right, though: Mark would get stuck at Mohawk. That's what happens there, she'd told Phil one night in the kitchen. She never insisted, never pressed, like his friends' wives. She would say something just once and leave it up to Phil, who hated making decisions. He'd never had to decide Mark's future, though, because right around that time, Sue got lymphoma.

She was sick for so long, death dragged itself out to the point that Phil just wished it would come. Sue had quietly—almost apologetically—endured chemotherapy, a bone marrow transplant, blood transfusions, and a bevy of medications. The lymphoma had gone into remission, but three years later it returned. Sue had inquired about the bills, but Phil patted her bruised hand and convinced her that the insurance was covering it all. Her survival was the sole thing he considered, and so he blindly agreed to every treatment and medication the doctor recommended, never really checking to see if his insurance would pay. Perhaps Sue knew this about Phil—that he could be hard-headed and foolish about certain things and was thus prone to making poor decisions.

On the night they learned her cancer had returned, Sue had told him that this time they should skip the treatments. She had looked so healthy, Phil remembered. She was putting on weight again; her thick, brown hair was coming in. She had touched her fingertips to his, eyes bright and confident, and said, "I don't think there's anything we can do." Maybe she had been looking into Mohawk's lousy insurance coverage to discover that there were significant things it wouldn't cover. Or maybe she had found the bills that Phil had tried to hide in the truck's glove compartment. Maybe, too, she was tired of fighting. Phil had tossed a kitchen chair and yelled that he would not give up on her. Mostly he was angry at her for giving up on him. Ultimately, she agreed to undergo the treatments again. Three agonizing years later, she was gone.

As if waking from a dream, her death brought Phil back to reality. His son was grieving, and Phil had no idea how to console him. There was $75,000 in expenses, which Phil couldn't handle alone. The latter seemed the easier fix: he volunteered Mark to work the extra hours with him. The former he had spinelessly left to time to assuage. Now, however, moving away from the court, Phil couldn't help but see that he was standing between Mark and the first real excitement his son had experienced in a long time. That was where Phil had always stood.

They reached the landing and Phil called Mark to stop.

"We're staying," Phil said.

"What?"

"We're not leaving before the game's over."

Mark moved closer and put on his jacket. "Dad, come on. You know better than I do what'll happen if we're late. Now let's go." He turned.

"Mark!" He shouted louder than he'd intended. His son looked startled. The horn sounded in the court below, and the ball pounded on the wood. He was about to assure Mark that he'd speak to Fleming in the morning, that all would be fine. Instead, he repeated, "We're staying."

Mark's eyes took on pleading. "This is crazy. We can't afford to lose our jobs for a game."

The crowd roared, and Phil glanced at the scoreboard. UConn was up six. It all might be over soon anyway. He looked down at his stained boots. He'd had these five years now, a Christmas gift from Sue and

Mark. Mark wore Phil's old ones, God knew how old. The T-shirt Phil had just bought Mark still had its creases.

"Listen to me." Phil got ready to say it and felt his voice failing. It took him two attempts to get it out. "I got nothing . . . Your mother—" He put his fist over his mouth. When he continued, his voice still rattled. "Your mother knew how to give . . . even when there was nothing. I . . . I don't know what I'm doing. I just . . ." Phil squeezed his throbbing temples. "We're staying."

Another eruption from the crowd, near deafening. Phil grabbed Mark by the shirt to pull him closer. "You hear me, you stubborn bastard?" He pushed Mark away, then laughed and wiped the tears. "We're staying until it's over. Okay?"

The fight in Mark vanished and he laughed nervously, but Phil could see he wasn't totally convinced. "Dad, we can listen to it on the radio."

"The radio?" Phil walked down the steps, jingling the car keys over his shoulder. "Can't go anywhere without me." Halfway down, Phil looked back to make sure Mark was following. He was, and grinning.

The game was in a time-out when they made their way back through the row to their seats.

"Well, look who it is," Wall Street said, happy to see them. "Forget something?"

Phil turned to look at the man, studied his eyes for a solid moment. Then he said, "I still got a little hair left to lose."

Wall Street laughed and patted Phil's back. There were only twenty-one seconds left to play in the third overtime, and Syracuse was down by three.

"Whose ball is it?" Phil asked.

"Syracuse's. They won't give up."

Everyone was standing and cheering. Mark was rigid, quietly watching.

"Let's go Orange!" Phil called loudly and kept at it until Mark loosened up and began cheering along.

Flynn dribbled up the floor, confident and calm. He crossed half court and immediately passed to their sharpshooter, Rautins, coming off a screen. He lifted into the air and took the shot despite the four hands in his face. He made it and tied the game. Phil and Mark jumped up and down like fools. Eleven seconds left, UConn hurried to get a shot off, but missed, and sent the game into its fourth overtime.

Exhausted and incredulous, the UConn players folded their arms over their heads and looked skyward for explanation. Those wearing orange found the game's endlessness funny. Flynn was leaning on a teammate, hobbling, but laughing back to the bench. Coach Boeheim rubbed his forehead, a cockeyed smile dimpling his cheek. Phil laughed at the absurdity of so many overtimes, as though they were targeted at him.

The burn in his legs, and now his back, clipped Phil's smile. He'd been standing since the end of the game, and all day at work, a total of thirteen or fourteen hours. He took the opportunity to sit and rest. He squeezed his calves to massage the cramps.

"You gonna make it?" Mark asked, his hand on Phil's back.

Phil stuck his arm under the seat, pretending to search for something in his coat pocket. "Thought I might have some gum. Guess not."

The next overtime began, and Phil stood, fighting hard not to grunt or wince. The pain reminded him of Mohawk and the repercussions of his decision. He shook it off. He was here; he would have a good time. Syracuse scored, and Phil clapped. It was too late to change his mind anyway. Besides, this was for Mark, whose voice was now frayed to a growl. He was pumping his fist at the players. Incredibly, time ran out again and the game was still tied.

A fifth overtime.

This was not only for Mark. It couldn't be. Phil watched the players on the court, waiting for the next period of play. The players' eyes were glazed as they glanced at the jumbotron, as if attempting to puzzle out another way to get ahead. *And what if they lost?* they must have been thinking. *What if they went through all this and still came up short?* That fear had to keep their legs strong. Otherwise, they would have all collapsed and stayed down. Maybe it wasn't fear, but a will to win. What did that feel like, Phil wondered, to fight for a win and get it? Or just to fight?

A sudden pain jolted up Phil's back, causing him to yelp. To cover it up, he cupped his hands around his mouth and called at the court. He focused once again on the heart of his team. Flynn was pouring sweat, eyes squinting pain as he sucked air, but he was still charging the ball at the hoop, making shots.

At 1:04 a.m., the game was going into a sixth overtime. It might go on like this all night. Wall Street looked something up on his phone and informed Phil and Mark that this was now the second longest game in college basketball history. A UConn player was laid out on the court, exhausted in disbelief. Other players' legs wobbled as they shuffled to the bench. Phil wanted to sit, could have, but resisted. His feet were numb in his boots, but his knees and hips throbbed. And if he moved his back even slightly, turning to one side or the other, the pain would be there to bite him back.

Phil stuck his thumb and finger into his mouth for the piercing whistle he'd perfected as a teenager. He accomplished little more than air and spittle, and Mark laughed at his failure. Phil demonstrated the mechanics, and Mark tried the whistle. He got it the first try, the strength of the noise surprising him, and he whistled again.

The horn sounded the beginning of the sixth overtime. Flynn high-dribbled as he orchestrated his teammates with his free hand. Rautins reacted, dashing to the top of the key to free himself; Flynn threw him the ball, and Rautins sunk a three pointer. Syracuse was ahead, the first time since overtime, 113–110. After UConn turned the ball over, another SU player had it near the basket, butt in his defender's stomach, backing him toward the hoop. Suddenly, he spun free, leaving his man to watch as he put the ball in the basket. They were up five. Then they were up eight.

Phil and Mark leapt and shouted, high-fiving anyone they could reach. It was easy for Phil to yell, to almost howl.

It was 1:22 a.m. Ten seconds remaining. Flynn had the ball once more, a shaky hand in the air all he could do to celebrate. His teammates clapped for themselves feebly, then hugged each other in near collapse. The seconds now on their side simply fell away.

Phil was doubled over, holding his knees, the horn around them echoing in him. His eyes were squeezed shut and he tapped his forehead with his fist. His entire lower half seemed amputated, completely numb. He suddenly called out as loud as he could, flung himself upright, jabbed his fists skyward, and tossed his head back to scream. Mark grabbed him and hugged, and they jumped up and down, hollering stupidly into each other's faces.

Mark slept against the window. He'd balled his jacket into a pillow, and Phil's jacket was draped over his shoulder. Phil's ears rang and his voice was gone. His hands were raw on the steering wheel, but he was still riled with the thrilling memory of the game. The pain was roaring in his legs and back. He hadn't been able to walk out of the arena on his own. Mark had tracked down a lady wearing a yellow vest who brought a wheelchair.

Phil felt a vibration in his pocket and wedged his hand in to look at his cell. It was Fleming. Phil slipped the phone back into his jeans. It was well after six a.m., over an hour late for their shift. Phil passed the exit for Mohawk and instead turned onto the ramp toward Chittenango.

Just then, a blazing white flash snuck up behind the truck. The sunrise blinded Phil for a moment until he adjusted the rearview mirror. He squinted his vision clear and saw that the road ahead of them was washed in sun except for the long shadow of the truck. Phil cranked the window and put his arm into the morning air, watching his skin take the light. He put his hand on Mark's leg and gave him a gentle shake. For too long he'd been driving his son through the dark of predawn; he needed to see this.

SNOW MAN

Winter, 2014

————◆————

10.1 OZ. ACRYLIC LATEX caulk plus silicone
   ½" x 8'4" moisture-resistant drywall
   10 oz. liquid nails, heavy duty construction adhesive
   12 oz. foam sealant
   1 qt. spackle paste int/ext
   Four rolls of self-adhesive, fiberglass drywall tape
   61.7 lb. pail of all-purpose joint compound
   9½" x 15" x 25' continuous roll fiberglass insulation
   6" x 75' butyl rubber with polyolefin film facer flashing tape
   30-year, three-tab charcoal shingles
   150 sq. ft. roll granular surfaced leak barrier
   5 gal. asphalt flashing cement
   10' traditional white vinyl-style gutter
   6" x 3' mill hinged gutter guard
   3" x 10' rust-free aluminum round corrugated downspout
   9 oz. white advanced gutter and flashing sealant
   He can fight infinity by building the finite. He can fill in the gaps,
plug up the darkness. He can pretend real numbers, real measurements
exist, because there's his proof: a wall, a roof.

"You plan on staying for a while?" asked Angela, a smirk dimpling her
cheek. Brett had no idea what she was talking about. Still smiling, she
nodded to the oak stand beside him. The first thing he'd done when
they entered this house-for-sale—an old Colonial just outside town
that he'd never been in before—was place his wallet, cell phone, and

keys on the stand. Then he noticed his socked feet. He must have also removed his slushy boots, which he never did in unfamiliar houses.

"Isn't that something?" Brett replaced his wallet and phone as calmly as possible, but the key chain he held onto. His fingers sifted through the collection of keys and tags and trinkets and located the rubber boxing glove, its red worn white. He began chomping it between his teeth.

"Brett," Angela said, squeezing his elbow and leveling her gray, wolf-like eyes on him. "Don't freak out. You said you'd give this place a serious look."

"I'm good. Let me just—" and he gave the glove a few more good chews before stuffing the key chain back into his coat pocket.

Angela had vetted the house already, so she directed the tour. "You'll love this place," she said, marching toward the kitchen. "Everything's been renovated, so you won't have to worry about . . ." She flipped her hand to indicate the rest. Probably the only succinct way to communicate it.

The kitchen appliances were old, but the floors were bamboo-hardwood, and the backsplash sparkled with emerald-green tile. The January sun coming through the window reflected the silver flecks in the granite countertops. Brett ran his finger along the line of grout filling the counter's seams—a flawless job that sent a shudder of pleasure through his bones.

Angela twirled, her brown braids swinging around her head like helicopter blades. "Gorgeous, right?"

"It's okay."

She punched his shoulder.

"I love it."

Her knuckles pressed his chin, promising more of the same. "Come look at the other rooms."

Brett tolerated the tour, politely nodding when Angela pointed out the crown molding and recessed lighting and new stone fireplace.

When they went upstairs, he was disappointed to discover further perfection: fresh carpeting, a remodeled bathroom, and, in both of the bedrooms, rosewood ceiling fans with gunmetal mounting.

"So," Angela said, biting her nails, "what do you think?"

He pulled the key chain from his jeans like a clown drawing an interminable length of handkerchiefs. He located his mini flashlight, the LED that blasted from the feet of a LEGO man. "I'm just going to check some things out."

Angela groaned and collapsed on the fluffy beige carpet.

He began with the upstairs bathroom, getting on his hands and knees and aiming the flashlight into typical problem areas. There wasn't a crack or anomaly or infelicity anywhere. The grout job on the tile was expert. The caulk sealing the toilet base to the floor was precise—a smooth, hairline bit of gleaming white. No hidden gaps showed where the baseboard or bathtub met the floor, or in the corners of the shower. Even under the sink, where no one would care to look, a foam sealant was used between the hole cut into the back of the cabinet and the plumbing. Whoever had done these renovations was no doubt a fellow obsessive.

Brett rushed back through the other rooms, eager for evidence that there was not another person out there with the same level of perfectionism as him. With each flawlessly measured and sealed room he grew more intrigued—and terrified. He found himself back in the kitchen, shaking and exhausted. Angela was there, leaning against the counter, playing on her phone. He must have had a look on his face.

"What is it?"

"There's not a goddamn thing wrong with this house."

Angela erected from her slouch. "You actually like it?"

"I'm just saying it's flawless."

She took his hand and petted it like you would a puppy. "There's one more thing." Her smile twitched at the corners. "It's no biggie."

She led him back through the dining room and family room. A window to the backyard revealed an expanse of snow and sentinel of pines just beyond the creek that ran across the back of the yard. The tops of the trees bent with the wind, spraying snow from branches like fine sugar. The scar on his forehead began to throb like heartbeat, its usual behavior when the weather changed.

Angela went to an unassuming door at the bottom of the stairs, which Brett had previously dismissed as a coat closet.

"Remember how much you love me." She inhaled, turned the knob, and pushed.

The room—apparently an addition—was in absolute disrepair. A stack of two-by-fours and a pair of sawhorses cluttered the center of the sawdusty plywood floor. The walls were skeletal, just a frame and exposed air ducts and electrical wiring. Something was flapping above. Plastic sheets covered the beams where a roof should have been. The arctic wind sucked the plastic in and out as if the room were hyperventilating.

"I thought this could be the baby's nursery," Angela said. "You know, whenever we start to try."

Brett stood in that spatial chaos, fluttering in the blizzard of possibilities, deciding.

Home repair was his most recent fixation. Since rehab he'd mastered the accordion, learned all of the constellations, and acquired his ham radio license, among a few other "hobbies," as Angela teasingly called them. For Brett, these were necessary to fill the gap left by the pills. This was the gap that always loomed, taunted, had an insatiable appetite. He couldn't fill it ever, just feed it and keep it fed.

Two years ago, just after he and Angela were married, they moved out of their apartment and rented a house outside Rochester. It was a shithole but all they could afford on their teachers' salaries. At the time, Brett was an adjunct at a small college, teaching the introductory philosophy courses that the tenured professors wouldn't stoop to. But

Brett was proud of himself for getting his shit together. His students actually called him Professor Pratt. He wore a blazer with jeans and got to talk about Leibniz and Locke and Kant—a far cry from his years as a fuckup in Chittenango. He often shuddered looking back on that gloomy, angsty teen whose main objective was to treat everyone around him like shit, especially himself. This was the kind of insight his years of rehab and therapy—and a high dosage of antidepressants—afforded him.

On the third night in the shithole, a downpour left a puddle of water near the front door. Brett tossed down a bunch of towels, soaked it all up, and there it stayed, in his head: *Where'd the water come from? How long has water been trickling into this house? If there's water, there's mold. Mold spores can nestle into the lungs, causing respiratory disease. What if Angela gets a respiratory disease?* He investigated, found the problem's source, taught himself to solve the problem (cement, drywall, spackle, lots of caulk—trial and error mostly), and discovered doing this kind of work calmed him in a way that—well, not in the same way the pills had, not even close. But it did calm him.

Then there was nothing more to repair, nothing else on which to focus his obsessions. He had re-caulked the same cracks and re-drywalled the foyer and re-flashed the chimney—there was absolutely nothing more to do, and he felt the gap swell.

The news came at just the right time. Angela's mother had called to inform them that there was a house up for auction in their hometown. Since there were no known inheritors, Madison County took over the house and was planning on auctioning it, most likely at a price Brett and Angela could afford.

Brett had his reservations. It had taken him twenty-eight years of scars and family dysfunction and a severe opiate addiction to get out of 'Nango, and now they were moving back. Also, they'd both have to find new jobs, though Brett didn't voice this since he knew as well as Angela that adjunct work would be plentiful for him in the Syracuse area, and with her experience and teaching awards, any elementary school would hire Angela on the spot. To his main concern, Angela had patiently explained that this could be the only chance they had of being homeowners. She then repeated her desire to have a child, and that Chittenango was the perfect little village to raise a family. Neither of those was as convincing as: "You owe me this, Brett." God knew he owed her quite a bit, and she wasn't shy about reminding him of that.

The upside was, now he had a new project to temper his restlessness. He was anxious to get started renovating the unfinished room, which, for now, would be the baby's. But there was the other thing, too, honestly, the main thing—the inexplicable familiarity of the house and its renovator. The old saboteur in him felt the need to dirty his hands getting to the bottom of that mystery.

Angela was lying naked on an air mattress in the middle of the unfinished room. She looked like a porn actress, propped on an elbow, legs open and hand fiddling between her thighs. Two space heaters going full blast made the room bearable; regardless, her breasts were prickled with goose bumps. Brett played the part of the unsuspecting oaf, except instead of walking in with a pizza, his arms were full of bags from the hardware store.

She said, "My vagina's slimy."

"Fantastic!"

"I'm ovulating."

"Fantastic?"

"It's prime time to knock me up."

"So you got the job?"

She nodded seductively.

His hands didn't have common sense: they continued to clutch the plastic bags.

"This is what we want, right?" She abandoned her sultry role and sat up. "We got a house; I'll be working again; you will be soon. Did you change your mind?"

Say no, Brett. Hurry up!

"No."

Say something else, idiot.

"I was just caught off guard, is all." His hands finally got the message and dropped the bags, then began working on unbuttoning his jeans. "Let's make a baby." He shuffled toward her with his jeans around his ankles like a prisoner in a chain gang. Then he got the connection.

". . . In the nursery. Of course. Where else would we conceive a child?"

"I thought it'd make a good story." She yanked his underwear down and popped his unprepared penis in her mouth.

"Right," Brett said. "What child wouldn't want to hear that his parents boned in the room he sleeps in?"

She muffled, "Screw you."

He couldn't help but scan the walls while she was working on him. He saw himself beginning the job: rolling out the insulation, measuring and cutting it, stuffing it between the beams. Prepping the drill, then fastening the drywall.

He noticed near the door, just over his shoulder, that a single panel of drywall was already affixed. How had he missed this? It made no sense to insulate and cover only one segment of wall. You insulate everything first, and then move on to the next step. More perplexing: if the renovator was anything like Brett—and the evidence was piling up that he was—he wouldn't be able to walk away from something he had just started. Unless he was met with a sudden demise, which just brought Brett back to the former issue of doing everything in steps.

"Ready to do this?" Angela asked, lips swollen and temples sweaty. Brett followed her eyes to his dick, shrunken into his pubic hair like a shy mushroom.

"Sorry."

Angela sat back on the air mattress. She hugged her knees to her breasts, looked at him accusingly. She was waiting for Brett to speak, which he discovered too late. She sighed and dropped her head to her knees. Just when he thought he was relieved, her head popped up in a dramatic flinging of hair.

"If you're having second thoughts, just tell me."

"I'm not. No. I just, it's just so cold in here, and I'm, the medication is, you know."

Angela rolled off the mattress and stomped toward the door.

"You're not going to let me explain?" he said.

"You sound like a retard when you're lying."

"You're not supposed to use that word."

She stopped and turned. Her eyes narrowed and nostrils flared. A vein popped from her neck, and her chest inflated with spite.

Brett crouched, stepped back for leverage, but his underwear still bound his ankles.

She came at him roaring. Brett grabbed the flesh of her sides and used her momentum to hurl her behind him. She thudded on the floor, grunting. Brett went to leap, but she kicked her heel into his stomach. She squeezed him around the neck and twisted him down. She mounted him, hooking her thick legs under his thighs, and proceeded to slap his face. He grabbed her wrists, and then noticed his erection stabbing at her belly.

"So now you're ready?" she asked, heaving. She wrenched free and stood up. She pulled her mass of hair from her face, blew him a kiss, and then took her round ass out of the room, trying to hide her limp.

God, he loved that woman.

Brett avoided her for the rest of the evening and into the night, holing up in the cold room made unnaturally hot, slicing the insulation with a killer's determination. Two Coleman lanterns gave him enough light by which to work and enough shadow to now and then spook him. When he had packed the last of the insulation into the walls, it was well after midnight. He wasn't close to tired; he was just getting going. And there was that lone panel, taunting the entire time. It was begging to be removed, and he didn't have the will power to refuse it any longer.

He loosened the screws with a twelve-inch Phillip's head, then used the drill to unscrew them completely. It took a swift yank to free the drywall. He pulled out the insulation. Despite the icy air penetrating the plastic overhead, sweat dripped from his nose and chin. He toweled it with his shirt, which was flecked with insulation dust. His face itched. He aimed the LEGO man into the gutted wall. There was nothing. He had the feeling of someone hovering over his shoulder, pressing him on, or warning him away. But from what?

From the six-inch horizontal gap of pure blackness in the back of the wall, near the floor. He stuck his hand in, breaking a spider web barrier. His fingers knew immediately.

Orange prescription pill bottles—labelless, nameless, and thank God, empty.

10 mg/650 mg oxycodone and acetaminophen (Percocet)

10 mg/660 mg hydrocodone bitartrate and acetaminophen (Vicodin)

8 mg hydromorphone (Dilaudid) tablets

80 mg oxycodone (OxyContin)

100 mg meperidine (Demerol) tablets

65 mg propoxyphene (Darvon)

60 mg sulfate (Codeine)

90 mg morphine sulfate extended release capsules (Avinza)

Fentanyl citrate lollipops (Actiq)

And, preferably, 75 mcg/h fentanyl transdermal patches (Duragesic) until the walls fall away.

These were how he fought infinity, by floating above it. Or within it. The drift. The cool wave. In 2009, life was beautiful.

The day would begin with Brett slapping on a Fenny patch, which he kept beside the bed, and lighting a cigarette. Then he'd have his coffee, more of a mixer for the Wild Turkey. By that time, he was in the right mood to get his dad ready for the day. Changing his diapers didn't bother Brett; neither did bathing him. His dad liked for him to sing *Wizard of Oz* songs in the tub. The unparalyzed part of his face would curl into a smirk. His blue eyes—brighter and clearer post-stroke—would follow Brett's, a look of perpetual thanks. No matter how high Brett got, he couldn't meet them.

However, his dad's stroke brought Brett and Angela together. He'd always known Angela. She was his neighbor since childhood. He couldn't have predicted they'd be married, since he'd done some pretty awful things to her when he was a teenager. Regardless, Angela began dropping by after work to help when she heard that he'd taken a leave from grad school to care for his dad. Why, Brett couldn't say. Perhaps she interpreted his assisting as selfless, which softened her. If this were the case, it would have been a colossal misinterpretation. He did it because there was no one else to do it, and there was no money to hire someone else to do it. As his father's sole caretaker, Brett managed his scripts, his pain. The stroke left him with daily, debilitating migraines, and all Brett had to do was call the family doctor, a friend of his dad's, and tell her he needed something stronger. When Brett was at the apex of his addiction, he was also hitting up his dad's neurologist for meds.

He'd give Angela one of the Percocets when she came over, and they'd cook dinner. She couldn't have known the extent of Brett's addiction; to her, this was just a recreational thing. They had an amazing time preparing Italian meals, feasts really, even though his dad was the only one eating. They'd roll meatballs in the kitchen while listening to Dean

Martin, the raw meat gooping their hands, keeping them from groping each other the entire time. His dad would often hang out at the kitchen table, moving his clumsy hand to the music.

Once his dad was in bed, they'd smoke cigarettes on the back porch, chatting while the lightning bugs made trails of cursive nonsense. Later, they'd have dirty, aggressive sex, where it seemed Angela was finally acknowledging the shit Brett had done to her. She'd bite his nipples and pound his chest and call him motherfucker—and he took it because he deserved it.

The crowbar is an honest tool. A solid length of iron, a violent curl of rabbit teeth at the ends, used solely for deconstruction. It was liberating and frightening to stab it into the wall at the bottom of the stairs, just outside the unfinished room. Angela was at her mom's again, otherwise she wouldn't approve of his disassembling the wall. He dug the crowbar in and ripped out another sheet. He pulled away the fluffy insulation and stared-down another gutted space. His hands were eager, groping fiendishly into the cool, dark gap. Of course they found something, they knew they would. But this? A small, rubber basketball, its orange faded to creamy-white by worried rubbing, and its tail a delicate chain attached to a key ring.

He felt around for more, this time hoping for nothing. But there was more, a nylon loop. He pulled and pulled to find a black, frayed leash. It was attached to a collar, as if the animal it belonged to had simply vanished. The tarnished, bone-shaped tag gave name to the mystery dog: *PADDY.*

In April of 2010, Brett's dad died. Doctors had said it wasn't uncommon for stroke victims to endure a second stroke. Not uncommon. That wasn't good enough. Brett blamed himself, assuming he had neglected his dad since he was perpetually high. He also suffered the guilt that came from resenting his dad so hard for so long for being a lousy father. What remained when he passed was all of that unresolved hatred swirling around like a galaxy.

Brett hardly remembered the funeral, being out-of-his-skull high. His mom was there, Angela of course was there, and nearly half of Chittenango was there, too. After all, the village owed Mayor Pratt. While his political ambition broke up their family, it saved the town. He'd single-handedly brought the Oz Festival back, and with that, some actual revenue. During the eight years he was mayor, two new restaurants went up on Genesee Street. He'd pressed the owners to make them Oz related, but they weren't having it. Sure, his dramatic enthusiasm annoyed Brett—he pictured his dad at the top of the bleachers during a Friday night Bears game, screaming for the defense to rally, even though he hated football—but when the stroke overcame him, something in Chittenango went dim.

Angela later told Brett that he'd tried to get into the coffin with his dad—he was only one leg away from achieving it. When he was pulled out, he still held onto his dad's blazer, so that the body was wrenched upright.

Brett had fled the funeral home. He checked into the only motel in the village and locked himself in a room with two half gallons of vodka and a bottle each of Percocet and OxyContin. He didn't set out to *exactly* kill himself, since he could easily have downed all the pills in one sitting, but he intended to waste away, to fall into the hole, the glorious freedom of seeking rock bottom. Two days later—the vodka gone, most of the pills swallowed—the motel owner found him laid out in the center of the gravel parking lot, an inch from death.

His stomach was pumped at a nearby hospital. Then they sent him to detox. The nightmares, the internal earthquake, the screaming and crying and the begging of nurses to kill him, he'd done it all.

Angela came to visit when he was nearing the end of the withdrawal.

"You can leave me," he told her from the sweat-soaked bed. "I won't blame you."

Her hands balled to fists. She was dressed for teaching five-year-olds: loud colors and chunky jewelry. "You put me through this," she said, voice quavering, "and then you force a decision on me?" She sucked air into her lungs and relaxed her hands enough to put one on Brett's arm. "I want you to tell me the whole thing. How long it's been going on. How much of our happiness was just the pills. And what your retarded intentions were in that motel room."

"I don't think you're supposed to use that word."

"Then, you're going to make a decision."

"What's that?"

"If we stay together, and you feel that urge again, you fight it. Understand? If you can't fight it, then there's no us. Think about it."

Brett did. There wasn't much else to do but think. Without deliberately deciding, he began the slow, embarrassing process of recovery. The first and most important step was leaving Chittenango. If there was any hope for staying clean, he had to get the hell out.

Rochester seemed like a good place. The Buddhist temples and meditation centers were all over the area, a good omen for someone trying to calm his mind. As much as he wished for them to be lame, the NA meetings and support groups helped. They were always handing out cheap, plastic tags to attach to key chains, reminders of their dedication to sobriety. Brett preferred more symbolic toys to clutter his key chain, which he began to collect. He also started seeing a therapist who prescribed antidepressants and suggested taking up "hobbies" in order to focus his energies. And he recommended that Brett not engage in any relationships for at least a year. He understood the rationale—to cut off all dependencies, and relationships are big ones for addicts—however, he didn't heed this. Quite the opposite. He devoted himself to Angela.

After two years of sobriety, Brett proposed, and the very next day they visited the justice of the peace, and then celebrated their marriage at Dinosaur Bar-B-Que. It wasn't long after that they began talking babies. Angela persuaded him that it was a good idea, that Brett would be okay. When he allowed himself to believe her, he was met with hope. Maybe he had a future as a father and family man rather than an ex-pill-fiend. Maybe.

Brett learned, going through an intense opiate addiction and coming out on the other end alive, that the heaven he had experienced was poison, and that he could never return to it. He'd tasted bliss. He knew how it felt in his mouth. He even knew where to find it and approximately how much it cost, but he could never, ever return to it. If this wasn't bad enough, they told him that he was able to find this happiness again, only sober. He knew it was not the same and he felt like shit that he had an amazing wife and the promise of a family, but neither could make him feel as good as a 75 mcg fentanyl patch. That was why they called it a disease.

When any normal person wanted information about his house, he'd go to the neighbors, usually while they were shoveling the driveway, their kids tunneling holes through the snowbanks. Beers would be offered from a garage refrigerator, the family dog scratched behind the ear, et cetera. Brett was avoiding the neighbors, though he would've loved a beer. He didn't want them asking him a bunch of questions about what happened to him, about why he left. And he didn't want to endure the judgment in their eyes, the kind leveled at someone who leaves his hometown, only to return. *So you didn't think we were good enough for you? And now you've come crawling back? Want a beer?*

Brett tried Google, lazy man's research, and discovered that the house had belonged to the DeMartanos. This was an unpleasant surprise, since Brett was aware of their ostensible curse. All three of them had died unnaturally within a four- or five-year span. Mrs. DeMartano battled cancer for years and years. When Brett's dad was mayor, he'd held fundraisers to help with her medical bills. It wasn't enough, and Mr. DeMartano killed himself trying to pay them off. He worked his whole life at Mohawk Steel & Die until he croaked right there in the factory—a brain aneurysm was what Brett had heard. Mark must have inherited this house and then, according to his online obituary, had died only three months ago. The details of Mark's death were hazy; Brett and Angela were in Rochester at the time, distanced from small-town gossip, and the obit gave him nothing. Brett rummaged his memory for more information, but Mark must have been a senior when Brett was still in the third grade. He'd had the reputation for being a bully, but Brett couldn't place where that came from; he certainly had no experience with it. The only evidence Brett had about Mark was this house and the pill bottles. That they were hidden inside the wall suggested that Mark was the renovator. That the bottles were there at all gave him nothing but haunting guesses.

Brett needed more. It looked like Mark had a Facebook page. It was his name, but there was no other information, and no photo, just that cartoony blue outline of an anonymous bust.

So Brett sucked it up and made a phone call.

"Hello, may I please speak to Chief Bell?"

"Yup. Got him."

"Hi. This is Brett Pratt."

"Well ho-ly shit, Brett Pratt. Until I heard you bought up DeMartano's house, I was certain you were dead."

"No. Didn't die. Close call, though."

"Probably should've though, right?"

"I'm sorry?"

"What I mean is, all them illegal substances in your body, might've served you right."

Brett shouldn't have been surprised. Bell had always been a dick. He'd hated that because Brett was the mayor's son, Bell had to take it easy on him. He considered hanging up but instead got to the point.

"I'm actually calling about Mark."

"Got what was coming to him."

Brett gritted his teeth. "And what was that, exactly?"

He expected him to say the clichéd, *What, you don't know?*

"What're you, writing a book?"

He should have talked to the neighbors.

"My wife, Angela, she wants to know. She's superstitious."

"Mhm." The answer seemed to make sense. "An autopsy was performed. State law, otherwise, who would've cared? Medical examiner found enough painkillers in him to kill an elephant."

Brett's hands began shaking, so much that he had to use his shoulder to pin the phone to his ear.

"So I take it he was found in the house."

Bell laughed. "You didn't know?"

There it was.

"Just one more question, and then, unfortunately, I'll have to terminate this pleasant conversation. Was it a deliberate overdose or accidental?"

"Hell, son, I don't know that. I can't see that it matters much."

It absolutely mattered.

"You know how many gobs of cash we found in that house?" Bell continued. "Turns out, Mark was a serious dealer. But I'm sure you were well aware."

Brett missed his chance to speak.

"Some people get all emotional about death," Bell said. "They call it a tragedy and such forth. Your father, that was a tragedy. Mark's mother and father, that was a tragedy. People like Mark, though: good riddance. When he died, the high school was drug free for almost a year. So when you call up and ask how he died? Well, I'm just biting my tongue on this end. Since I respect your father and what he did for this town, I'll refrain from chewing your ass out."

"For the record, Chief, I'm clean and sober. I've been for four years now."

"If you say so."

Angela wanted ice cream. She required it, and Brett was granted permission, at eleven p.m., to get it for her. This was her way of allowing him to begin the complicated process of apologizing for ruining their attempt at reproduction. They hadn't even brought it up again. The problem remained that he did not want to go out into public for fear of being interrogated about his past. Still, he couldn't refuse Angela, not now. He knew of a convenience store that sold ice cream. He could duck in, hopefully without being noticed, and get the hell out.

The plan was going splendidly. There was no one in the Nice N Easy, except the female clerk, whom Brett didn't recognize. He paid for the vanilla bean Häagen-Dazs and headed out the door swinging the bag. The night was clear and bitingly cold, assaulting his scar and swelling his skull like ice in a balloon. His eyes teared and his nostrils felt frozen shut. Just as he was stepping off the curb, a purple pickup jerked into a parking space ten feet from him. The little warning people have in their guts that alerts trouble was going off.

The driver got out of the truck, a cigarette pinched in his lips. He was tall as ever, face lean and hard edged. A knit hat was pulled low on his forehead, hiding the eyebrows that would otherwise signal the extent of his meanness. It was Dean, a high school friend, in the loosest of terms. He'd ridiculed and bullied Brett, given him the scar on his forehead. As for Brett, he wasn't blameless either. But that . . . that day on the bank of the creek—no, he wouldn't allow himself to acknowledge it. That wasn't him; that was another Brett, someone who was confused and angry and lonely and strange. He'd been trying to sprint away from that kid for a long time and had gotten a good distance going. Now, seeing Dean, brought him closer than he'd been in a while.

The intense fluorescence of the overhead lights cast Dean in an eerie glow like a Ghost from Christmas Past. Their eyes met as Dean brushed by, and not knowing whether he recognized Brett, and fearing he'd come across as rude for ignoring him, Brett foolishly said, "Hey."

"Hey," Dean repeated flatly and thankfully kept moving toward the entrance. But then he backed up and narrowed his eyes. His face suddenly opened into a wide smile. "Brett, holy shit!"

Brett flexed his mouth into what he hoped resembled a smile. "Good to see you, Dean."

They shook. Dean patted his shoulder with his free hand like a big brother might.

"You came back?" At one time, back in high school, that slanty smile would have been laden with danger and vitriol. Now, it seemed literal. Otherwise, he still looked the same, a style best described as grubby.

"I guess I did. Wasn't really the plan."

"Where you live? Still on Jill Street?"

"We actually moved into the DeMartanos' house."

"You mean Mark's?"

"Yeah, Angela and I."

It seemed important for Brett to inform him that he was married. Dean didn't seem to care, though.

His lips directed smoke upward and he asked, "Where's Mark?"

"Oh, he's . . . well, he . . ." The cold was still drawing out tears, and here Brett was trying to say someone had died while looking like he was broken up over it. To counter that, he said, "He croaked."

Dean seemed genuinely distraught. He dropped the cigarette between his feet and mashed it out. "I didn't know."

This little reunion was off to a bad start. They were both bouncing around on the pavement now, trying to stay warm. It appeared that the temperature would be a good enough reason to flee.

Brett said, "Well, it's cold as shit out here . . ."

"I know." Dean thankfully returned to his truck. But before opening the door, he said, "Come on."

"What?"

"We'll talk inside."

Brett grumbled to himself but got into the passenger's side, competing with empty Coke Zero cans for foot space. Dean turned the ignition and blasted the heat. The ice cream was on Brett's lap. He should have left it outside to stay cool, but it now seemed too late. Being in Dean's truck, sitting side-by-side with the heat roaring in their faces, made Brett self-conscious. This right here was exactly what he'd been trying to avoid since moving back.

"I live out in Utica," Dean said, lighting a Camel Wide and offering Brett the last one from his pack. His hand took it before he could refuse. "Been there for . . . I guess six years now? Visiting my dad this weekend. Hoping to get a job at the casino."

He lit Brett's cigarette, and they both cracked their windows.

"Casino?"

"Yeah, man. The Indians are opening a casino right over there in the Tops Plaza. Apparently they still own that land."

"A casino in Chittenango?" The cigarette made Brett pleasantly light-headed. He hadn't smoked in years and he almost instantly decided he'd start again.

"It's going to open sometime this summer. They're doing interviews this weekend; thought I'd give it a shot."

Brett could see the plaza lights from here. It was beyond his imagination to picture something as vibrant as a casino in a place as tired as Chittenango.

"You know what they're calling it?" Dean said. "Yellow Brick Road Casino. Your dad would've gotten a kick out of that."

Brett tensed, rattling the plastic bag the ice cream was in. It wasn't the mention of his dad but of the past, because he and Dean had a past, a strange one that Brett didn't want acknowledged any more than it had to be.

"Look, Brett." Dean swiveled to face him and instinctively, Brett drew back. His head slammed on the window.

"Sorry," Brett said. "The nicotine's got me jumpy."

"I can't blame you," he said, sadly. "The shit I did to you back then. That's the point, man. I got to come clean and apologize."

Brett's fingers went impulsively up to his scar. Goddammit, there was no part of himself he could control.

"For that." He nodded at Brett's forehead. "And for treating you like shit in general. I mean, you were my only goddamn friend."

Brett kept his eyes on his shell-top boots, shrugged. "That's cool."

"Really. I . . . Here's the thing, I was into drugs pretty hardcore for a while, and then got clean. One of the steps in NA is apologizing to all those you fucked over. You were always on my list, but I wasn't sure how to track you down."

His eyes were so earnest, desperate; they demanded something genuine from Brett. "It's no problem. I, you know, forgive you." Brett had the good sense not to perform a papal air-blessing, though he really wanted to.

Dean looked off toward the plaza lights. "Mark was someone else I needed to apologize to."

Dean went into his coat for another cigarette, but his pack was empty. He looked back toward the Nice N Easy. This was obviously the time for Brett to share his own addiction story, his time in NA, and his reaching out to those harmed by his drug use. Brett didn't believe in fate, but even this coincidence—this bringing together of old friends with strangely similar struggles—hardly seemed random. So he should honor this cosmic opportunity; he should say something.

"Whatever happened to that dog?"

Dean squinted his eyes.

"Remember the one, white and yappy, kind of a pain in the ass?"

"I know the one," he said slowly. "It wasn't yours, was it?"

"No, it was actually . . . Angela's."

He raised his eyebrows. "Did you ever tell *your wife* you tried to kill her dog?"

"Actually, you tried to kill it."

Dean postured for the argument but remained in good spirits. "I saved that thing. I took care of it. I loved that dog."

"Well then, where is it?"

Dean gave Brett an unpleasant look. Brett held his eyes, unwilling to back down, a kind of unintended revenge for years of submitting to him. But Dean didn't seem to have the fight in him, and when he turned away, he was clenching his jaw, eyes flickering with the lights. What the hell was Brett doing, picking a fight with an addict in a vulnerable moment of his recovery?

"Want some ice cream?" Brett lifted the lid of the carton, displaying the bean-flecked dessert.

Dean looked at the container. "Shit yeah." He laughed. "Do you have spoons?"

"Oops. No spoons."

Dean reached between Brett's legs. Brett tensed. He opened the glove compartment, fished around through the papers, receipts, napkins. He slammed it shut and sat back. He was disheartened, as if the lack of proper utensil was the last straw.

"Let's just use our hands." Brett pulled off his gloves and demonstrated, forming his fingers into a scoop. The ice cream had softened perfectly, like Cool Whip. Brett fed himself. The sweet, silky vanilla coated his tongue. He offered the pint to Dean who shook his head and smiled as he dug in. He hummed as he held it in his mouth. He looked at Brett. "Goddamn that's good."

They sat there in silence, passing the ice cream back and forth, little smiles on their faces. They were like kids sneaking a treat, though they'd never been as innocent as the kids they were acting like.

A knock on the window on Dean's side, and they both jumped. The windows were too steamy to see through, but there was a fuzzy light trying to penetrate. Dean cranked the window to find Chief Bell's flushed face.

"Well shit," he said, smiling. "Dean Fleming and Brett Pratt." His flashlight landed on the near-empty ice cream container. "What the hell is going on in here?"

"Just catching up," Dean responded neutrally.

Bell flashed the light in Brett's face. "Your eyes look kinda glassy there, Mr. Four Years."

"I'm sure it has nothing to do with a light blasting directly into my eyeballs."

"I think you'd both better step out of the vehicle."

Dean seemed used to this, pushing open his door immediately. Brett preferred to grumble and whine as he exited the truck.

"Hands on the hood, please."

"This is stupid," Brett said.

"Just let him get his kicks." Dean bent over the truck, stuck out his butt farther than necessary. Brett put his hands on the hood, which was warm from the engine. The cold air, however, bit into his cheeks and ears.

Bell patted Brett down first. He found his key chain, pulled it out and clanged it on the hood. "The hell is all this?" Dean also seemed alarmed.

"It's just . . ." But Brett wasn't sure how to explain. The assemblage of toys and trinkets and tags displayed in this light looked suspicious, even to Brett. He was more worried that Dean would recognize the clutter as the tokens of a former addict.

Nothing more was said, and Bell moved on to Dean, patting him down more forcibly. He extracted from Dean's pockets lighters and pens and chapstick, a tin of Altoids, loose dollar bills and receipts, and an iPod. The only thing incriminating, according to Bell, was a small, glittery-pink pony figurine. Bell set it up on the hood in between Brett and Dean.

"You both got a thing for kids' toys."

"It's my niece's," Dean shot back.

"Either that or—"

"I said it's my *niece's*!"

There was the anger Brett remembered, still sizzling, just more restrained.

Feeling as though the situation was getting increasingly tense, Brett said, "Why don't we all go to my house and I'll show you my Star Wars LEGOS?"

Neither of them budged.

"I just put together the Millennium Falcon," Brett said over his shoulder. "Took five straight hours. It's badass."

"Alright," Bell finally said. "Stand up."

Brett snatched his key chain and worried the glove. *Pump pump pump.*

"I don't know what the hell you lovebirds were doing in there. Eating ice cream in the parking lot in the middle of the night? Quit giving me reason to get suspicious, 'cause the two of you together is bad news." Bell looked at Brett. "Especially for you, Pratt. If you're really going on four years sober, I'd stay the hell away from Dean."

Brett felt Dean eyeing him. He passed the key chain from one hand to the other, trying to ignore Dean naturally. Brett's icy breath was too copious, filling the quiet space between him and Dean. Another car pulled into the lot, breaking the awkward silence.

"We done here?" Dean said, righting himself to tower over the squat officer. Bell didn't respond, just headed toward his cruiser. Dean got back into his truck, calling, "See you, Brett."

Brett's words were a peep. "Alright." He pressed the key fob's unlock button to his salt-frosted Volkswagen, embarrassed to announce that he drove a foreign car.

"Hey," Dean said. "You want this ice cream?"

"Oh, uh . . ." What was the right thing to say? What would undo all the ways he'd just messed up their reunion? "No, thanks."

Dean disappeared into the truck and pulled away. Brett waved, but he wasn't looking.

Inside his car, Brett dropped his head on the steering wheel, pressing the scar into the cold vinyl until he couldn't stand the pain. He drove home slowly, and it wasn't until he pulled into the driveway that he realized Angela had been waiting for the ice cream that he and Dean had just eaten.

Brett lay on the air mattress in the unfinished room, face up, watching the late morning shadows of the overhead beams inch along the walls. He was thinking about how badly he'd handled last night's unplanned meeting with Dean. What chewed at his conscience the most was withholding his own addiction and recovery.

Brett hadn't really apologized, not to the extent Dean had. There were three people on his "Amends List," and one of them, the one he most needed to apologize to, Dad, was dead. So that left Mom and Angela. He liberally interpreted the wording from Step 9 to avoid talking to his mother. The fact was, he felt Mom needed to apologize to him and Dad for abandoning them. And while he had treated her like shit the few times he'd seen her, Brett knew that if he tried to make amends with her, he'd end up saying things he'd regret. That conveniently left only one person on the list. And if he was honest with himself, he'd done a pretty half-assed job apologizing to her.

When Brett got into funks like this, he had this waking nightmare of a tape measure. The tiny notches became extremely close, and he got stuck in the yellow space between the numbers. This made it impossible to move even an inch, because, as Zeno pointed out, movement is a paradox: for anyone to get from point A (the air mattress) to point B (the kitchen where Angela was eating her Grape Nuts with raisins), one must first go half the distance from the mattress to the kitchen (say, to the bathroom, where Brett couldn't look into the mirror), and to travel to that halfway point, one must first traverse halfway to the next halfway point (inside the wall, where he kept Mark's pill bottles, which, to tell the whole truth, he had swabbed with a wet finger last night just before crawling onto the mattress), and before that, halfway to that halfway point (from his sweaty back to his side, lying in perhaps the same part of the floor that Mark's convulsing body lay), et cetera, et cetera. There are an infinite amount of halfway points, and therefore, movement was impossible.

He wanted to escape himself. He wanted not to obsess over abstract numbers and philosophical tenets. He wanted not to fixate on types of caulk and the best methods for flashing. He wanted not to have his fate dictated by his past. All he wanted was to be light, to go lightly into the kitchen and brush Angela's hair away and kiss her neck without thought or hesitation or shame.

Found in the wall so far:

Silver pewter Syracuse Orange logo

Brown rabbit's foot

Blue and orange boondoggle

Plastic green alien holding up two-finger peace sign (one finger broke off)

3 in. rubber Tweetie Bird

Gold horn, gold crucifix, and silver, oval St. Francis

Numerous gnawed pieces of rawhide

Clean and Serene for 30 Days (Red)

Clean and Serene for 60 Days (Green)

Clean and Serene for 9 Months (Yellow)

Clean and Serene 1 Year (Blue)

Clean and Serene 18 months (Orange)
Five different rubber basketballs, the orange worn away.

The National Weather Service has issued a Severe Blizzard Warning . . .
Potentially historic storm expected to impact the area . . . which is in effect
from 4 p.m. Thursday to 2 p.m. EST Sunday. Accumulations . . . up to
thirty to forty inches of snow are forecast. Winds . . . with gusts up to sixty-
five mph. Impacts . . . blowing and drifting snow will produce whiteout
conditions. Wind chills from twenty degrees below zero to ten degrees below
zero will produce extreme cold impacts. Preparedness . . . make sure your
house is secure.

Timing . . . horrible.

A clap of thunder rocked the house. It sounded like a bomb had
exploded a few yards away. Brett went outside to investigate. The arctic
air lashed at his nose and cheeks. The ponderous atmosphere was firing
off an intense static electricity, which perked the hairs off his neck and
agitated the scar. He walked around to the side of the house, hand in
his pocket, squishing the boxing glove. The ladder he'd left leaning on
the addition was an obvious invitation. He climbed it and carefully
perched on the icy beams of the unfinished roof.

Their house was on Falls Boulevard, the elevated, southern part
of the village. He could make out the contours of the still-wild land
from this vantage, how it sloped like a white, leafy wave toward town,
through which the creek sliced a northward vein before continuing
through his backyard. The first settlers and the Natives before them
might have seen just this, a land full of promise. It was spiritual to
imagine observing this view as if for the first time. Perhaps that was
how his dad had seen it every day—that was what kept him in love
with this place. Contrary to what Dean had said, he didn't think Dad

would've gotten a kick out of the Oneida Indians' casino, Oz-themed or not. That wasn't how he'd want Chittenango to rise to prosperity. And this place could never seem new to Brett. Chittenango's luster had already been dulled by everyone else's hopeful gazing.

Not including Mark's. Brett couldn't imagine Mark looking hopefully at anything. Had he been able to, he'd be up here on the roof, firing a nail gun into cold shingles, finishing what he started.

Mark was doing so well for so long. He had found a project that would distract him from his addiction for a good while—at least eighteen months, according to the key tags. He'd renovated the entire house, and when he neared its conclusion, he decided to build an addition. One night, however, after getting the foundation down and the frame up— the hard part—Brett imagined that Mark had realized this too would end. And soon. It doesn't take long to insulate a room and put up the wall and put down the floor. Doesn't take long to put on a roof. For a healthy person, all this might take two months. For people like Brett and Mark, working feverishly through the night, three weeks tops. And what about when he finished? The answer to that was the gargantuan, hairy monster heaving and drooling just beyond the completed addition. It was the crushing thought of needing to find another distraction—fine, *hobby*— that itself would be finite. So he'd made a phone call and gotten a couple bottles of something good. Brett was confident there was no sadness in the occasion, certainly no regret. The decision must have been freeing. And it must have been a hell of a ride leaving life on the long cool wave.

Another jarring crack of snow thunder. The trees in the distance were thrashing, as though being shaken by their trunks. Just above town, a mass of sinister clouds collected themselves into an army, dumping snow.

A state of emergency has been issued for Cayuga, Chenango, Cortland, Herkimer, Madison, Oneida, Onondaga, Oswego, and Otsego Counties, and remains in effect until Sunday. Snow drifts and dangerously high winds could lead to significant damage. Do not leave the house. If possible, take cover in a lower-level corridor or basement free of glass exposure.

The unfinished room is not an ideal place. His wife will come in soon to tell him the same thing. "Did you hear the news?" she'll say, and he'll lie and say he didn't. The lie comes easy. "We should go to my mom's," she says. "Snow will come in through the addition. It could pour into the family room. That's the best-case scenario."

He doesn't want to go to her mom's—that's exactly how he says it: "I don't want to go to your mom's."

Angela confronts him. "We have to leave right now." He can see her patience vanishing, leaving behind a quivering jaw, flexing neck. "Stand up," she growls. He pretends it's more difficult than it is getting off the half-deflated air mattress. He's up, and his eyes skitter over hers, as though they are repelling magnets. "This has gone on long enough. I know you know that, which is why I've backed off." She is giving him space to explain himself, but he feels emptied out. The only sensation is on his forehead, the scar aching at the changing air pressure. Angela's eyes are now shimmering with tears. He remembers when she was twelve, standing on the doorstep of his childhood home, asking about her dog. She used to chew on her pigtails, and it was so cold that the ends of her hair were frosted white. There's so much she doesn't know. Too much, really. He's been trying to protect her from the truth, but it's only now that he realizes the truth is not the issue. It's him that he needs to protect her from.

The good news is that informing her of this is easy, because Angela's readying for a fight. It's how they work, their little game. Her nostrils widen and she makes a sound like choking and then comes at him. She pushes him backward. She pounces on him and punches his arms and chest, then grabs his hair and yanks his head around. He is barely present, hardly defending himself, just watching the room spin.

Finally, Angela notices. She stops. He can see her heart cracking. It's in the same place that he had cracked it before—far too many times—and then sealed it up with promises and notes, key chain trinkets and hobbies. This time, though, the fissure in her heart is gaping, like a vacuum yawn wherein her own fight is being sucked.

She stands, flimsy and phantom. She keeps her hair over her face and says through it, "I'll be at my mom's." Before she leaves the room, she says, "Be careful, Brett."

When she is gone, the house deflates a little, which he feels in his tailbone grinding the floor through the mattress. *Strong winds may down power lines and trees. Have a winter survival kit with you.*

Why isn't there nothing? There was a conception of the universe, a galactic birth, the birth of something. But there could have just as easily been nothing. Just a tiny, quantum nudge one way or the other, and the universe would have failed to be born. It seems like the chances of this, of nothing, are just as good as the something.

To think of himself now, armed with a crowbar, digging it into the wall, wrenching free a panel, and compare that to the just-missed chance that the crowbar, the wall, the violent wind, the Brett never came into being puts everything into perspective. It certainly helps with the guilt.

Brett didn't invent this concept. It was Leibniz who asked, "Why is there something rather than nothing?" And Wittgenstein was rightly awed at the concept that anything, meaning something, should exist at all. Heidegger, too, was amazed that, we are rather than are not. Everyone else chooses not to think about this for good reason: it's terrifying. But people constantly battle against the nothing. They create structures to contain themselves: cars, cubicles, coffins, buildings, and, of course, houses. It's not shelter that they're seeking—it's not keeping the elements out, not warmth. They need controlled space, walls and a ceiling, to reflect their thoughts and vision. Otherwise, what would they see if they peered into the infinite? How far could their vision go? How far their thoughts?

The other question is: can you turn something into nothing—can you birth nothingness and then will into existence a new beginning? Brett was going to try. After all, he'd committed himself to it—first by investigating Mark, then lying to Dean, and pushing out Angela, to now: crowbar and sledgehammer and arms of fury. As he rips off the walls on the inside, he hears the blizzard tearing away the shingles and shutters outside. The house hiccups and convulses. The windows explode. Then, in a colossal crack, the roof is detached and sucked up into the sky, where the snow has taken the shape of a twirling funnel, the center of which is directly above his head. He holds fast to the banister on the stairs as the snow twister inhales all these loosed panels that flutter high like slips of paper. There's a terrific jingling, and a swarm of key chains shoot into the cone of swirling white. There's a tug at his pocket, and he feels his own key chain slithering out of his pants and darting into the sky. *Take it. Take it all away.* And it abides.

ROGERS ROCK

During a brief delay among the red men, arising from the loss of his trail, [Major Rogers] had time to throw his pack down the slide, reverse his snow-shoes, and go back over his own track to the head of a ravine before they emerged from the woods, and, seeing that his shoe-marks led to the rock, while none pointed back, they concluded that he had flung himself off and committed suicide to avoid capture. . . . He had gained the ice by way of the cleft in the rocks, but the savages, believing that he had leaped over the precipice, attributed his preservation to the Great Spirit and forbore to fire on him. Unconsciously, he had chosen the best possible place to disappear from, for the Indians held it in superstitious regard, believing that spirits haunted the wood and hurled bad souls down the cliff, drowning them in the lake, instead of allowing them to go to the happy hunting grounds.

—Charles M. Skinner, *Myths and Legends of Our Own Land*, 1896

Late Spring, 2014

———◆———

SHE CALLS HIM BOY. She says, "Boy, get here." He's learned to call her Mama.

Skin and long bones, he stands up from the floor, where he's been looking at a greasy *Archie* comic. A fire going in a metal drum, its smoke sucked out a hole in the rotting roof and hovering over the hunting cabin like a blank thought. The boy sheens with sweat. The lady's face does, too, but with her eyes always watering it's hard to tell.

She says, "Time to eat."

He kneels between her knees where she sits on crackling whicker. She reaches into her Knicks jersey and pulls out her breast. It puddles from her hand. He's a good boy who makes his mouth an o, knows by now how to suckle without teeth. No longer does she need to pinch his nose to fill him. As he sucks, she notices something treacherous on him. She yanks at his ear.

"Stand up," she says.

He does.

"Raise your arm."

He does.

"What's it you got under there?"

He puts his fingers into his armpit where the down has turned black. "Hair, Mama."

She frowns. "Pull down yer pants." She jerks his arm so the firelight casts him orange. She lifts his penis, palms his testicles, rolls them around in her hand to find more wiry hairs. "You been hiding these from me?" she asks, voice thick like blood-sludge.

"I don't know, Mama. I'm sorry."

She shoos him away, looks up at the hole in the roof, tears slithering down her plump cheeks. She sighs. "You're not my boy no more. Get in yer bed."

He walks slowly to a bunk fastened to the wall, gets under a dusty blanket. His eyes are wide and white with fire.

"Stay there," she says.

"Okay, Mama."

She gets up, holds her side and groans as she straightens. She stands beside the blazing drum, tells him again to stay.

"Mama?" he asks, but she ignores him. He puts the blanket over his face.

She kicks the drum over, spilling fire in the boy's direction. The flames move like water over the dry floorboards. The lady exits the cabin, standing just outside the door in case he tries to escape. The woods scream with crickets. The heat pushes her back and back, always watching the cabin being consumed by a fire that lights up the forest. Always listening beyond the crackle and hiss. But the boy's a good boy. He makes no noise, accepts his immolation with dignity, just like she taught him. He's been a real good boy, but now it's time to find another.

EJ followed Dean around their apartment, from family room to kitchen to bedroom, demanding that he answer. "How do you know it's her?"

Dean rubbed at the stubble of his head, moving through rooms just to move, trying to sort through his thoughts. He was already far beyond that question; that had been answered immediately. Now he was fighting through his shock, nearing an inevitable conclusion of what he was going to do about it.

Turning from the back wall of the cramped bathroom, he bumped into EJ's flabby chest. EJ grabbed Dean's shoulders and pushed him down on the toilet, big brown eyes serious. "Get your mind right and talk to me."

Dean pulled his hands down his face and moaned. EJ was ten years younger than Dean, headstrong and naive in his midtwenties but better experienced with relationships. This was Dean's first, and he still wasn't convinced that he had to abide by all of its obligations.

Remaining distant, for example, wasn't an option. He had to let EJ in. Their relationship was built on that, on sharing everything. They'd met at an NA meeting in the basement of a library, discovered a kinship in their mutual loathing of group hugs and the pushed spirituality. So while they'd hardly spoken in group, they had to each other. Against every other member's opposition, EJ and Dean became each other's sponsor.

EJ's drug of choice was crystal meth. He'd been using for about six months while holding down a steady job as a UPS driver and maintaining a serious relationship with his boyfriend. Then he went on a seven-day binge. At the end of it, he was living in the boiler room of an apartment complex, he'd been raped repeatedly by his dealer who knew EJ was desperate for ice, and his boyfriend put a restraining order on him because EJ had threatened to cut out his lungs if he didn't loan him money. He only checked himself into a hospital because his kidneys ached and his urine was a brown sludge. He'd lost twenty pounds in that long week of not eating, drinking, or sleeping. When Dean first met him, EJ was continuously at the snacks table stuffing his face with doughnuts and cookies, guzzling one bottle of water after another.

It didn't take a genius for anyone to guess Dean's poison, considering the fresh scar that gnarled the bend of his arm like silly putty. Still, Dean shared his own stories with EJ, because what the hell else was there to do when shit was this bad? He began with the easy ones, his dad kicking him out of the house, living on the streets of Buffalo not too far from EJ's boiler room, the blister that had turned into a serious, oozing infection. Eventually, after months of meeting privately at a Starbucks, and then dating, and then moving in with each other, Dean told EJ about how he and his brother were kidnapped as kids, and how his brother was murdered. The last thing to come clean about was how Dean had most likely pushed his mother to suicide.

Despite the "higher power" propaganda of group, Dean and EJ committed themselves to completing the twelve steps. They moved to Utica, EJ's hometown, where they'd lived a contented coexistence for six years.

"Okay," Dean sighed, rubbing his knees. "Just give me a minute." He was deep-breathing himself away from the panic attack. EJ rubbed him briskly between the shoulder blades, moved his rough hands up and down his back. "It was her," Dean said. "It had to be."

"Alright, take your time."

The coincidences were too obvious. Local news had put out an Amber Alert for two missing boys, brothers, taken from a festival in Lake George, a hundred-some miles west in the Adirondacks. But it was more than coincidence that convinced Dean. This he couldn't disclose to EJ, but he *felt* her. He'd always felt her, his abductor, felt her mothering continue to nurture and hex him. He couldn't share during one of those slobbering, wake-you-in-the-night confessions that as a child, he'd never given the police any information about his abductor out of this primal, maternal bondage. And what he was just figuring for himself, which lay waiting on the other side of the panic, was that through this recent kidnapping, she was calling out for him. She wanted him to find her, and he didn't have the strength to refuse.

"Dean, be cool. Be cool." EJ crouched beside him, his forehead to Dean's, his dark hand on Dean's, the touch almost getting through. "If it's her, we call the cops. When you're ready."

"No." Dean stood, freed himself from EJ's tenderness. He said from the hall, "I'm going after her."

The Lake George Forum was packed with every age and type of Elvis. Most were dressed as the bulging seventies Elvis, the one with the white jumpsuit, big collar, lots of rhinestones. Many of these were busting out of their tight costumes in all the wrong places. The handsome Elvises were the ones who took on his fifties persona: powder-blue blazer, black shirt and pants and white socks, guitar over the shoulder, and *ooh* that hair. On the other end of the expansive hall, a child was screeching the lyrics to "Hound Dog" from the stage. The youth competition for the Ultimate Elvis Tribute Artist was underway. Carol was there to scope out the contestants.

She wore the festival's official T-shirt, which she'd decorated with thirty-some Elvis buttons she'd collected over the years. *Keep Calm and Love Elvis, It's an Elvis Thing, The King of Rock n' Roll,* and her favorite, *Nobody Knows I'm Elvis.* She kept her long gray hair in a braid that swung down her back. Thankfully, nearly everyone else in the building wore aviator sunglasses, though hers had a darker tint.

She snaked through the crowd in her ghostly way, blessed or cursed with the kind of ordinariness that allowed her to go unnoticed. Toward the back of the forum, lingering near the bathrooms, were two boy Elvises practicing their lip curls. The younger one sported a gold blazer with a butterfly-collared black shirt, black pants, black shoes. The other was jumpsuit Elvis, adorable sideburns taped to his cheeks. Both boys wore their hair like a black, shiny helmet. Carol watched them while pretending to browse the leather goods at a vendor's table. More than a minute had passed, and they were still alone, goofing around. She took a tissue from her pocket and dried her eyes. It was time to make herself noticed.

"You two! Oh dear, we've been looking all over for you. I'm Carol, events coordinator. You two've qualified to move on to the final round of the competition! Isn't that so exciting! We just need you to come with me so we can register you for tomorrow's event. Don't worry, it'll be quick, and I'll send someone here to tell your parents where you are. Where are they?"

"At the café," the younger one said defensively, "getting lunch."

"Perfect. I'll let Debbie know. She runs the café. Okay, quick, let's go! I'm so excited for you two. You're my favorites!"

Putting a hand on their backs, she lightly directed them through the crowd, toward the stage. "You're brothers?" she asked.

"Yeah," said the young one.

"How old?"

"Seven."

"I'm ten," Jumpsuit finally spoke. "But I don't think we should go nowhere. Dad said he'd be right back."

Carol kept ushering them forward. "It's fine. Debbie will let your dad know. We need to get you registered right now, otherwise you won't make it into the finals."

As the area got denser with people, Carol hugged the boys closer, pressing them into her body, so she could feel the jack-rabbit thump of their little hearts.

Twenty years after losing his only sibling, Dean was a brother again. Even if it was only a "half" brother, a perplexing title. He didn't *half*-love five-year-old Sara; he didn't *half*-teach three-year-old Ethan how to write his name. What was true was that he'd only known them for half of their lives. It was only recently that his father and stepmother had allowed him into their home and around their children. He understood their reservations. He'd been a shit most of his life, his heroin addiction only part of it. The majority of his existence had been like a rusty plow scouring the earth wherever he went, ruining those he came into contact with.

The hardest part of the Twelve Steps was reaching out to those scarred people to try and make amends. Kathy, his stepmom, hung up on him the first few times. It wasn't until he sent her a letter that she agreed to hear him voice his apologies. She was easier to talk to than his dad, who in the past twenty years had acted as if the abduction never happened or, worse, that he didn't care.

Still, Dean had called him at work. Dean read from a prepared script that EJ had helped him write. "I don't ask forgiveness, because I know it's too much to ask. But it's important for you to understand that I have many regrets." His voice rattled with shame and anger. "I'm not asking to see you again, because I know that's too much to ask. But I don't want your last memory of me to be what it was." His dad didn't respond, which Dean was thankful for. He wasn't ready to have a conversation.

The worst was visiting his mother's grave back in Chittenango where she was buried beside his brother. The two stones, side-by-side, that he had erected with his wretchedness. His knees in the snow, butting his head on one stone and then the other, tears turned to frost on his cheeks. He couldn't apologize; he didn't feel worthy of freeing himself of that guilt. He'd hold onto it, blacken himself with it, show her and Jason that he was human again, someone whose heart could break over and over.

It was Kathy who reached out to Dean, inviting him to dinner. There he was again, at the doorstep of his childhood home, knocking on the door. When he first saw Sara, who skipped to him in a Dorothy dress, brown hair in braids, he sat on the floor and wept, right there in the family room. The child put her arms around him, her love immediate and unconditional. She said, "S'okay. S'okay." They knew each other. She understood the roots of his pain. Her touch was the only one that healed.

After that first visit, Kathy was convinced that Dean had turned a corner and should be a part of the family. His dad probably only agreed because Kathy called the shots. It didn't matter to Dean. He was hungry for time with the children. He visited them as often as he could, which was most weekends and a few Thanksgivings and Christmases. EJ never accompanied him. One surprise at a time.

Dean put together elaborate LEGO sets with Ethan. The boy enjoyed Dean's company, but he was just as content with his blocks or watching cartoons. It was Sara to whom he became most attached. He'd play in her room for hours, dressing up and acting out scenes from *The Wizard of Oz* and *Cinderella*. He read to her. She told him long, labyrinthine stories. He bought her books and art sets, believing she was gifted and needed more encouragement. She needed more of everything.

The closer he got to the children, the more protective he became. When he couldn't visit, he called Kathy daily to see how they were. He became especially anxious when she'd tell him that his dad had taken them out. EJ didn't think this was healthy, kept telling Dean that he was being paranoid. But then, just last month, Sara was left alone by the pool, fell in, and nearly drowned. Luckily, Dean was nearby to save her. But he was furious. "Who was supposed to be watching her!" he shouted to his dad and Kathy as they came sprinting from the house.

So many dangers in their small world, so many ways for them to be damaged.

The drive to Auburn Correctional Facility wasn't long, a quick hour and a half east on the thruway. He wished it were longer. He needed to prepare himself emotionally for being face-to-face with Wayne LaFleur, the other half of the husband-wife team who had stolen Dean and his brother. Both Wayne and Dean separately made sure his wife was never found. At ten years old, Dean had refused to give the authorities any information about her for reasons he was only now beginning to comprehend. Wayne was simply protecting his wife.

But while Dean tried to rehearse the questions he'd ask Wayne, that morning's argument with EJ dominated his thinking. As was EJ's hard-headed way, he'd followed Dean around the apartment shouting at him as Dean shirked and dodged.

"You're not ready for this. As your goddamn sponsor I'm telling you not to go."

"I got to. I'm sorry if you don't understand, but I got to."

"You ain't fuckin' James Bond. You can't just go chasing after criminals."

"I'm the only one who knows the lady's face. To sit around here while I know what she's doing to those kids, it'd mess me up."

What he didn't tell EJ was that years ago, when he was in the beginning stages of recovery, he had received in the mail a visitor request form from prison. It was from Wayne. At that time, Dean was vulnerable and exhausted and cloaked in the spirit of forgiveness. So he filled out the form and mailed it back, and for the longest time, was too distracted by his recovery to think about it. Since he'd heard about the recent abduction, however, he'd immediately recalled the form. Dean called the prison, they confirmed that he was on inmate LaFleur's list of visitors, and before he had the chance to think it through, he made an appointment.

"Going will mess you up. You got serious shit you need to sort out, and you ain't even been to see that therapist yet."

"It'll have to wait."

"If you walk out that door, you're walking out on me."

"EJ, come on."

"Don't fuckin' '*come on*' me. You ain't taking me serious. I'd rather you be alive than us be together."

"I *got* to do this. I ain't done a goddamn good thing in my whole fuckin' life."

"Well that's some bullshit right there, 'cause you don't think you and me is a good thing?"

"That's. Not. What. I. Meant."

"Just get on. I'm tired of talking to you."

Hours later, Dean was still angry, still believed in his side of the argument. That quickly disappeared when he neared the entrance gate of the prison, saw the daunting, castle-like façade looming ahead. The guard checked his clipboard, confirming Dean's appointment. Dean parked, walked in the shadow of the brick walls, gazed up at the fences topped with coiling barbed wire. As he entered the front doors, passed through the metal detector and was patted down, he realized how lucky he was to have never entered this place in handcuffs. The sum of his crimes—arson, vandalism, theft, assault, drug use and dealing, not to mention indirectly killing his brother and mother—should have amounted to significant time.

He was given a visitor's pass and then escorted through heavy doors that unlocked with a loud buzz. Dean was jumpy. He began to believe the CO was taking him to a cell, that Dean had been tricked into turning himself in, punishment at long last for his overlooked transgressions. But they finally arrived at the visitors' room where a row of inmates in khaki sat opposite of their spouses and mothers and cousins and lawyers. Then Dean got it, an embarrassing reality. All the inmates were black. Dean was white. That was how his crimes had gone unnoticed.

The only other white person in the room had to be Wayne, otherwise, Dean wouldn't have recognized him. Seeing him seated at the table, praying or speaking into his clasped, tattooed hands, Dean realized his memory of Wayne was more feeling than physical. This man here with his long, scraggly goatee and shaved head had no approximation to anything in Dean's memory.

Wayne's eyes lifted as Dean sat. His face brightened and he held out his hand.

"Praise God, is that you?"

Dean allowed Wayne to shake his hand, more of an impulse than a decision. Wayne cupped and patted it.

"Yeah, it's me."

"The Lord brought you to me, that's for sure."

"No, he didn't."

"I was just praying on you the other day," Wayne continued, childlike with excitement, "and then I got told you wanted to see me. Praise God."

"God's got nothing to do with you and me." Already, Dean was veering from his strategy of remaining emotionally aloof. "I'm not here for you or your conscience, either. I'm not your ticket to heaven, so don't waste your time apologizing or explaining. Understand?"

"Course. You're here about my wife."

Dean quit adjusting in the chair and saw the light in Wayne's green eyes. "How'd you know that?"

"You suckled from her, she's inside you. You miss her."

Dean took a deep breath but barely found air.

"That and the FBI already done asked me about her." Wayne laughed, rubbed his forearms, which were slathered in prison tats: Christ-and-fire themes.

"What'd you tell them?"

"Just what you'd want me to tell'm. Nothing."

"Now that's changed."

"Nothing changes."

"I want her found."

"Then why don't you talk to the cops? Tell'm everything you never told'm before when you was a kid? But you won't. 'Cause like me you love her, that's why. You don't want her found; you want to find her yourself."

"So tell me where I can find her."

"Nobody finds Pumpkin. She finds you."

Sweat trickled down Dean's spine, into his ass. There were two rotating fans going in either end of the room, volleying hot air. "What do you know about Lake George?"

"Ha ha!" He pushed his big face across the table. "Need a vacation? Then let me suggest Fort Ticonderoga. Really pretty this time a'year. You can stock up on pencils. They's even got a nice campground round there." He rapped his knuckles on the table and laughed some more.

Dean looked around the room, just now hearing the chatter. On his right was a large-bosomed woman looking drowsily at her man, bored with whatever he was insisting. A CO leaned on a podium in the corner of the room, moving his eyes down the row of visitors. Dean was close to quitting this interview. Wayne had been in here over twenty years; Dean was merely his entertainment. He tried one more angle. "Why does she take two boys, and then kill off the other?"

Wayne shrugged. "Nobody leaves one by himself. But they do leave two, one to watch the other."

"Why won't she keep both, then?"

The light in Wayne's eyes dimmed. He pressed his palms flat on the table. "It was an accident. I forgiven her. The Lord's forgiven her. *You* forgiven her. He was a real good boy, obedient. But I know it was an accident. She took him out fishing for his birthday. He was reeling in his first big catch." Wayne's eyes took on that verdant green again. "I bet my boy snagged a twenty-pound bass, I'm sure of it. He still in that lake rasslin' that motherfucker, praise God."

Dean suddenly shivered as though something had drawn its ice finger up his rib cage. "He was about ten years old?"

"How you know that!" Wayne slammed his fists on the table. The room hushed. The CO marched to them, loomed over Dean's shoulder.

"You causing trouble, LaFleur?"

"No sir. Sorry sir. I got the Spirit in me is all."

Those nearby giggled.

"Keep it down or I'm sending you back." The CO returned to his podium and then called out, "Five more minutes!"

Wayne looked Dean straight in the eyes. "It was an accident."

Five more minutes and then Dean would never see this man again. So he laid it out, the question that had always nagged him about Wayne.

"Why do you protect her while she steals and kills children? How does that sit with your God?"

"My God is your God."

"That's a pathetic answer and you know it."

"Then how's this: I protected her for the same reason you did."

The heat shot up into Dean's ears, sizzled in his face. "There is no fucking God. As long as your whore of a wife goes on kidnapping and abusing kids, and nut jobs like you bash in little boys' heads." His eyes prickled, his vision speckled red. "You and your cunt wife killed God off, and you drag his corpse around with you."

The people on either side of them took notice, leaned away to get some impossible privacy.

"She'll get you, you shit punk." Wayne spoke this through a smile. "She'll reclaim what's inside you, what's hers."

"Look around you," Dean said with a growl in his throat. "This is the best it's going to get. When you die, you'll rot in the ground like the rest of us."

"Time's up!"

Everyone began shuffling, the metal legs of the chairs scraping the floor.

Dean continued, "I want you to think about that truth tonight in your cell. There's no heaven, no other existence but this one."

"You apologize for stabbing my Pumpkin."

"Time's up!"

"When I find her," Dean leaned forward, "I'm going to cut out her heart and piss on it."

"Hey!" The CO grabbed Dean's shoulder and pushed him away from the table. "I know you're not going t'cause trouble on my watch."

Dean paid the guard no mind. He stared Wayne down, hoping he would make a move so Dean could hurt him.

But the inmates were filing out of the room, Wayne falling in line. Then he began to sing, *"Go wash at His bidding, and light will arise."* And then, strangely, all the other inmates joined in. *"The light of the world is Jesus!"*

Dean didn't remember walking back to his car. He was gripping the wheel, heaving and seething. That old ugly anger was crawling around inside him again, that which he'd worked so hard in the past seven years to contain. How easy it was to give himself over to it, how free and easy it flowed.

He got back on I-90, racing west toward the Adirondacks.

The Legend of Rogers Rock—of Major Rogers's mythical "leap" off the mountain—meant little to Carol, probably less to the hundreds of campers who pitched their tents or parked their RVs on Rogers Rock Campground. This was her second week there, having arrived well before the Elvis Festival to make sure she was settled beyond suspicion. She had reserved the ideal spot, the one closest to the base of the mountain and adjacent to the water. She was returning from a hot shower at the nearby bathroom, hair wrapped in a towel, toiletries in hand, sensitive eyes protected by sunglasses, when two uniformed state police and a lean bloodhound met her at her campsite.

"Morning, ma'am," the female officer said. "This your site, I take it?"

Carol almost said *Yessir* to the lady cop, whose body was shaped like a brick, no hips or breasts. "Yes, it is."

"Mind if we take a look around? We're checking everyone's."

"Go 'head." She sat down at the picnic table, didn't look at the lady cop when talking to her. "I'd put coffee on for you all, but the fire's down."

"Don't worry 'bout that, ma'am. We're plenty coffeed up."

"Does the hound need a drink?"

"She's all set." The male cop handling the dog spoke a command, calling her "Girl," and she set her nose to the ground, heading toward the tent.

Carol removed the towel from her head, commenced the task of combing out her long hair.

"You're Carol Flowers?" The female officer waved an oft-folded list of registered campers.

"Everybody calls me Candy. All except my husband, God bless'm."

"What'd he call you?"

Carol halted her brush and glared at the lady cop. "Ain't that our business?"

"Of course, sorry." She penciled something on the list. "You been here since May 23?"

"If that was a Monday, then that's right. I do this every year, camp out here on the lake for two weeks. Been doing it since '95. Gets my head right."

"Where you from, Mrs. Flowers?"

"Well, that's a long story. If yer asking where I now live, that's Watertown."

"Guess you heard about the missing boys."

"Course. Didn't think you were here just to look through my underwear."

The male cop had taken Carol's duffel bag from the tent, and the hound was sliming it with its nose.

"We'll be done soon, ma'am. Can I ask you your whereabouts the day they went missing?"

"That was Saturday or Sunday?"

"Saturday."

"Let's see . . . went for a short walk in the morning on the trail, there." She pointed toward the mountain. "Try to get a little exercise in. After, took a swim. Came back to the site, made some coffee and my instant oatmeal. I believe I might've taken a nap, I can't be sure." She sat with the brush in her hand, staring at the dirt and thinking.

"Did you go anywhere, off the campgrounds?"

"Oh yes. To Martha's."

"Martha's?"

"The best ice cream in Lake George. It was pistachio day. That's my weakness, and they don't always got it but a few days a week."

"So you went into town?"

"I ain't a fool going into the village on a weekend, no. Martha's is just outside the village. You don't know it?"

"I know Martha's," the other cop said, pulling his head out from Carol's Pontiac Sunfire. "It's over by Great Escape."

The dog had been sniffing the tires of Carol's Pontiac when it was seized by a sneezing fit. Four, five, six in a row, and counting. Its handler crouched beside the hound and palmed its big head. "What's wrong, girl?" The cop got a massive sneeze in his face, a spray of saliva and mucus.

Carol called, "If your hound's sick, I'd appreciate if it didn't sneeze on my vehicle."

"I think I better get her a drink," the handler said, leading the spasmodic dog toward the lake.

The lady cop watched them leave and then eyeballed Carol. She finally asked, "Did you go anywhere else?"

"While I was in the area, I went to Rite Aid to pick up my pills." She rested her hand on her side. "I got this kidney thing, so I take these steroid pills. And then I got to take calcium and Vitamin D for my bones. They's in my pocketbook."

"You go hiking and swimming with a bad kidney?"

"If I don't exercise, them pills'll grow me fat."

The lady cop squinted but said nothing. Carol couldn't control the image of pulling a rusty blade across the lady's throat. Instead, she sharpened her words: "I may not be as manly as you, but I ain't infirm."

The lady cop folded up the list and said to it, "You an Elvis fan, Candy?"

Carol pulled her brush through her hair, flinging the excess water on the dirt. "Maybe when I was a teenager. Now I'm partial to that Carrie Underwood gal. I like her anger in that one song."

The lady cop smiled. "I know the one." As she walked by Carol, she said, "You remind me of my mom."

"That right?"

"I hated her guts."

Carol's hand seized, and she dropped her comb. The lady cop picked it up, handed it to Carol and said, "Have a good morning, ma'am."

Carol continued to comb out her hair when she caught a knot. With an effortless jerk of her wrist, she yanked the knot free. Her scalp stung, and a bloody piece of it dangled from the clump caught in the brush. The loosed hair was copious enough to choke a bitch.

Dean drove through busy Lake George village, trafficked by four-wheel-drive vehicles tethered with bikes and coolers and canoes. It was a late Monday afternoon in June, and the T-shirt shops and wax museums and pizza joints teemed with tourists. Yesterday's visit with Wayne felt like it had happened in a different time, in an alternate universe.

The van with Jersey plates in front of him stopped suddenly, no traffic light or pedestrian to be seen. Dean slammed on his brakes, then laid on the horn. The driver was oblivious, a hairy arm pointing out the window in the direction of the lake. Dean shouted, "Yeah, there's a fucking lake here, asshole." He was mentally exhausted, famished, and had no clue where to begin his search. The entire three-hour trip he'd tried to come up with a strategy. He thought he'd first drive along the shore, looking for abandoned motels or lodges. But he was no detective, and surely the authorities had already scoured the area, investigating places Dean would never even think to search. He'd never even been here before, knew Lake George was a popular vacation spot, but that was about it. In his mind, he thought it would be a quaint little lakeside village that he could walk the length of on foot seeking out clues. He was pissed at himself for how stupidly wrong he was. It had already taken him ten goddamn minutes to drive past two blocks of shops, what with these dumbass tourists inching and gawking at their leisure.

He finally made it through the village and pulled over at a Stewart's. He buried his face in his hands, bit down hard on his palms to keep from sobbing. EJ was right to try and discourage him, and now Dean wanted to hear his voice. He shimmied his cell from his pocket, and noticed a text from EJ. *FBI came looking 4 u. Didnt tell them anything but u shuld. I done worrying bout u.*

Dean wiped his eyes and controlled his breathing. Cops. He couldn't talk to cops. Didn't like them, didn't trust them. Besides, what helpful information could he give? His memories of the abduction were emotional, not physical. He just needed something to eat and a place to stay the night. One thing at a time.

Inside the Stewart's, he quickly spotted the newspapers by the door. No surprise, the headline was about the kidnapping: "Parents of Lost Boys Make Tearful Plea." Dean took a copy and read the caption underneath the photo of the mother and father. *After four days and still no leads, the parents of the missing boys appear on television to appeal to the alleged abductor.* Dean folded the paper under his arm and continued through the aisles looking for a decent meal.

The guy at the register looked like one of Dean's ilk. He had the hard, resentful eyes of a townie who had to sell gas and beer to out-of-towners and, worse, to those from high school who were home visiting their parents. His ball cap was frayed and low on his head, blond facial hair wild and patchy. He punched the items into the register with crooked, stained fingers. His appearance was the kind of severe that compelled you to imagine what he would look like if he'd been given a better lot in life. But Dean's imagination wasn't up for the challenge.

"Nice sleeves," the guy said, nodding to Dean's tattoos.

"Thanks, man."

"I get mine done in Saratoga." He pulled up the sleeve of his T-shirt to display the extent of his ink.

"Damn, they do good work. I got all mine in Syracuse. I'm from around there."

Putting the newspaper into a bag, the guy said, "Those kids are fucked."

"What do you mean?"

"There's no way they're going to find them. They already searched every person at that Elvis thing, put up checkpoints on every road out of here, and looked at all the hotels and motels on the lake. So what does that mean?"

Dean wasn't prepared. He was about to try a stupid answer when the guy went on.

"That means they're in the mountains." He made a face as though that was the definitive statement. He then went back to bagging Dean's food. "Those kids're fucked, bro."

Dean stood there with his wallet open, staring at the cash, unable to find the appropriate bills.

"Hope they do find'm, though," the guy continued. "Goddamn po-lice everywhere make me nervous."

This nudged Dean from his trance, and he handed over the money. As he received his change, he thought to ask, "I'm looking for a place to stay, but," he leaned in, "somewhere far away from these pricks."

"Ha ha, I hear you. The farther north you go on Lake Shore—that's Route 9—the quieter it gets, especially up near Hague. That's where I'm from."

"Thanks, man." Dean took the bag from the counter.

"Hey, dude." The guy's eyes got wide, desperate. "If you need a place to drink tonight, my cousin's band is playing at a bar, George Henry's. It's in Warrensburg, north of here."

A place to drink, Jesus Christ that sounded like a good idea.

"It's a good band. None of that gay shit."

Dean laughed to himself. "I might." He put out his hand. "Dean."

"Cliff. Nice to meet you, man."

A drink sounded like a good goddamned idea.

An hour after the Staties left her campsite, Carol went into her tent with a spade and zipped up the door behind her. The goddamn pig and his hound had tracked dirt all over the air mattress and plastic flooring. She applauded herself for thinking of the cayenne pepper spray that she coated her car with. That had retarded the hound better than she hoped. But she wasn't about to stick around to see if it would work twice.

She lifted the mattress and rested it on her shoulder. Her fingernails found the tiny seam in the bottom of the tent. She lifted the flap, which was secured by Velcro, until a three-by-three square of ground was exposed. She dug at the earth with the spade, careful to keep the dirt out of the tent. About a foot down, she found the white plastic bag, the one handed out at the Elvis Festival. She pulled this out of the ground, shaking the excess dirt back into the hole. The contents clattered a kind of horrible music as she set the bag down inside the tent. She refilled the hole, resealed the floor, and lay the mattress back down, neatly arranging the sleeping bag and pillow on top.

Back out in the cool of the late morning, she secured the bag under her arm so to restrain the noise. She got into her two-door Sunfire, stuffed the bag under the passenger's seat, and drove down the gravel road toward the exit. She went north on Lake Shore with the windows open, the breeze drying her tears. Before entering Ticonderoga, she turned right, crossing the bridge over the very northern tip of the lake. She then drove south again, along the lake's quieter eastern shore. About five miles down the wooded road, she saw her marker: a macadam, closed off with a chain and a rusty sign, PRIVATE PROPERTY. She idled the car just in front of this, off the road, checked for coming vehicles, then snatched the bag and got out. She stepped over the chain and walked five yards into the brush. There, she emptied the bag. Scorched bones and a small, blackened skull clattered to the ground; a soiled jumpsuit missing half of its sequins; a lacerated blazer. She scattered these around with her foot, and then stomped them into the weeds.

With the bag around her hand, she unlatched the chain and extended it until it reached the shoulder of the road. She got back into the car and did a U-turn, inspected the chain as she passed. Someone would definitely notice, hopefully soon.

On the drive back to the campsite, she heard the familiar thrashing of a helicopter somewhere overhead.

A helicopter chopped the cool blue sky as Dean drove with the window open. Cliff was right; once he got past Bolton Landing, Route 9 was mostly peaceful, the lake on his right sparkling through the trees. He'd eaten half of the pre-made egg salad sandwich and a handful of Combos. But what he really wanted was to tear into the paper bag on the passenger seat, get a good swallow of the Jack Daniel's he'd purchased along the way. He had enough sense to wait until he found a room.

He remembered Hague, kept driving until he found it. After twenty miles, he passed a couple buildings and parked cars and some lampposts with flags—all in the span of a yawn. He suspected he might have gone too far. He turned around, and sure enough, there was Hague. The motel was about the only structure in town. It was a quaint little place, white clapboard, trimmed hedges, bright flowers along the walkway and brimming from flower boxes under the porch. Thankfully, one room was available.

The bottle of Jack was open before he got all the way into the room. He'd downed a neck's worth by the time his boots were off and he was sitting on the springy bed. He would get ripped, and he would enjoy every minute of it. There was nothing else he could do here. What had made him think he could do anything the authorities hadn't already thought of? The paper confirmed Cliff's information that there were roadblocks set up, that all guests of every hotel, motel, cabin, and lodge had been checked and cleared. They'd closed off the lake to boats while they swept it; they had at least five helicopters canvassing the mountains, covering a fifty-mile radius at any given time. But there was one thing they hadn't thought of—Dean Fleming! His zero years of investigating experience, coupled with his lack of familiarity with the area, made him essential to the hunt.

Really, all he had was a faint memory of the lady and an intimate knowledge of her abuse. It was now four days that she'd had the boys, three days of her forcing them to suckle from her dried tit, of making them eat and wear God knew what. And at this point, only a miracle would have kept the unwanted one alive. It rattled him to imagine those boys, but it was irrational for him to think he was giving up on them when there was nothing he could do. Except get drunk one last time before hopping back on the wagon as if nothing had ever happened.

The windows were open, a breeze swaying the curtains. He checked his cell to see if EJ had called or texted. He didn't get reception up here. All the better. He tipped up the bottle, let the warmth fill his face and throat as he enjoyed the faint scent of a campfire coming in through the window.

The fire was going strong now. Carol scattered the kindling across the pit with a stick, and then placed the grill over top. She set the skillet on the grill, watching its black bottom for smoke. She dropped in a spoonful of lard. It screamed. Then the days-old meat scraps she asked the butcher for at the Price Chopper. She'd found some celery stalks in the trash barrel that afternoon, broke those up and in, stirring until they were blacked with the meat fat. Next, two handfuls of rice, water from the lake, and a generous heaping of salt and garlic powder. She sifted through her purse and found her pills. For herself, she crunched a

Prednisone and Vicodin, knowing soon she'd have to hike Rogers Rock and couldn't be saddled with pain. She dropped two more Vicodin in her hand and with the sheer force of her leathery palms, ground them into dust and sprinkled them into a bottle of water.

Tonight was the night. She hadn't heard a helicopter in a few hours. The radio confirmed that children's bones and clothes were found on the east side of the lake, so most likely the authorities were focusing their search over there. She rolled up her tent, packed up the cooler, put everything in the back seat. The trunk she had to keep free.

Carol returned to the skillet and scraped the bottom and sides, freeing the burnt rice. Nothing left to do but stir and wait for the stars to appear in the blue sky.

There were Venus and Jupiter, and then came Arcturus, Vega, Deneb, and Altair. Her daddy had taught her the stars, taught her to wish on them so hard, so long, until your eyes water. Only then will they hear you out.

Dean was driving. When had he gotten in the car? Where was he going? *That's right, George Henry's, look for it on the left.* Someone in the motel parking lot had given him directions, he couldn't remember who now. Jesus, he shouldn't be driving. He rolled the window down, sat up, clenched the wheel and got serious. It got cold quickly in the mountains. *Good thing,* he thought. Where was he even going? *Oh right, a bar. To do more drinking.*

There it was, on the left, a small place on a corner, bunch of people smoking outside, the band's drums thumping. *They call that place the Duck and Punch,* the man who'd given him directions had said. *Just so you're warned.*

Dean parked on the street and walked fast toward the bar to hide his stumbling. The smokers eyeballed him as he moved past, and he stared right back. He'd be ready for a fight if it came down to it. But it wouldn't. This was a locals' bar, and though he wasn't a local here, he was a local. He belonged. If there was anything he could depend on, it was always belonging in places like this. The greasy walls, the dark wood, blinking neon, cheap beer, and yes, even the stares, because you understood the people behind the eyes. It's the outsiders who mistook that hard look for antagonism. Dean understood it's how you test a man—how a woman tests a woman—to determine their breed. It's the outsiders who look away or who respond with shit talk. It's other locals who answer with the same hard stare like flashing a badge. *You're in. You're welcome here. Pull up a seat.* Once you're in, you still might get a fist to the temple when you're at the urinal, because that shit happens in places like this. *Nothing personal.*

Someone shouted to Dean through the fog of faces and flannel and wall of electric guitar. Cliff was leaning back in his stool, smiling, and looking more like himself here than at Stewart's. Dean and Cliff slapped hands as if they were old friends. Cliff shouted introductions to his boys, who barely nodded.

Cliff got up from his stool and stood beside Dean. "They're good, right?"

He was talking about the band that was spitting distance from the bar, not on a stage but on a large piece of plyboard set up in front of the pool tables. They were as good and as bad as any bar band, playing the '90s grunge that they had grown up listening to.

Dean needed a beer or, better, a shot. But the dude behind the bar had his back to everyone, looking up at the TV. It was impossible to hear the report, but the ticker scrolling across the bottom of the newscast said that bones and clothes believed to be the boys' had been found. Dean squinted to focus the blurring words, to be sure he'd read that right. But Cliff hit his arm.

"You want to take a bath?" Cliff said, grin as shit-eating as Dean had ever seen. Cliff elbowed him and laughed. "You thought I was fag there for a second, didn't you?"

"Um."

"Follow me."

Cliff walked past the band, but not before punching the guitarist in the arm and headbanging to the song. Behind the pool tables was the men's room. If Cliff didn't intend on Dean taking his previous invitation as a come-on, then he had no idea how to interpret his beckoning him into the bathroom. Dean still followed him, because he was drunk, because Cliff expected him to, because Dean wanted to know what he had to show him, even if it was bad. Maybe especially if it was bad.

The graffitied bathroom was empty; they were alone. Cliff leaned against the door to keep it secure. He reached into his pocket, and Dean's racing heart cut through the drunken fog. Cliff pulled out a vial of white powder.

"Bath salts," Cliff explained, shaking the vial. "You ever try this shit?"

Leonard, a guy from his NA group, had messed with MDPV and came out on the wrong end. He didn't eat anyone's face like that dude in Miami, but the stuff he got was cut with a bunch of other chemicals that fucked with his kidneys and his head. He'd told the group he was never the same after, as though a door to a dark world had been opened and there was no shutting it.

Dean's throat was suddenly dry. Swallowing felt like trying to squeeze a stone down a sandy hose. He shook his head.

"It'll make you feel like God." Cliff uncapped the vial and sprinkled the small crystals on the edge of the sink. "We'll get all jacked up, and I'll show you a good time while you're here." Cliff looked up while cutting lines with his driver's license. "You down?"

The bathroom was hot, the unflushed urinal putrid and nauseating. Dean wanted the hell out. He tried to call on EJ's voice, not his boyfriend but his sponsor, to talk him off the ledge. But his brain was muddied by the hot urine, by the band screaming a Danzig tune, and the cells in his skin yearning for the drug that prettied the filthy sink.

"Hell yes."

Cliff's eyes grew to happy circles. "I knew right when I saw you that you got down with the hard stuff. My boys are too chickenshit. They just want to hang with weed."

He pulled a cut straw from his back pocket. Dean watched his greasy hat as he bent over the sink and snorted a line. He immediately lifted his head and growled at the ceiling while holding out the straw. Dean didn't hesitate. He'd committed himself to whatever dangers might come, and he wanted it badly. He took the straw and sniffed the tiny crystals. They burned his nose, nothing like cocaine or heroin. His eyes watered and he shuddered. The drip down his throat was acrid. Then he looked at Cliff, smiling and shiny-eyed, and there it was. The warmth. The euphoria. The strength. He stretched his arms out as if casting off chains and he howled. Cliff laughed and did the same. Someone pounded on the door, tried to come in. Dean's muscles leaped to attention. He shoved the door closed so hard, he heard the dude on the other side of it fall on his ass and cuss. Dean was alive again, living.

"Let's get the fuck out of here," Cliff said. "We'll save the rest for later."

They exited the bathroom, and Dean felt like Clark Kent emerging from a phone booth all Supermanned up and prepared to kill anyone in his path. The dude on the floor was the bartender. He got in Cliff's face and told him to get the hell out or he'd call the cops. Dean was ready to clock him, but Cliff tugged on Dean's T-shirt and the next thing they knew, they were out in the cool of the night.

Dean circled the parking lot, unable to stand still. He yelled at the sky which was teeming with more stars than he'd ever seen. Cliff was laughing at him. Then he handed Dean a cigarette and the smoking focused his energies some.

"What're you doing here?" Cliff asked eagerly. "Like, what are you really doing here?"

Yes, talking. He was in the mood for talking. "I came to find those boys, the ones who were kidnapped. I came thinking I could find them, but this fucking place." He looked around, saw the mountains darkly outlined against the sky. "Way too big."

"What the hell you want to find them kids for? You Batman or some shit?" Cliff started singing, "*Doo-doo doo-doo doo-doo doo-doo, Batman!*"

"I know the lady who took them." Yes, it felt good to talk. "You know how I know her? I was kidnapped by her when I was a boy. She took me and my brother. She held us in a cabin; she molested me. But I escaped. I stabbed that bitch in the stomach with a pair of scissors. My brother was murdered though. But I didn't leave him there. I swam his body through Oneida Lake until we reached the shore and someone found us. The lady, she got away." There was no emotion to the words; it was like telling a story about someone he used to know.

Cliff kept saying, "Are you kidding me?"

"I know it's her, dude. I fucking know it. And she's going to kill one of them boys because she only needs one. She needs one to replace the son who died a long time ago." Dean watched the smoke he exhaled dissipate into the sky. "Shit, she probably already killed him. She's probably long gone by now."

"Fuck that, let's go find her." Now Cliff was the restless one. "Yeah dude, let's find her. I know these mountains, you know the lady. We'll find those kids and get a reward and be fucking heroes!"

Dean wanted to succumb to the idea, give his energy and optimism over to something big and reckless. But the drug wasn't strong enough to quash his common sense. "You're crazy. How the hell we going to search these mountains?"

Cliff was pacing, a cigarette in his mouth as he pulled out another. "You got to know something the cops don't. Think, goddammit."

Dean didn't like the way Cliff was talking to him. His arms needed something to do. This shithead had twice uttered *fag* in his presence, and while that usually didn't rankle him much, it added to the reasons to hurt him.

But then there was something that kind of speared its way to the forefront of everything else. "Ticonderoga," Dean said, suddenly recalling what Wayne had told him. "The lady's husband told me he used to camp near Ticonderoga. Maybe it was with her. I don't know . . ."

Cliff's excitement quickly turned Dean's doubt into confidence.

"Come on." Cliff trotted to a pickup.

"Where?"

"The only fucking campsite near there," he said, laughing. "Rogers Rock."

Carol made her way up the mountain. The heat from the food seeped through the Tupperware so she kept moving it from one hand to the other. When she did, she had to swap her walking stick, a strong limb she'd kept hidden at the base of the trail for her trips. The pills had both numbed her and doubled her strength, though she still felt the distant bite in her side at each step. Thankfully, she didn't have to go even halfway up.

By this point, she had memorized the place. In the beginning, the sudden chill was the signal. A cold, wet exhalation of air that seemed out of place. She left the trail and made her way through the thick brush. The partial moon provided enough light, and her eyes performed well in the dark. The rocky ground dipped, then rose like an errant tooth. At its crest, she shivered for the icy breath coming from a slender opening beneath a massive slab of limestone. It looked as though there had once been a cave here, until a quake or blast collapsed its entrance, leaving only a slivered gap in the rock.

Carol climbed down to the narrow mouth of this cave. She reached her arm into its frigid shadows and felt the rope. She tugged on it, called, "Boy." She tugged again, "It's Mama. I got dinner."

There was a rustling, muffled whimper. The rope slackened. The face that emerged frightened her. In the pale light, the boy was ghoulish. The gag in his mouth cut his face in half, and the weight he'd so quickly lost made him look elderly. She untied the knot on the back of his cold head and freed his mouth. His chin began to tremble, as though the gag had been securing a faulty jaw. The boy tried to make words, but there was only gibberish.

"Eat something, here." She opened the lid, and steam and a bitter scent rose. The boy's hands were tied, so she dipped her fingers in and fed him the rice. He was hungry for it, humming as he licked her fingers. She then pulled the bottle from the pocket of her sweatshirt and poured some water into his mouth. "You and I are leaving," she said as he gulped. "We're going home."

The boy's eyes were heavy-lidded, but he managed to look at her, the first time. His chin still quaked, but he was finding his tongue. The first word was a long stutter, but the second was as clear as the night sky. "My brother?"

"He's not your brother no more," she said, pushing more food into his chattering mouth. "He's staying here."

If he had any water left in him, he'd be crying. How pathetic crying eyes were when there were no tears. She couldn't look at him anymore. She tied the gag back on him. Once she had the boy safe, in a cottage in Vermont she'd reserved, she'd fix him up with her love.

"Time to go." She hooked her hands under his armpits and tugged. The gap in the rock was so slight, his hip bones wouldn't clear. His kicking and squirming didn't help either. She moved him along the lip to try to find a wider spot. But there was no part of it that was wide enough. She tugged again at the boy, but his muffled scream said she might seriously damage him if she persisted.

"Shit!" How could this have happened? If he went in, he should come out. His bones couldn't have grown. If anything, he'd lost weight.

It's the temperature, she settled on. It was colder the night she'd fitted the boys in; the warmer weather must have swelled the rock.

Her heart beating furiously, she brought her hands to her face and screamed into them. She smacked the heel of her hand into her head over and over, beating herself for being so stupid. She returned to the boy, yanked at him again, convinced she'd missed a way the first time. She hadn't. He wasn't coming out.

"You stupid fuck!" She fell to her knees, mouth agape in a soundless sob. She punished herself again, this time butting her head against the rock. The third time knocked her out.

"I smell something. Food."

Carol opened her eyes, unsure of where she was. Until she saw the collapsed cave, the top of the boy's head in the dark. It was a good thing she drugged his water; he hadn't the strength to make a commotion.

"Why's it so cold all a sudden?"

The voices were close. She rolled over, her head aching. She toppled a nearby mound of stones, unearthed a grocery bag. The voices were closing in, two men and their bodies parting brush. Her panic pushed aside the pain; she was in survival mode now. She kept her eyes focused on the direction of the men as her hand slipped into the grocery bag and found the handle of her Colt .45.

"It's over here. Hamburger Helper or something."

"Goddamn it's cold."

She raised the gun up the slope that she'd descended. Cocked the hammer, waited. "Be careful" was the first thing she heard before she saw the form overhead. The gunfire was an explosion of light and sound. The Colt's kick nearly knocked her backward. The whole mountain seemed to thunder. Tumbling down toward her was the man's body. He settled just at her feet, hissing and gurgling from the space that used to be his right cheek. She stood over him to get a better look. He was just a townie, probably drunk and wandering. But there was another. He was looking down from the crest of the slope, so silent and motionless she at first doubted his reality. Then he turned, and she fired.

It was like that dream where someone was after him, and even though he was running so hard, Dean was going nowhere. The brush was thick, the tree branches low and dense, the trail gone. He fought through it, taking lashes on his bare arms and across his face. The only thing he could trust was the incline of the mountain. Instead of going down, his instinct was to climb. The drug was working against him, a lull in the high or a complete crash, and his boots felt leaded. He was using his hands like an animal, clawing at root and rock, bending fingernails back. When he felt the need to stop, his knees and thighs screaming, he heard her behind him. "Wait," she was calling through heavy breath. "It was an accident. I need your help. Wait."

That voice crawling through his spine, chewing on the back of his neck. It gave his body the strength to climb: not the gun but that voice, which had awakened the memory and sharpened all those details gone interminably fuzzy. The voice saying she wanted him, not his brother, ordering him to change his clothes, telling him to eat, and when he wouldn't, saying she knew what he wanted, and there was her breast, and on his tongue now he tasted it, the taste of betrayal.

Dean heaved, the bile running down his chin and shirt as he continued to climb. Then he noticed he could more clearly see his hands clutching the rock, a lighter shade of violet. He raised his head, noticed the sky through the trees was the deep blue of dawn. The trees themselves were thinning and ahead he could see smooth, bald rock. In an excited rush, he fought more desperately; his only goal now was to get to the top of the mountain. If he died, if he was shot, at least it wouldn't be in the back. The only thing that mattered was to get her out from behind him.

He stood on the summit. The mountain under his feet was bald rock like a giant's stony head, a smattering of trees here and there. To his left the mountain gave way suddenly and steeply, the lake beyond the precipice so still in the morning's gloom it resembled gray land. Dean stood facing the trees from which she would emerge, wheezing desperately, arms tingling for lack of oxygen. But he regained control at each breath, and in that, discovered a new power, as if the climb had emptied him of weakness, and on the peak, he was being filled with strength. It felt like an ancient rite of passage, the mountain's gift.

Her aggressive panting preceded her. When her round face broke from the shadows, she looked an inch from unconsciousness. The gun she waved might as well have been a limp leaf. Dean had the higher ground, the stronger breath.

"Hello, Pumpkin."

Her eyes went stupid with fear. The Colt fell to her side, then dropped from her hand. "How?" she breathed. "How?"

"I'm one of your boys." Dean approached her, feeling the euphoria of fearlessness. When he got within arm's length, he extended his hand as if to help a lady out of a car.

"It's you?" She took his hand, not taking her eyes off him. She let him walk her up to the summit.

"You never saw us grown up," he said.

"Time don't look good on nobody." Her breath was more controlled. "Especially not on boys."

The sun was coming up on their right, touched Dean's wrist with warmth. He looked out over the lake and saw in it the undulating shadow of the mountain. She was just beside him, their arms touching. He wanted to hate her more, wanted her to pulse with his anger. But he felt nothing from her, as if there was nothing to her.

In the distance below came the unmistakable wail of police sirens. Of course someone would have heard the register of that powerful Colt. Carol worried the loose skin of her forehead with her hand, looked like she might start crying. She had tears running down her face, and then he remembered how her eyes had always leaked.

"You picked the wrong one." This came out of him without warning. "People always thought I was the good one. But it was my brother who was better. He'd do a better job hating you right now."

"My boys never hate me," she said to the lake, a breeze catching her hair. "Once I give'm my milk, I'm their mama."

Dean wanted to disagree. More than that, he wanted this not to be true. But he couldn't find the evidence in him to dispute it. Then he felt her leaning into him, wrapping her big arms around his waist, resting her face into his chest. And his arm went up to hug her shoulder.

Their sneakers were orange with sunlight. They both looked out to the water, the slow, easy motion of the lake like a giant, living epidermis.

"Mama," he said, "Tell me where the boys are."

She didn't speak. Her shoulders rattled, a chill or a sob.

"Tell me, and I won't take you down this mountain to the police. I'll let you go how you want."

"You saw where I was at."

"It was dark. I don't know how to get back there."

"They's a cave more'n halfway down. You'll feel the cold of it. Just keep to the trail till you feel the cold of it."

"Are they both alive?"

"I only ever wanted one. I only ever wanted you. If you'd stayed, they all'd be alive."

There it was, the heat in his eyes, the clench in his throat, the hatred. He took her face in both hands and pulled it into his. He was afraid he would kiss her or bite her. He just wanted to go to the boys, to leave her, put his back to her for good this time. But his hands held on, squeezing her face so that her hands clutched his wrists.

"I hope to God there's a hell." He pulled her face into his chest, sobbed into her campfire hair. The higher power he'd been asked to acknowledge, that he'd tried to deny, was opening itself up to him.

There was no comfort in it, just an honest desire and a willingness to make himself small for it.

Dean finally turned his back to her, not another look or word.

The angle of the mountain pulled him quickly down the trail. He made his skin too sensitive to temperature, so that every hundred feet he'd think he found the cave and would go off searching. Then he realized he'd have to trust himself to know, either that or fail. It was only a few minutes after this decision that the icy breath licked his arms. He rushed toward its source and soon came to Cliff's body. Red ants had swarmed the meat of his face. A trail of blood ten feet long told he'd died slowly, painfully.

Dean hurried past the body to the gap in the rock that resembled a smirk. He pushed his face into the cold darkness. "Hello? Are you there? I'm here to help."

He heard rustling. He put his arms in, afraid of what he'd find. He felt a shoulder and thankfully, it moved. He pulled and there was a face, deathly but alive. He tried to get the boy out, but he couldn't loosen him. So Dean clawed at the canvas gag, freeing the boy's mouth. He ran his hands over the boy's damp hair as if to rub life back into him.

"Is your brother down there?"

The boy chattered uncontrollably. The pale skin pulled taut on his face, making his eyes appear lidless, huge. Dean hugged him to his body, rubbed his spiny back. Then he tried again.

"Where is he?"

"He's my brother. My brother."

"I know, I know." Dean wiped the boy's hair from his damp forehead. "Is your brother still down there?"

The boy nodded.

Dean plunged in his arms, then his head, until his ribcage stopped him from going farther. He groped the limestone until he felt a cold lump. If he hadn't been looking for a person, his hands would have mistaken this for a sweatshirt stuffed with sticks and clay. He grabbed hold of anything, pulled. This one easily slipped through the opening. When he did, Dean saw that the boy was unconscious, but he was still holding fast to his brother's legs, so that now, both boys were freed from the rock.

She watched the mountain's shadow in the lake, maybe saw herself atop. But her vision blurred. Even though the light was at her back, her eyes were sensitive to the sun burning the periphery. *Never take your eyes from the light and you'll always be guided right.* Her daddy'd gone blind abiding that mantra. She didn't have his fortitude, her vision a testament to her failures.

The boy was the biggest of them, come back just to insult her with his growth. Adulthood had scarred his arms, ruined his spirit, just like it did everyone, but him more. If only he'd let her love him the way she'd wanted, she would've protected him from age. That failure codified suddenly in her chest like a tumorous bone, tugged her off the mountain moments before she was ready. The plunge sucked the air from her, stole her ability to scream, the tremendous urge instead filling her with a pressure that was released as a terrible burst when her body smashed onto the surface of the lake.

Dean refused to look the boy in the face as he pried his arms off of his brother's legs. As soon as he did, he pulled the boy into his arms. He hugged and swayed and begged for a heartbeat. He reached out for the brother, pulled him in to join the prayer, an embrace of bones. Suddenly, there came a distant but startling *pop*, like the explosion of a big balloon. It made them jump, all of them. When they recovered, Dean felt on his chest a weak, remote thump like a voice calling from the past.

WHERE THE SUN

SHINES OUT

Summary, 2014

———◆———

SARA SQUEEZED HER EYES shut and pulled her blanket over her head, leaving a small gap to breathe out of. She hugged her lamby tight to her chest to calm her hammering heart. It was still night. When would it not be night anymore? She rolled over in her bed, to the other side of her pillow, but it was still waiting for her.

An old dog got into their yard. It was sniffing around their pool, putting its splotchy nose into the blue water.

Sara said, "Hey doggy." It looked up, the white hairs dripping off its face like an old man's mustache. Sara laughed and walked barefoot over the hot porch boards to it. The dog looked sick, missing hair on its butt and on one of its shaking legs. "What's your name, doggy?" It sniffed her hand. She looked back at her house so nobody would see her touching the strange animal. "Want a drink?" Sara cupped her hand and reached into the cool water and lifted it to the dog. It licked and licked and she laughed. "Is that good?" She got more, this time with both hands, a real good cold drink for this poor dog. But the water jumped up at her and pulled her down.

Her toes reached for the rubbery floor, but the floor was gone. She grabbed for the sun, but the pool had gulped it, turning it greenish and silent. Her scream went inside instead of out. Water packed her ears and all her banging insides roared. The pool filled her mouth. She felt her tongue swell, bulging against her teeth, her throat. The water was growing her like a balloon and she would explode. Bubble clouds swarmed and netted her; light shimmered blue and green, and then went black. Her scream sounded like herself, but a roboty and faraway version. Sara was losing herself, oozing into the water, forever gone.

Then, a whoosh of air and a blaze of light, and she heard the clean noise of birds and breeze and neighborhood cars, and Uncle Dean.

"I got you."

He was holding her above the water, his strong hands in her armpits. His green eyes were quiet and warm, making her sleepy. The whiskers around his lips prickled her forehead. She wrapped him up the monkey way, and over his painted shoulder, Mama and Daddy were bursting out of the house.

When Sara woke up, she looked out of her bedroom window and saw his purple truck in the driveway parked under the rusty basketball hoop. She had been afraid Uncle Dean wouldn't come to visit as he sometimes did on weekends. She'd waited up for him, but it got too late and Daddy told her to go to bed and that was when she got afraid he wouldn't come. But he came like he said.

Sara leaped off the bed and ran into the kitchen. Daddy was in his bathrobe drinking his coffee and reading the paper. Mama had the red bowl out and was pouring a box of cake into it.

"Where is he?" Sara asked.

"Sleeping," Dad said.

"Aw, man, still?" Sara climbed up on the stool next to Dad. "He'll sleep all day."

"He didn't get in until late." Mama put the bowl in front of Sara with a whisk. "I'm making his birthday cake. Want to help?"

"Can I lick the spoon?"

"First give me a kiss."

Ethan danced into the kitchen with no underwear, tugging his penis.

"Ethan, stop pulling your noodie," scolded Sara.

"But it's getting dead," said Ethan.

"Your noodie can't die, stupid."

"Yuh-huh, look." He stretched it out, then let it go like a rubber band and it hung purple.

"Sara, leave Ethan alone." Daddy folded the newspaper loudly. "Jesus, Ethan, put some underwear on."

"Karl," Mama said. "It's too early to be in a mood."

Daddy sighed. "Ethan," he said, trying hard to keep his voice quiet, "put your underwear on or you can't watch cartoons."

Ethan went into his room and came out a minute later wearing Spiderman underwear but backwards. He ran into the living room and turned on the TV and sat on his knees in front of it, bouncing.

"Keep mixing," Mama said to Sara. She slid open the new glass door to the back porch. "We'll put the cake together when I get back." Out the window, Mama lit a cigarette. She sat on a chair looking at the pool or the creek beyond the fence, breathing smoke.

"Daddy," Sara said. "Did Dean ever pull his noodie when he was a boy?"

Daddy stood and poured his coffee down the sink. He tightened his bathrobe. "I don't remember. But if you're asking if it's a normal thing, then I'd say that some little boys do what Ethan does. Is that what you're asking?"

"No."

"What are you asking?"

"How he was a boy."

"How he was?"

"Er . . ." She looked to the ceiling, then to Daddy's face. "What he was like."

Daddy got a plastic cup from the cupboard and filled it with milk. He put it in front of Sara.

"I don't want milk," Sara said, moving the cup away from her. "I want juice."

"Juice has too much sugar. You need to drink milk."

"But I don't like it."

"Dammit—"

"Mama's gonna yell at you again," Sara whispered, twisting her head.

He sighed, and then smiled at her. "Just have two sips, okay?"

She thought that a fair compromise, took two quick sips, and then returned to the cake mixing.

"He was kind of like you," Daddy said. "He asked a lot of questions. And then he was like Ethan. Kind of . . . strange."

"He was like two people? How was Dean like two people?"

He leaned on the kitchen island. He didn't say anything until he said something quickly. "Sweetie, I need to get ready for work." He kissed Sara on the head and went toward his bedroom. "And call him Uncle Dean, okay?"

"But he's not my uncle." She licked the vanilla goop from her knuckles. "He's my brother."

"Half brother."

"Is a half brother the same as an uncle?"

Daddy shook his head as he often did with her. It looked like he'd say something else but instead he went into his room.

Sara got off the stool and went to Ethan and kicked his fanny.

"Hey!"

"Want to sneak into Dean's room?"

"Yeah."

"It's a game, okay? We can't wake him up, but we'll just go in super-quiet."

"Super-*duper*-quiet," Ethan kind of whispered.

They walked to the door that was Dean's room, back when he lived here. Sara put her hand on the knob and looked at Ethan, her finger to her lips. Ethan copied her. She pushed open the door oh-so-slow and saw Dean in bed. She smelled his boy sleep smell, which was like farts and made her almost laugh. One arm was out of the blanket and it was covered with the strange tattoos that were like cartoons and nightmares. On the wall was a fuzzy photo of Dean in a newspaper that Mama had framed. Sara couldn't read what it said but she knew it was for the time Dean was a hero and helped rescue some boys.

Sara and Ethan tiptoed farther in. Ethan was being good at the game, but Sara felt giggles butterflying her belly. Their faces were close to Dean's face, noses almost touching. He should wake up now. His eyes should pop open and see them, but he was still sleeping.

Sara screamed, "Wake up horse cheese!" and Ethan squealed.

Dean's eyes jumped open, not seeing, and then he saw and smiled and licked his lips. "Horse cheese?" Dean said with a throat full of pebbles.

Sara laughed and climbed in bed on top of him and Ethan did, too, but she had a better spot on Dean's chest. He was hot like an oven and there were sweat dots on his forehead.

"Are you sick, Dean?"

He cleared his throat. "Are you sick?" he said, "Because your ears are melting off your head."

She grabbed her ears, but they were still there. She got in his face. "You're a liar. It's not nice to lie."

"Liar liar pants a-fryer," Ethan said wrong, stuck near the wall.

"It's time to get up so we can play a game," Sara ordered.

"Okay, but you guys have to get lost so I can dress."

Sara had the checkerboard out on the kitchen floor with the right pieces on the right squares. Dean had taught her checkers last time he was here, at the beginning of summer. He had given her the game for her birthday. Ethan was in the other room watching TV; if he saw the checkers, he would want to play and ruin everything.

Dean came into the kitchen. He looked happy, like he might have candy in his mouth. He was wearing what he always wore, dirty jeans with a fat brown belt and a tight T-shirt. You could see all the tattoos on his arms, like he had dipped his arms in paint.

"Sorry the kids woke you," Mama said to Dean, touching his shoulder strangely.

Daddy went into the refrigerator and took out his lunch cooler but didn't say anything to Dean.

"Karl," Mama said.

"Good to see you, too." Dean made a funny face at Sara, and she covered her mouth to muffle her laugh.

"Karl," Mama said again.

Daddy turned toward Dean. "Thought you were getting in at nine."

"I said I might be here at nine, but I had to see about work."

"So you couldn't call?"

"Karl."

"Sara was waiting up for you."

Sara said, "It's okay."

"I'm sorry about that," Dean said. "But I got called in to work."

"Goddamn Indians don't respect a day off."

"Karl, language."

Dean was still cheerful, his eyes wide and glassy. "They own the casino. They don't manage the bar. Besides, who was the last person at Mohawk you gave a day off to?"

Daddy slammed his cooler on the counter. "Don't you dare compare me to those . . . heathens."

"You do remember how we nearly destroyed the entire population of *Native Americans*, right?" Dean looked at Sara to say, "They're not called Indians." Then back to Daddy, still holding a smile. "And now you're all bent out of shape as if they're some kind of oppressive regime keeping you down."

"Don't give me your liberal BS. They brought gambling into this town. Worse, they brought *gamblers* here."

"Let's just end it there," Mama said, a hand on Daddy to settle him the way only she could. "We're happy you're here," she said nicely to Dean. "Can I get you some coffee?"

"No thanks, Kathy."

"Karl," Mama said, calm and steady. "We'll see you this evening. We're going to have a nice dinner, right?"

"Of course we are."

Daddy left, and Mama took Ethan swimming because he was starting to get crazy. Sara grabbed Uncle Dean's fingers and pulled him to the checkerboard.

"Do you remember how to play?" Dean sat like a boy, cross-legged.

She was lying on her stomach. "Yes. But this time can't you let me win just one game?"

"No." His light eyes were serious but kind. "If you want to win, you got to beat me."

"Aw, man. You stink."

"You go first."

She moved her red piece, and he moved a black piece, then she moved a red piece the same way he did, with one finger. He jumped it and took it.

"Hey, no fair."

"Course it's fair. It's how you play."

They kept playing and he kept jumping her pieces and taking them. A pile of red chips grew next to him, and there were none by her. Even though he never let her win, she liked just sitting quiet with Dean. But sometimes there were things she wanted to know, and he always talked to her like a normal person.

She asked, "What's that?"

It was bubblegum skin, stuck in the bendy part of his arm. She saw it last time but didn't say anything because Daddy told her not to, but Daddy didn't say not to this time.

"A scar."

"What happened?"

He looked at it. "I fell out of a tree and a branch stabbed me. Worms and eggs started growing in my arm, so the doctor had to go in with a knife and cut it all out."

"That's not what happened. Besides, you're too big to climb trees."

Dean put a checker in his mouth and crossed his arms, then spit the piece on the board. "What do you think about that?"

Sara laughed from her belly, then climbed over the checkers and took his arm in her hands. She wanted to touch the gum scar but was afraid it would be gross.

"Are you better now?" she asked.

Dean put his hand on her fingers. His palm was wet and hot and his fingernails were like rips of paper. He was gentle, petting her hand, but he wasn't talking. She had said something wrong and was sorry.

Outside in the pool, Ethan squealed as Mama twirled him. "Motorboat, motorboat, go so fast!"

"Have you been in since last time?" Dean asked.

"No."

"Why not?"

"Guess what? Daddy said we might go to an amusement park this summer."

"It won't happen again." Dean's voice was soft.

"I don't want to."

"You love the pool."

"I just don't want to."

"We'll go in together. I'll hold you."

"Just *don't.*" And like balloons, her tongue was inflating in her mouth. Her hands were getting bigger. Faraway things were closer and sounds nearer and she saw that green sun. She cupped her big hands over her ears and squeezed her eyes shut.

"Okay, Sara, okay." Dean held her face and kept saying "It's okay" until, like magic or God, it was. He sat her on his lap and hugged her from behind and swayed. She was safe and warm and her heart felt quiet. A spinning coin stopped spinning.

"Did you know," Dean began, but didn't start again until he breathed a few big breaths. "When I was a boy, I had a brother. We were stuck in a big lake, at night. He couldn't swim, and I had to carry him across. That night—" A big breath came out, rattling him. "I got . . . changed. Like I didn't come back. Like who came out wasn't me. Know what I mean?"

She felt her head nodding, though his words were swimming through her, not really settling anywhere.

"But you're strong, much stronger than me. When you're ready, you'll go back into the pool. And I'll be there, if you want me to."

She put her hands on his arms and traced the swirling tattoos. She imagined the skin unstained and unscarred. "You have a brother?"

He stretched out the y of the "Yes" as though he didn't want to free it.

"Then that means . . . I have another half brother."

"Sort of."

"Should I call him uncle, too?" Sara craned her neck to look at him.

"No. You shouldn't even call me uncle."

"What is his name, our brother?"

She wasn't sure Dean had heard her. She was about to ask again, when he said, "Jason."

"Jason." She looked back down at Dean's hard, thin arms. "Where is he?"

"Gone."

"Because you didn't save him?"

She turned her head to hear his answer, but cheek to his chest, heard only his heart drumming. The question *why not* itched her tongue, but she knew that she had already asked too much. Sara stood and moved behind him, draped her arms around his shoulders. His spine rippled down her body. His heart still banged through her. She couldn't stop his spinning coin.

Daddy brought home lobsters that night for dinner. He was in a better mood. Ethan was angry at the adults for boiling the lobsters alive. He wanted to keep them as pets or let them go in the creek. Sara didn't like it either, but since Dean was the one who put their fighting bodies in the pot, she thought it was okay. She sat next to Dean, and he showed her how to crack the claws and pull out the white, shimmering meat. It was so sweet, and dunked in butter, she decided it was her favorite food. When everyone had finished, Ethan told Dean to eat the lobster's antennae. Dean immediately plucked one off and rolled it up and put it in his mouth. Sara and Ethan and Mama squealed. Daddy said, "Aw, come on Dean-O."

Dean chewed and chewed doing silly things with his eyes. Finally, he swallowed. "Okay," Dean said to Ethan. "Your turn."

Sara and Ethan had to go to bed after ice cream. Sara lay in bed listening to the hum of the adults' voices echoing from the nearby kitchen, which made her drowsy. She wasn't sure if she had fallen asleep, or if it was immediately after, but the voices suddenly became loud. Sara got out of bed and pressed her face to the door.

"What in the hell's gotten into your head?" Daddy said. "How could you think it's a good idea to tell Sara about Jason?"

"Settle down," said Dean. "I didn't tell her everything. Besides, she's smarter than you think."

Sara's stomach ached with guilt. She had asked her daddy about Uncle Jason when he was tucking her in. She didn't know it was something she shouldn't have said.

"It wasn't your decision to tell her that. You can't just come in here, unload that on a five-year-old, and leave. Now Kathy and I have to do damage control."

"You mean, now you have to talk to your daughter."

"How dare you." Daddy's voice was jagged and violent. It wounded Sara to hear it. "I'm trying to start a new family here."

"New family. That's interesting."

"Dean," Mama said. It surprised Sara that she was there, like she had suddenly come into existence. "Obviously you are part of our family."

"I don't think that's obvious to him."

"The only reason we're letting you visit here on the weekends is you got your shit together," Daddy said.

"Thank you for your generosity."

"Despite the fact you're working for the goddamn Indians."

"Enough with that already."

"What he means," Mama said steadily, "is your dad's worried about you in that kind of environment."

"I'm having second thoughts," Daddy continued. "Maybe you're not ready to be back. Maybe the tough love was better for you."

"Tough love." Dean laughed, but not with humor. "I remember something like that a long time ago. Weren't you trying to toughen me up? Teach a ten-year-old how to be a big man and look out for his little brother. How did that turn out, again?"

"Shut up."

"Dean," Mama warned.

"Oh, that's right," Dean continued. "Some freaks snatched us up and stuffed us in the trunk of their car."

"Shut the hell up," Daddy screamed.

Sara heard a kitchen chair crash and there was pounding on the floor, and Mama yelled, "Karl!" Tears sprouted from Sara's eyes, and she began to shake.

"You know," said Dean, "I don't give a shit what you think about me. You and I are nothing. But what you got with Sara and Ethan you better not fuck up. Keep them close."

There was a strange silence that came on suddenly, like a giant glass lid had been placed over them. Then she heard Dean, at least she thought it was him, his voice bent and twisted. "Just don't let it happen again." Footsteps stomped toward Sara's bedroom, and she jumped back in bed. A door slammed down the hall. The house was quiet again, but Sara's head rang with the fight.

The next morning, Sara stayed in her bedroom and made Dean a birthday card. She was on the floor with her markers and crayons and glitter, staring at a drawing of a dog. It was brown and white and it stood on green grass and had a volcano behind it because one time Dean taught her about volcanos. The card needed something else, so she taped to the top of the volcano one of her old toys she didn't play with anymore, a small, glittery pony. She held out the card in front of her.

The dog was okay, but it didn't look like the one in her head. She wanted it to be perfect. She wanted the drawing to repay him for all he'd done for her, for the feelings he filled her with, and for the things she didn't get from anyone else. These thoughts just made her want to see him, because she believed he'd understand, just with a look, what she wanted to give.

She went out of her room with the drawing in both hands. The house was quiet. Daddy was at work. Mama and Ethan weren't in the kitchen. The door to Dean's room was closed. Angry music thumped out. She pushed the door open and held up the card and called, "Happy birthday!"

Dean was nodding over a picture frame with cocoa powder on it. The blinds were down, but a bar of light fell across his back. He was in his underwear and looked skinny like Ethan. He jumped to hide the picture frame. It was the one from the wall, the one of him as a hero. He looked at her like he hated her with his eyes, turning the powder into something terrible.

"Sorry," she said, dropping the picture at her feet.

"Wait." He put his hand out. He was like a boy.

But Sara was scared, and she backed out and closed the door.

His purple truck was gone after that. He had sneaked out the house and didn't come back for his birthday dinner. Mama still put frosting on his cake and all thirty-two candles—Sara had counted them twice. Daddy came home with a bag filled with Burger King cheeseburgers, which he said were Dean's favorite.

It was late and he still wasn't home. Daddy called Dean's cell phone. "It went straight to voice mail," he said. He called the bar where Dean worked. "They said they haven't seen him."

"I don't know," Mama whispered to Daddy.

"He's probably angry about last night."

"I don't know, Karl."

"He probably went back to Utica."

Mama looked steadily at Daddy like she did when she wanted him to do something.

"Okay," Daddy sighed. "I'll call Bell. Then I'll drive around." He grabbed the keys from the counter.

Sara thought about it all night, about what she saw. But this time she didn't tell on Dean.

Two days later, Sara, Mama, and Ethan were on the way home from the hardware store. The cell phone rang and Mama looked at it, then pulled the car off the road. Sara sat up in the car seat to hear. Ethan dropped his Spiderman and wanted Sara to pick it up, but she told him to hush. Mama kept saying "No" in different ways, the last ones shaky and stretched out. There was the taste of green sun fat on Sara's tongue. "What's wrong?" Sara asked so carefully. But Mama wasn't talking, and Sara fell back in her seat to cry. Mama turned around, her face bunched up, and put her hand on Sara, but Sara almost couldn't see and almost couldn't breathe.

"Sara, look at me."

Mama's eyes were brown, and Sara turned her head away.

Ethan put his hand on Sara's head, and echoed Mama's order, "Look at Mom," but she looked at Ethan and saw her own eyes, green, like Dean's.

Dean was sick, but maybe he would be okay. The order of the words from Mama and Daddy was always the same: the *sick* was like the truth, the *maybe* like a lie. Sara wanted to know what happened, but Mama wouldn't tell. She had talked to Daddy on the phone at the hospital. He said how the police found Dean's car at the Erie Canal, and he was in it, sick. No one was saying it all, Sara could tell.

She was on her bed, staring at the wall. The balloon was in her hands and her tongue, and the dirty sun in her eyes. The farthest-away thing out the window, the line of blue-green trees after the creek, became the closest thing, right up on her nose. God from church or from inside her heart was punishing her for not saying what she saw Dean doing but instead was making her see what seeing is like when you die, when you can see into forever and ever, and there was no way to stop it; even if you told God that forever was too long to see, it still would never end.

Sara squeezed her eyes shut and turned away from the window. She tried to calm her body. Bright blue seeped into the darkness behind her eyelids until it was everywhere. Then there was hot sun and wet feet and water sounds. She was standing in a lake. The water was black. Dean was there, far away but close, staring at her. Barks and hisses pounded from him in a slow, uneven rhythm. Dean's tattoos shimmered. He screamed, and his tattoos moved like snakes. They turned liquid, back into the paint they were made of, and the black snake paint was oozing off his body, filling up the lake. The water moved up his legs, his stomach, his chest, his face. The lake was up to his eyes. He watched her, then the water went over his head. Sara wanted to rescue him but she couldn't move. She looked down, and a piece of the paint lake was on her hand—a tattoo stain the shape of a spider.

Sara sat up, sweaty and trembling. The spider was fluttering up her arm, and she yelped and smacked at it, but it wasn't there. She ran downstairs, afraid of behind her. Ethan was pants-off twirling, watching TV.

"Ethan, where's Mama?"

"Um . . ." He pulled his noodie. "She's at Spiderman's house."

"I'm here, Sara," Mama said from the kitchen.

"I want to see Uncle Dean."

"Sara, I don't think that's a good idea."

Ethan said, "You can't see him. He's dead."

"Ethan," Mama said, "don't say that."

"But he is. I saw it on the show."

"Ethan, hush it!"

"He's just dead."

A pop happened inside Sara, and she exploded on Ethan. She screamed fire at him and raked his face and smacked his noodie over and over until Mama pulled her off. She screamed "Let me see Dean!" until she couldn't talk anymore.

The smell and lights and shiny floors of the hospital reminded Sara, for the first time, of when Ethan was born. Daddy had carried her through the halls to see Mama and her new brother. Then she was in the hospital bed with Mama and the baby, and she was allowed to touch Ethan's hand and he grabbed her finger. Now, walking the halls with Mama and Ethan, dinosaur band-aids on his face, she waited for other memories. Once they got to the huge elevator, the sick was turning in her belly like gymnastics, and she was breathing in gulps.

"Sara?" Mama said. "Are you okay?"

"Can you pick me up?"

Mama grunted as she lifted Sara. The elevator stopped and they walked down another bright hallway.

"Listen," Mama said, "you know you don't have to see Dean if you're too scared."

Ethan fiddled with something in his pocket as he walked alongside. Mama said to him, "What are you messing with?" He held up his hand, showing something furry.

Mama squinted. "What is this?"

"It's just a foot." It was a paw, like from a rabbit or another small animal. Little claws curled out from the dirty white fur.

"Jesus!" Mama flopped Sara down. She slapped the paw from Ethan's hand. "Why do you have this? Where did you get it?"

"It was in the road." Ethan was getting upset. "I didn't kill it, I just took the foot."

"But *why*, Ethan?"

He began to cry and Mama changed her tone. "It's okay, just come here." She scrubbed his stained hand with three different wipes from her purse. She made him use the stinging sanitizer on the wall. "Don't ever touch anything like that again, understand?"

He nodded but Sara knew he didn't understand; he'd never. This sudden awareness about her little brother bothered her. Or was it what she was going to, Dean, that bothered? She couldn't tell the two apart.

They came to a room that looked like all the other rooms. The door was open, and Mama leaned inside the shadows and whispered, "Karl?"

Daddy came out. His eyes were swollen red, and his face was silver with whiskers. He didn't look at Sara or Ethan. He only put his forehead on Mama's, and his shoulders went limp.

A nurse walked by. "Hello," she said to Sara. Sara pressed herself into her mama's legs.

Mama knelt down in front of Sara with sparkling eyes.

"I'm going in with Daddy to see Dean. I want you to wait with Ethan right over there." She pointed to chairs that were a few feet away, just across the room. "I'll only be a minute, and then you can come in with me to see Dean if you still want to."

Some of the weight around her heart lifted, and Sara nodded. She took Ethan's elbow and pulled him toward the chairs.

"Do you want a magazine?" Sara asked Ethan, going through some on the table. She held up one with giraffes on it. Ethan said, "No." She held up another one.

"I just want you to find the cartoons," Ethan said.

A TV on the wall showed the news. There were angry people with signs shouting outside of a building. The news lady pointed a microphone at one of the angry men and he said something about a casino and gambling and Indians. Sara recognized the place as Chittenango, the funny name of the place where she lived.

"Hello." A lady with a bulging stomach and a man stood in front of Sara. "Are you two all alone?"

"Yes," Ethan said.

"No," Sara said.

"Where are your parents?" The lady was pregnant, and that made her probably okay to talk to.

"They're in there."

"That's where our uncle is dead," Ethan said, bouncing in the chair.

"Hush up, Ethan! Besides, he's our brother, not uncle."

The man said, "Is your brother Dean Fleming?"

She wasn't sure about the man, about men in general. This one had something ugly on his forehead, like a belly button knot. But he seemed okay, too small to be dangerous.

"That's who we came to see," the man said. "Dean."

"But maybe this isn't a good time," the lady said to him. She then looked at Sara, her eyes wet and kind. "We're very sorry about Dean. Very sorry."

"Was he your friend?" Ethan asked.

"He was my friend, yes," the man said.

"I have a friend named Watermelon."

"No you don't, Ethan. Don't lie."

The man said, "I have a friend named Jelly Bones."

"I have a friend named Jelly Mellons."

Ethan was laughing and Sara didn't like the lying and the lady pulled the man's arm and said something into his ear and the man nodded.

"We're going to let you and your parents visit," the lady said, hand resting on her stomach. "We'll come back some other time."

The man said, "Can we get you guys anything?"

Sara said no, but Ethan asked for a toy. Sara smacked him. The man went into his pocket and took out his keys. He removed something from his little key chain, and handed it to Ethan. It was a LEGO man.

"Push his stomach."

Ethan did, and blue light shined out of the toy's feet. "Whoa, that's cool!"

"Say thank you," Sara said.

"Thank you."

"You're welcome."

The two strangers waved and then walked away. Sara wanted them back, but she just sat quietly, picking her thumbs.

Ethan whispered to Sara, "That guy had a weird head."

"I know. I thought it looked like your belly button."

"No it didn't!"

Sobbing came from the dark room. The sound was like a cat at first. It then turned wild, like an animal wailing. Daddy scrambled out of the room as if something were chasing him. He was crying hysterically. Mama was trying to hold him up by the shoulders, but Daddy was bent over and fleeing down the hall. "Karl!" Mama was shouting. Nurses were trying to help him, but Daddy kept moaning and flailing his arms and moving away.

"Mama?" Sara called.

"Just wait there," she yelled without looking back. Then, she and Daddy were gone around the corner. There was nothing left of their voices.

A small, old nurse came from around the same corner, walking quickly toward them. "Your parents will be right back," she said in a firm voice. "Your mother said to wait here for her, and if you need anything, I will be right over there." The nurse pointed to a desk a few feet away.

"Is my daddy turned crazy?" Ethan said.

"Hush it," Sara said, elbowing him.

The nurse smiled, then walked off.

Sara wanted to go into the dark room and see Dean. She wondered what he looked like to get her daddy so upset. Was he sleeping, or was he all broken with bones showing? She tried hard, but she couldn't stop shivering.

When Sara woke shivering almost every night, slapping dreams from her arms, Mama would tell how Dean had saved her. The story helped put her back to sleep. It was Sara's birthday and Dean just got there and they were going to have a little pool party. Sara was supposed to wait on the porch steps until everyone put on their bathing suits. Mama was making sandwiches and Daddy was packing the cooler when Dean came into the kitchen. He asked for Sara because he was scared and knew something was wrong. He looked out the window and saw her hair slithering on top of the water. He ran to the sliding glass door but he couldn't get it open because since the big snow storm it was always stuck, so he stepped back and put his shoulder down and smashed right through the glass. He dove into the pool and scooped Sara up before Mama and Daddy could even get outside. Mama never said anything about the white dog. Nobody ever said they saw it.

And then there were the boys Dean had saved. And then there was Jason, who Dean hadn't saved. But who would save Dean? She knew he was lost now, blinded by dirty sun and oozing out into forever.

The nurse was at the desk, on the phone. Sara slipped off her chair, still shaking, and sneaked to the door. She leaned on the cold metal doorframe, listening.

"Don't," Ethan whispered. "You'll die if you go in."

"Hush, Ethan."

Sara stared into the dark room, hearing machine rhythms. She felt a sticky hand. Ethan was holding onto her, his twiggy body on hers.

"It's not a game this time," she said, pushing Ethan away. Sara was surprised by how she sounded.

Ethan bounced back and grabbed her hand again. "I'll just go in with you," he said, "so you don't die." He shivered, like her.

She squeezed his hand. The dark room kept getting darker the more she squinted, and her heart bumped in her ears the more she listened; and there in the bumping, in the dark squinting, she could hear Dean, splashing.

Ethan pushed the LEGO man's stomach, and he and Sara followed the light into the room.

Inside, machines blinked and wheezed like robots, and computer screens cast green light on everything. Tubes went from the machines and computers to the bed where sleeping, just sleeping, was Dean. He had a tube between his swollen lips and his face was thinner and hairier, and both his arms were wrapped with bandages at the elbows. But he was just asleep was all. This loosed her feet, and she walked right up to him.

She tapped him on the shoulder. "Uncle Dean, wake up."

There was only the beeping and wheezing from above her. She said it again, louder. Then again. She shook him. He was just so close to waking. His face right there turned to her, the lips and eyes and nose of him sleeping, and all he had to do was open his eyes.

But he wasn't, and maybe he wouldn't.

No fair, she thought. But he said from inside her, *Of course it's fair.*

Sara put her hands just over the tattoo puzzles on his arm. She traced them with her finger, wishing she could solve them like math or sound them out like words so she could understand him, the big part in him that was quiet, his lake, what got him sick. But they were all just dark, strange swirly things.

"Sara," Ethan whispered. He was still near the door, only a few feet inside the room. "Come on." He was serious, his whisper edged with fear and urgency. His silhouette in the doorway looked so small, his light shining on the floor so puny. He motioned to her with his hand. "We have to go."

ACKNOWLEDGMENTS

As I WRITE THIS, I realize how misleading it is that only my name is on the cover, since so many people have had a hand in helping me get this book published.

Like my generous mentors (and friends): Michael Parker, Lee Zacharias, Paul Lisicky, Patricia Bender, Alice Elliott Dark, Tayari Jones, Jen Arena, and Jayne Anne Phillips. Like my friends and classmates from the MFA program at Rutgers University–Newark; my friends and colleagues in the Rutgers Writing Program; and my inspiring students of composition. Like the Berkeley Heights and Long Hill Township public libraries where I wrote much of this. Like these beautiful people who read early drafts and chapters, who published excerpts, or who took the time to offer guidance: Richard Thomas, Kris Saintsing, Zach Herrmann, Amanda Whiting, Jaime Karnes, Brian Panowich, Saeed Jones, JJ Koczan, Brian Walker, Andrew Brininstool, Jason Cook, Leah Angstman, Joseph Gross, Joyce Duncan, Matthew Sheehan, and Robert Stapleton. Like my hometown, Chittenango, a village that, despite my often-fictional portrayal of it in this novel, is a nice and magical place and home to wonderful people. (Go Bears.) Like my great friend, Sam Starnes, who continually supports my writing and inspires me with his talent, work ethic, and friendship. Like Erin McKnight from Queen's Ferry Press, who gave my first book life; my tireless, wonderful agent at Prospect, Kirsten Carleton, who took a chance on no-name me and my bleak novel; and my brilliant editor at

Skyhorse, Chelsey Emmelhainz, whose edits were so smart and incisive. Like my big brother David, who helped develop and authenticate the factory details in "Overtime"; my sister, Jennifer, an excellent reader who gave heartening feedback and encouragement on early drafts; and my brother Brian, who inspired this story of the inextricable bonds of brotherhood. There's so much of you, and us, in this; there'd be no book without you. Like my incredibly supportive parents who, despite the novel's depiction of family dysfunction, raised me and my brothers and sister in the most loving, fun, and creative home we could have ever hoped for. I love you, Mom and Dad. Like my beautiful, silly, and kind children, Cameron and Sammy, spirited warriors for joy and love who battle the darkness with their mighty hearts; and like my teammate, my steadfast wife, my hilarious friend, the sun and light and beauty of my life—endless love and thanks to you, Megan.

I am so very grateful to you all.